GIFTED

AWAKENING BOOK TWO

Jacqueline Brown

Also by Jacqueline Brown

The Light, Book One of The Light Series
Through the Ashes, Book Two of The Light Series
From the Shadows, Book Three of The Light Series
Into the Embers, Book Four of The Light Series
Out of the Darkness, Book Five of The Light Series
"Before the Silence," a Light Series Short Story
Awakening, Book One

To receive your FREE copy of "Before the Silence,"
please visit www.Jacqueline-Brown.com.

To the Church Militant:
Take heart—the war is won.

One

My father held the gas can on his right side. The black tip of the long plastic lighter protruded from his coat pocket. The rest of us kept still, watching as he made his way through the snowdrift that had gathered at the base of the inn. The snow covering the inn reminded me of Thomas, of how quickly something or someone could change. In a little over a week Thomas had changed from the boy I had gone to church with my entire life, to someone who allowed evil to take control of his whole being. The inn built by my great-great-grandparents had done the opposite. It had changed from a place of evil—to a place of empty history. Now draped in snow and the smell of fresh salt air, the inn reminded me nothing of the place that held the terror of Thomas's last moments on earth.

Luca and his aunt, Sam, stood beside me, motionless. Their gifts were beyond what any of us could fully understand. Each felt evil and good with such intensity that the evil dominating the inn for generations had almost killed Luca. Now neither one was cringing in pain or sickness, the evil of the inn no longer crippling their bodies. My father unscrewed the cap of the red gas can and splattered gasoline on as much of the desolated wooden structure as he could reach without stepping onto it. He refused to touch any part of it, even with the soles of his shoes.

Immediately after Thomas's death, my father wanted to burn down the inn. He wanted it gone, off our property. Jason,

Luca's practical, no-nonsense uncle, reminded us the inn was a crime scene. My father accepted his caution, waiting over a month until the full investigation was over—until Thomas's parents stopped outwardly questioning their son's last hours on this earth. After the questions and the investigation ended, the winds started. No rain or even snow had fallen since Thomas's death. The thirsty, barren woods would be kindling in high winds, so my father waited.

He had no choice.

Yesterday there'd been heavy snow. Today the winds were still. Today was also the day of Thomas's funeral. This coincidence at first made my father pause—to burn the inn on the day of Thomas's funeral in some ways felt wrong … in others, right. It was my grandmother, Gigi, who finally said there should be no more delays.

Thomas died six weeks ago. Since there was no body, there was no rush for a burial. His parents never thought they would be burying their son—no parent ever does. It had taken them this long to accept that he was gone, or at least to plan the funeral.

We all agreed with Gigi. It was fitting that we were saying goodbye on the same day to both Thomas and the place that led to his death. If his parents were in their right mind, they'd appreciate that we were burning down the place. Since they were not, we hadn't told them. We had not told anyone. Who would we tell? Thomas's death had made many things clear. Darkness is real; no amount of pretending will change that. And friends are rare. My family and I were ostracized every day, more and more.

Perhaps, as my father seemed to secretly hope, our lives would return to normal once the inn was gone. Whatever normal may be, or at least how things were before Thomas killed himself on our property. It was not our fault. I reminded myself of this often; rarely did I believe it.

Guilt hung over me and over each of us. No, we had not killed Thomas, and no, we never wished for him or anyone else to die, but somehow we were not quite innocent.

There was something about the splintered wood building in front of me that made us guilty, not of murder, but of something.

Gigi did not know the story of her grandparents. She didn't know what made them come here, to our small town, or why they were so vile. Only that her grandmother's parents had been innkeepers, and so her grandparents became innkeepers as well. The building in front of us was not large. The rooms, which I'd never seen, were tiny—big enough for a single twin bed, nothing more. The mattresses, Gigi assumed, were still in there, rotten from decades of damp ocean air.

Though how her grandparents came to our town was unknown, why they chose this cove to build their inn was an easy guess. The quiet cove had deep water where ships, large and small, could safely harbor. The inn, a place sailors could have stayed in, would provide a break from the sea. Later, the quaint, quiet cove gave respite to vacationers seeking the therapeutic sea air. With its view of tranquil waters, the building attained the status of a destination inn. How this happened was beyond Gigi's knowledge, but her mother said it was true. Great-grandmother Dorothy told her young daughter that strangers came from all around to stay in The Hidden Inn. Hidden because it was far removed from the dirt road—even from the sea, the building could not be seen. Not until you entered the cove could it be discovered, either by land or water.

When Gigi and her mother arrived, it was exactly as Great-grandmother Dorothy had told her: a destination inn with a grand hotel being built. It was so fully booked with guests during the summer they arrived that Gigi and her mother slept outside in a tent her great-grandparents had erected for cooking. It provided much needed added space to the popular inn. Now, it was hard to imagine it that way. So long had it been run down … so long had it been infused with evil.

"That's enough," Gigi called to my father, who was still pouring the gasoline.

Her voice had returned to normal a few weeks ago when the swelling around her nose subsided. Even the dark circles under her eyes have faded and were easily hidden by makeup.

Dad obeyed his mother … he always did these days. He screwed the lid onto the plastic gas can and carried it away from the building to ensure no flames would reach it. He was constantly cautious, aware of every threat.

After setting the can on the ground, he went back to the inn, taking the lighter from his pocket. He stretched his hand toward the building. Fire erupted as soon as the tip touched the gas-soaked wood. He stepped back, hesitating for a moment before coming toward us, picking up the red canister on his way. His features were difficult to make out against the bright flames behind him.

The day was cold and gray, the same as when Thomas died. But today there was no rain, nothing to stop the flames as they spread through the dry building.

Dad didn't look behind him until he reached his mother. She took his arm, leaning her head against his shoulder. He was a good man, a kind man. She'd raised him well—she'd be the first to tell you this.

The flames grew, the centuries-old wood snapping as it burned. The porch was already engulfed. The flames were now on the inside, growing brightest at the windows and doors. The fire climbed from the first to the second floor. The roof caught as the walls began to crumble.

Was this what Luca's house had looked like when Thomas set it on fire? By the time we saw it, all that remained was a skeleton of burned wood. Had Thomas hidden in the distance, watching it burn like we now watched the inn burn?

Unlike Luca's house, no one went to the inn … no one wanted to save it. In some ways, this was sad. Something that had been in my family for five generations had nothing good associated with it. Gigi's grandparents—their life—their memory was despised.

Perhaps that was what they wanted. In the end they created their legacy; they chose how they would live and how they would be remembered. They could have filled their home with kindness and love. They could have cherished their daughter, Dorothy, and later, their granddaughter, Gemma, but they didn't.

The roof collapsed, an eerie cry exhaling from the burning wood—as though all those who were once hurt by this place were calling out together into the billowing black smoke on this gloomy morning. Sorrow threatened to suffocate me.

"If this place had been different, you wouldn't exist. None of you would," Luca said as if reading my thoughts.

His amber eyes, set against his brown skin, were a bright spot in my darkening world.

He'd been told as much of the inn's story as I had. I leaned toward him, my thick coat brushing against his, the coat Gigi had bought for him.

"No," I replied, "we wouldn't."

Perhaps we were the good that God brought from the evil. I didn't feel that within myself, but I could not deny the goodness in Gigi or my sisters. Before all of this, I would have included my father in that list. Now … I was not as sure.

"It's done. That horrible place is gone," Dad said, with far more relief than I felt.

"Yes," Gigi said, squeezing his arm, "we are free."

"Are we really?" my littlest sister, Avi, asked, her young voice so altered since she last stood here—the place where we watched Thomas fall to his death.

"Oh yes," Gigi said, holding Avi's hand. "We are free, the darkness is gone."

My other sister, Lisieux, and I did not speak, but we caught one another's expressions. We shared the same doubt as our littlest sister.

Our father's face beamed a broad smile of triumph, one that made me uneasy. To smile about any of this felt fake. But many interactions with my father felt fake these days. Despite what Luca had told me about my dad recalling things while I slept, Dad hadn't remembered much … only that he'd spent time at the inn with his great-grandmother. He couldn't remember what they did or what they spoke of, only that he came often, despite his parents' insistence that he stay away. What his role had been, no one could say, but that he had played a role was clear. Even Gigi didn't doubt this. But where I placed blame, she did not.

My dad was not perfect. She realized that, while refusing to acknowledge anything except the good in him. This trait made her a loving mother, though seeing only the good was not realistic.

I wondered what part of reality she had ignored when he was a boy—and now, a man. There was something about him, something I didn't fully understand. He was different. I couldn't describe the difference nor explain it, but I felt it the same as I felt the burning flames in the distance.

The snow and ice between the inn and us had melted. It had no choice but to give in to the heat encroaching upon it.

Two

I dried myself and wrapped the towel around my dripping hair. The bathroom tile felt cold against my bare feet. I stood in my open closet, the steam from the bathroom creeping in around me, adding warmth to the space between me and the dress hanging away from the others. Gigi had picked it out, and the tags still hung from it; it was dark gray, with long sleeves and a gentle flair at the waist. I'd say it was a pretty dress—if it were not the dress I was going to wear to Thomas's funeral.

I lifted it from the rack in the closet and carried it into the bathroom. I didn't want to wear this dress; I didn't want to go to Thomas's funeral. The last funeral I had been to was my mother's.

I inhaled sharply.

"This funeral will not hurt as much," I said to the pale red-haired girl in the mirror. "There's no way it can hurt like that."

I opened the bathroom drawer and found the scissors. I cut the tags from the dress, throwing them in the trash. I hung my damp towel beside the dress, the bright yellow a stark contrast to the dull gray. I'd wear my hair down; it would add color to a colorless day.

Pulling the wide-toothed comb through my wet hair caused knots to form. Every few inches I stopped, using my fingers to separate the tangled strands—some snapping, most slipping free. From the bottom drawer of my vanity, I pulled out the hair dryer and plugged it in. The heat warmed my bare skin. My hair was already straight; I was drying it to keep it from wetting my dress or turning into icicles and breaking off in clumps.

After a few minutes, my hair was dry, or dry enough. I sniffed it; before my shower it stunk of burning evil; now it smelled like roses. How easily the past could be masked by the perfume of the present.

I stepped into the unzipped dress and pulled the zipper up. I stared at myself in the mirror. The elegance of the dress made me look older—perhaps not older than I was, but older than I felt. In a few weeks I'd be eighteen. An adult. Would that change me? Would the world be different?

I unscrewed the top of the waterproof mascara and gently ran its brush through my pale red lashes. I brushed on a thin layer of foundation powder and ran the lip gloss across my lips. In my closet, I slipped on the black tights that Gigi had suggested I wear with the dress. I carried the tall black boots back to the bathroom and sat on the toilet lid to zip my legs into them. I brushed my hair one last time, turned off the light, and left the bathroom.

I went to my window, a matter of habit that long ago stopped being necessary. Our yard below held only the movement of chickens. In a futile attempt to delay the inevitable, I watched them pecking at the ground. I lowered my gaze and turned from the window.

I forced myself to the door of my bedroom, then to the landing, then down the stairs. I had no doubt I'd be forcing myself to move through the rest of this day.

In the kitchen, Gigi was twisting Avi's flaming red hair into a tight braid. Typically, it flew out in all directions, like a physical representation of her personality. Now, like Avi, it was tame and quiet. She was the one most changed by the events of the last six weeks. She'd had the most innocence to lose. Deep within, the exuberant child still existed—we saw her from time to time—but mostly we saw a different child. She was no longer excited by life, only passively accepting of it.

"Your braid is beautiful," I said lovingly.

"Thank you." She didn't raise her eyes to mine.

Gigi kissed the top of her head. "You're done, my dear."

Avi slumped her shoulders against the back of the barstool.

Dad entered the kitchen from his office, which had gone from being a place used mainly by the family in the evenings to a cave he often occupied alone. He was handsome in a black suit with a dark red tie. His brown hair, speckled with gray, was combed neatly back. His eyes gave him away, the sleepless nights resulting in dark circles. His cheeks were not as full as a few weeks ago.

Though Gigi placed no guilt on my father, he assumed all of it. The truth, I sensed, lay somewhere in the middle.

"Are we ready?" Dad asked as Lisieux entered the kitchen.

Her brown hair fell in soft waves lying neatly against her dark purple dress—the perfect color for her. She looked beautiful. She was beautiful, and so was Avi. I wished we were going somewhere else … anywhere else.

Avi didn't move; she remained staring at the countertop. Lisieux walked dutifully toward the coats, like a soldier going to battle.

Silently I stood as Dad handed me my coat. I felt bad for my sisters. They were completely innocent in all of this, yet they were lumped in with us, the guilty ones.

"Where's everybody else?" Avi asked.

Dad was helping put her coat on. "They decided to stay home," he stated as he buttoned her coat.

Lisieux and I exchanged a look.

"Stay home?" Avi asked, her green eyes brimming with panic. "But Sam promised."

Gigi placed a hand on Avi's shoulder. "We thought it best if they didn't attend the funeral," she said firmly.

"Why not?" Lisieux asked our father. She sounded as upset as Avi at the prospect of being away from Luca, Sam, and Jason.

After Thomas burned down their house six weeks ago, they'd been living with us. Having them here made it feel as if they were part of our family. To my sisters, Luca was like a big brother, to me a best friend—an only friend. I craved his presence. He was like the air I needed to survive. He and I had never spoken of this, yet somehow we understood it. That was one of the many beautiful things about Luca; so much was understood without needing words.

After a glance at her son, Gigi answered. "We thought it would be too difficult for Brenda and Phil to see them today."

"Then why are *we* going?" Lisieux asked in an angry tone—which she used most of the time these days.

Gigi removed her new coat from the hook. She had purchased it to replace the one soaked with her blood on the night Thomas died.

"It's a difficult day for all of us," Gigi said. "Sam and her family don't go to our church. The connection they have with Brenda and Phil is that they were there when their son died. That is the only thing that will enter Brenda's and Phil's minds when they see them."

"Luca goes to our church," Avi argued.

She was right. He hadn't missed Mass in over a month and he was always seated next to Avi.

"Yes," Gigi said, "and have you noticed that Brenda and Phil no longer go to the Mass we attend? They are now going later on Sunday or on Saturday evening. Today will be the first time we've been around them since right after Thomas died, and we do not need to rub salt in their wounds."

Dad shrugged into his coat. "Today is not the day for them to be reminded how their son died," Dad said numbly.

I said, "*We* will remind them."

Dad spoke, his expression distant. "I discussed that with Father Luke. He said we should be there. We're part of the church family. It's our duty to support Brenda and Phil as much as we possibly can."

I wondered if my sisters thought the same as I did, that we failed miserably at whatever duty we owed our *church family.* We were not wanted there. We were the social outcasts; perhaps we always had been. Though, now … there was no pretending otherwise. Except maybe by Father Luke, who was as oblivious to the happenings in his parish as any pastor could be. His saying we should attend did little to convince me. Though in his defense, not attending also felt wrong.

"We need to get going. We can't be late," Gigi said, slipping her purse over her shoulder and opening the garage door.

We went to my dad's car without another word. He and Gigi had been trying for weeks to tell us it wasn't as bad as we thought, that people didn't hate us. That we were overreacting and being particularly sensitive because of all we'd been through. They said all of this, yet it had been Gigi's idea to suddenly start a new family tradition. Three weeks ago she decided it would be more fun for us to buy hot donuts from a bakery after church, instead of going into the parish hall and eating room-temperature donuts with the rest of the congregation.

Dad no longer set limits on how many donuts Avi could eat—though she rarely had an appetite for even one when eaten in our kitchen or the bakery. I was the same. Every Sunday I forced myself to eat one in a poor attempt to make my dad and grandmother feel better. Donuts and church were linked, in my mind, and the pain of one brought the distaste for the other.

Lisieux was the same as Avi and me; the one exception was Luca. He could easily eat a dozen by himself, and did that first Sunday when no one else felt like having any.

I stared at the closed kitchen door as we backed out of the garage, wishing, hoping, praying Luca would emerge from it.

The still, gray morning had turned into a bright, windy afternoon. The air was cold, the trees that had lost their leaves were bare except for the bits of snow clinging to each of them in different ways. Some sat on the branches, others on the bark, like it had been blown there and refused to leave.

The barren trees and chilled air were givens for November; the bright sun and snow were not. These were gifts. The sun brought with it hope, and the white veil of snow, beauty that covered the scars of the past.

"It's crowded," Avi said with trepidation as Dad parked in the gravel lot. The main parking area was full.

Lisieux begged one last time. "They won't notice if we aren't there."

"They will notice," Gigi said with an edge of exhaustion as she undid her seat belt and opened the door.

The three of us didn't move. She and my dad opened our doors. I squeezed Avi's hand and scooted out of the Range Rover.

Lisieux took my arm and I hers. The slick snow and loose stones made it difficult to find our footing in the heeled boots we wore. Avi leaned heavily against our father; she wanted to be carried though he didn't want to pick her up. Gigi walked alone at the front, like a general leading the charge. Her shoulders were straight, her gray hair pulled back into a sophisticated wrap.

We followed dutifully, the uneven gravel giving way to smooth asphalt. We were able now to walk faster, but we didn't. Or perhaps I didn't. Lisieux, I realized, was delicately pulling me forward. I allowed her to lead me; I couldn't think clearly enough to control my own actions.

When we reached the sidewalk, I raised my head. The side of the church was visible from where we stood. In the secluded parking area next to the church sat the long black car.

Lisieux said, "Why would they have a hearse here? There's no body."

I felt the blood drain from my face, my mind becoming fuzzy. Before I understood what was happening, the world faded and my body became heavy as it hit the ground.

"Oh my gosh, Siena!" Lisieux cried as she reached for me, trying and failing to keep me from hitting the concrete.

Dad hurried to us. "What happened? Are you okay?" he asked, helping me to my feet.

"She tripped," Lisieux said.

Did I trip? I didn't remember. I could remember nothing, my mind blank as I stared without blinking at the curtained windows of the black hearse.

"She's wet," Lisieux said as she took my left arm. My father took my right.

"She fell into the snow," Gigi said with practicality, her hand around Avi's. "Come on, we can't be late."

My dad and Lisieux helped, or more accurately, forced me forward.

"I don't want to go in," I said, my voice thick as they escorted me, one at each arm, up the stairs.

"This isn't about you or us," Gigi said under her breath as two men in black suits opened the doors in front of us. "This is about supporting Brenda and Phil and praying for Thomas's soul, something he certainly needs."

Before I realized it, I was inside. The church was dim compared to the bright daylight behind us. The sunlight streaming in around us reminded me of the day of the fall festival, of Thomas coming in, surprising Luca and me. The brightness had blinded me for a moment so that I wasn't sure it was Thomas. What would've happened if I hadn't been blinded? If I'd seen him, from the beginning, for who he was and what he wanted?

The nauseatingly sweet smell of fresh flowers overpowered the narthex. There was a four-foot standing bouquet on each side of a framed picture of Thomas. In the formal picture his hair was combed back, he wore a coat, a tie, and a subtle smile. I wondered what this picture had been taken for—his senior picture for the school yearbook?

Lisieux and I obediently entered the door our dad was holding open for us. Gigi and Avi were already in the back row. We quickly scooted in next to them. The pew in front of us contained another family from church. For the most part they kept to themselves and didn't join the chatter—good or bad—

that often happened when groups of people were gathered. They truly were at Mass every Sunday for the Eucharist and nothing else. The mother, Jody, offered me a sincere smile before facing forward again. Her kind gesture made tears prickle my eyes.

The church was full and smelled of the flowers covering most of the altar. The flowers were grouped in bunches, separated by multiple large framed pictures of Thomas. There was no coffin … there was no body to put into it.

Only the pictures.

At each picture, people gathered, dabbing their eyes with tissues. Some were holding on to each other; others stood by themselves—each mourning in their own way.

There were so many people my age, some I had gone to school with many years ago. Many others I didn't recognize. Their presence reminded me of how much Thomas was loved.

From her spot several pews up, Thomas's ex-girlfriend, Beth, turned and glared at me. Those around her took turns doing the same. The irony struck me painfully—Thomas was loved … I was hated.

A hush fell over the church. Everyone stood. I kept my eyes straight ahead, focused on the four dozen or so white lilies that stood on either side of the framed picture in the very front of the altar. In this picture, Thomas was sitting at the beach. The waves were crashing against rocks behind him, his brown hair falling gently into his eyes. He looked very much like he had the Sunday he first spoke to me. This picture was recent, taken a few weeks before his death. His eyes were bright and blue, with no hint of darkness. His smile was confident, as always. I wondered who he was smiling at, who was on the other side of the camera. I doubted it was either of his parents; from what he had told me, he wasn't typically around them. Friends were far more important to him, and that showed in the church being packed with people our age.

Heads gradually turned forward when Thomas's father practically carried his sobbing wife up the aisle. I lowered my gaze, focusing on the back of the oak pew in front of me. My hands rested against it, keeping me steady as my heart threatened to stop beating. This was too much. Too much to experience. Too much to feel. The sobs came again and again from Brenda as others helped Phil guide her to the pew reserved for them at the front of the church.

Beside me, Avi was holding on to Dad, her face buried into his jacket. I hated that she was here. I hated that any of us were here.

Father Luke's placid voice came over the speakers. It was difficult for me to understand his words, not because they were unclear but because my mind wouldn't settle. I mimicked the movements of those around me and sat.

A familiar voice spoke into the microphone. I raised my head. Beth was standing at the ambo. She dabbed at her eyes as she began the first reading. Her voice was strikingly strong. Her presence startled me for a reason I couldn't fully explain. She was friends with Thomas; they had dated last summer, and their parents were close friends, so why would she not be the one to deliver the readings at his funeral?

Somehow, her standing up at his funeral added even more hurt.

If she'd been the one with him when he died, would they hate her as they hated me?

Beth stepped down, bowing respectfully on her way back to her pew. Brenda grabbed onto Beth, pulling her in for a heavy embrace, each of them breaking down into sobs. Brenda held on to Beth until, finally, Phil gently helped his distraught wife sit back down. She fell against his chest. Beth's mother rushed out of their pew and took hold of her daughter, guiding her back to their seats.

Chastity, Beth's best friend, sat with her parents in the pew behind Beth's family. She turned dramatically in her seat, searching the rows behind her until her gaze fell on me. If looks could kill, I would've been dead. So much hatred, it physically hurt. Others saw what was happening and joined in. No one wanted me there; everyone despised me.

The young mother in the row in front of me sat taller, and so did her husband. Together they blocked most others from being able to glare at me. I slumped farther in my seat, so grateful for their simple heroic gesture.

The responsorial psalm was sung by the church's main cantor. Afterward, Father Luke stood. He wiped his eyes as he approached the ambo. It was unusual to witness much emotion from him, though there had been a great deal of it during these last few weeks. Father Luke was not a new priest, but this had been the first parishioner he had lost to supposed suicide.

He read the Gospel clearly, until he got to the words "Jesus wept," and then he, too, wept. He recovered and began his homily.

"Our faith demands that we view this world as testing grounds for our eternal life. Thomas understood that better than most. He and I had several conversations regarding the importance of choices made in this life, in preparation for the next. In fact, a week before Thomas died, he spoke to me of the supernatural, questioning my understanding of it. He was a young man who was searching, trying to understand all that this life and the next have to offer. He was wise to ask such questions. We should all ask such questions. Life is often not fair, which is clear in this case. Of all the parishioners I have, I never would have dreamt that Thomas's life would be the one to be cut short—certainly not in this way. He was so cheerful and helpful. Always willing to help at any of the church functions."

Father Luke wiped at his eyes. "How this happened, I do not understand. Life is a mystery, at times a tragic mystery. If we take any solace, it is that we can be assured that, like the good thief, Thomas is with our Lord this day in paradise because, as we are all aware, mental illness does not keep us from our Lord. Thomas's tragic actions at the end of his life do not negate or represent who he was. As the Scripture passage says, 'Jesus wept,' just as we all weep. There is heartbreak—

but it is short-lived for those of us who, like Thomas, focus our attention on eternal life."

After a few more minutes in which Father Luke extolled how virtuous Thomas was, the homily was over. I felt as though the last ten minutes had been about someone I'd never met. Did Father Luke actually believe those things about Thomas?

On his way across the altar, Father Luke removed a tissue from the pocket beneath his long robes. As he blew his nose, I was struck by his simplicity. There was no malice in this priest. He was good to an extreme and expected others to be the same. To realize that there was another side to Thomas would be nearly impossible for someone like Father Luke. Instead, he saw in Thomas exactly what Thomas wanted him to: someone apparently deserving of immediate sainthood.

As the muted sobs rang throughout the pews around me, I wondered if I was the one who was wrong. Perhaps Thomas was as holy as Father Luke believed, who all the people here—except my family—thought him to be. I wished I could believe that.

I followed the others and knelt during the Consecration of the Eucharist, using the opportunity to bury my face into my folded hands. The darkness of my hands brought me the briefest moment of solace.

When I raised my eyes, I saw Father Luke stepping down from the altar. He went directly to Thomas's parents and gave them the Eucharist. Thomas's mother received the holy presence of Jesus where she sat, too distraught to stand or kneel.

His father received while standing beside her. Others around them stood and went up to receive the Eucharist.

Our turn came sooner than expected since many in the church were not Catholic and didn't go forward to receive. I followed solemnly behind Avi. My skin burned as the whispers followed me up the aisle.

Finally, we reached the front, where Father stood. Directly behind him was the framed photograph of Thomas at the beach. He was so often laughing in life, yet in the end there was no laughter, no joy, nothing of the boy whose eyes danced in this picture.

Father Luke held the white wafer in front of me, the source and summit of our faith, as he often referred to the Eucharist.

"Body of Christ," he said solemnly.

"Amen," I stated, and he placed the thin consecrated Host in my left hand. My righthand fingers lifted it into my mouth and then made the sign of the cross.

I didn't chew the thin wafer; instead, I allowed it to dissolve in my mouth as I made my way back to my pew, careful to keep my eyes focused on the scuffed pine floor. I thought of what Luca had said after he came to that first Mass and sat where we now sat. He had felt the presence of God in the Eucharist and questioned me as to why the one at the altar, Thomas, had not received it. I felt the papery wafer dissolve in my mouth. It was easy to forget what it was, but the demons that surrounded or, perhaps, occupied, Thomas didn't forget. The sacred presence of Jesus repulsed them and therefore repulsed Thomas. Life would be so much easier if I could see the world as it truly was.

A prayer silently entered my heart: *Help me to see what is hidden.*

The time to kneel ended; we stood. A moment later, Thomas's funeral Mass was over. I should've felt relief, but I didn't. There was no way for us to slip out unseen.

Father Luke was waiting to escort Thomas's parents from the church. Brenda leaned clumsily on Phil as they made their sorrowful procession down the aisle.

My father, who was closest to the crowd streaming out of the church, remained seated. He must have felt the stares of daggers shooting his way, but he did not react. His gaze was above the emptying pews, transfixed on the crucifix. Dad was familiar with suffering; he had survived it before. He would survive it now.

Gigi said, "It's time for us to go outside now."

Her posture was commanding. Unlike my father, she was standing, her head raised, her shoulders back. She wasn't hiding. She was adamantly refusing the guilt others were assigning to us.

My father did as she instructed, Avi still clinging to him.

"Why did you make her come?" I whispered to Gigi.

Gigi's expression softened when she noticed her youngest grandchild. "Hiding is not our way," she said, turning from me and exiting the pew.

As we left the church, the fresh air felt surreal. Surreal that cold air would be stinging my lungs when Thomas was no longer breathing.

We stood to the side. The rest of the church was filing past Thomas's parents, in a sort of line of misery. How did his parents have the strength to speak to each of them?

"We need to say something to Brenda and Phil," Gigi said when the line was beginning to dwindle.

Avi clung tighter to Dad.

Lisieux's eyes became wide. I took her hand in mine. We'd face this together as we'd faced Mom's death together.

It was as if the crowd parted to allow us to reach Brenda and Phil.

"There are no words we can speak," Dad said, embracing Phil.

Phil didn't answer; he merely nodded, allowing my father to comfort him.

"We're so sorry for your loss," Lisieux managed to get out between tears.

"Thank you," Phil said, no longer being held by Dad.

Brenda sniffed. "What about you, Siena? Are you sorry for the death of our son?"

Her words were biting. I felt Gigi's arm tighten around mine.

"Of course she is," Gigi said lovingly. "None of us have stopped crying. His death,"—her voice choked—"it is tragic."

"I wasn't asking you, Gemma," Thomas's mother said coldly. "I was asking your granddaughter, the one who broke my son's heart, causing him to end his life."

"I … we …." I stumbled over the words. "We were never dating. He—he didn't care for me in that way. We never even held hands."

"It doesn't make sense, does it?" she said, glaring at me.

"N-no," I stammered, my face burning.

"That's what I keep thinking too. It doesn't make sense. Yet here we are. My son is dead, and you're standing here," she said, her voice acidic.

Everyone was staring.

My heart was racing, my body sweating. I felt as if I would pass out.

My father spoke, his words calm and in control. "We are sincerely sorry for the loss of your son. We pray for him and you both daily."

"And what about yourself?" Brenda said, her word laced with venom. "Do you pray for yourself?"

"Yes," my dad answered kindly, scooting me out of the way to block me from Brenda.

"That's good, Paul, because from what I hear, *you* need it."

In a flat tone, Phil stated, "You should probably go, Paul."

My father nodded. "We're all heartbroken by Thomas's death." He turned, ushering us between his arms.

After we were away from the crowd, he scooped up Avi and carried her to the car.

The car unlocked as we approached it. He opened the back door and slid a crying Avi inside. Lisieux slipped in behind her, and Dad shut the door.

"Get in," Gigi commanded.

I did as she instructed, and she shut the door behind me. Then she got in and shut her door. Dad started the engine and drove the back way out of the parking lot.

"You shouldn't have made us come," Lisieux said. "You definitely shouldn't have made Avi come! Why did you, anyway?"

"We thought it best," Dad said in a gentle tone.

"No, you didn't," Lisieux retorted. "You didn't want us to be there any more than we did. Gigi made the decision, and you didn't want to go against her. Just like you've been doing every second since Thomas died."

The car became silent; all that could be heard was Avi's soft sobbing. I put my arm around her and held her against my chest. Lisieux placed an angry hand on Avi's leg. The three of us had survived loss before; we would survive it now. The car made its way safely through the snow-covered streets. Our gates swung slowly open. The wind and snow had covered the tracks we'd left earlier. There was no longer a difference between our driveway and the yard around it. Both appeared exactly the same, yet Dad never veered from the path.

Four

Dad opened the garage door and pulled inside. Jason's rusted jeep sat in the spot where Gigi's car typically was. It was there at Gigi's insistence. She'd told them to take her place in the garage because she wasn't going to drive in the snow, so they may as well keep their car free of snow and ice. Sam and Jason refused her offer for the first few days they lived with us, but Gigi's stubbornness eventually won out. Her car now sat on the side of the driveway, covered in several inches of snow. The dry jeep reminded me that they had intended to go to the funeral today. It was the reason they were home on a weekday. Would their presence there have made things better? Probably not, but having Luca beside me would have.

We went into the house, and Gigi closed the door behind us, blocking the cold of the garage from the warmth of the kitchen. The delicious smells of roasting turkey, sweet potato casserole, and homemade rolls brought me joy—until I remembered I didn't deserve joy. Instead, the mouthwatering aromas brought additional guilt. I shouldn't be allowed to enjoy such good things, not so soon after Thomas's funeral.

Sam stood at the counter where she had been making salads. Jason was stirring a pot on the stove. Lisieux was sitting at the table, legs crossed, furiously pumping her right foot up and down, teeth gritted.

"How did it go?" Sam asked as we entered.

"The service was as nice as it could be," Gigi said plainly.

Sam said, "I suppose it was good we weren't there?"

Still fuming, Lisieux exclaimed, "None of us should have been there!"

"I don't think it would've mattered if you were there or not," Dad said, sounding exhausted.

"It was that bad?" Sam asked, coming around to where we stood, placing a hand on Avi's back as she clung to Dad.

Sam loved Avi, perhaps not as much as a mother loved a child, but certainly as much as an aunt loved a niece, and Avi felt the same for Sam.

"It was what I expected," Gigi answered, her voice void of emotion.

"You expected that?" I asked with frustration.

"They're hurting," Gigi stated.

"That doesn't mean they can be so cruel," Avi said, startling all of us with the loudness of her voice. Between bouts of crying she said, "Why … are they … so mean?"

Jason loved Avi as much as his wife did. "Honey," he said to Avi, "when people are hurt, they hurt others. I'm sorry you have to learn that so young."

There was a time—many times, if I was being honest—when I used to wonder what Sam saw in him. She was smart and beautiful, with her naturally blonde hair and joyful air. Jason, in contrast, wasn't particularly attractive or educated, but now I understood. He is definitely one of the good ones, as Luca's mom would say.

"Jason's right," Dad said, squeezing Avi and placing her feet on the wood floor while keeping an arm around her. "Hurt people lash out. Brenda's deeply hurt. I didn't expect her to lash out like that, but I should have. Maybe we shouldn't have gone today. I thought it was the right thing to do, but thinking about it now .... Brenda must see us and wish over and over that we'd done more and were somehow able to stop him."

"I wish the same thing," I said.

"Thomas did what he did. None of you can change that," Jason said. "It's the way the world works. People do awful stuff, and the rest of us have to deal with it. Doesn't make it right or fair, just the way it is. Thomas's parents—they have to deal with what their son did. That's the way it is. And you all are gonna have to deal with people blaming you. Not right or fair, just the way it is."

Dad lowered his head, his hand resting on Avi's back. "Yes," he said. "It is what it is. With time, Brenda will heal and her hatred for us will fade."

I crossed my arms, my heavy coat still on, offering the smallest amount of protection. "She wasn't calling all of you murderers, she was calling *me* one."

"Avila," Dad said, "why don't you go into my office and play on your screen for a little bit."

She replied, "I heard what Thomas's mom said."

"There's no point in trying to keep us out of it," Lisieux said. "You made us go today. You made us be in the center of this whole awful thing."

Dad groaned in frustration.

Sam went to the microwave and pushed a button. "If you're going to stay in here, you might as well have some hot chocolate. I have it ready to go. I figured you'd need some warmth when you got home. Avi, let go of your dad and sit beside your sister." The microwave beeped. She opened the door and took out two mugs of cocoa.

Avi released Dad as Lisieux scooted over to let her in beside her at the table.

Dad exhaled audibly and hung up his coat on a hook by the door to the garage.

Sam placed the hot cocoa in front of Avi and Lisieux.

"Thank you," Lisieux whispered as she held the mug but did not attempt to drink it.

"Would you like some, Siena?" Sam asked kindly.

"Hot chocolate won't fix being called a murderer," I said softly.

"Sit down," she said, leading me to the counter stool. "I'll make you some anyway."

I sat without thinking.

"How'd they get the idea Siena killed Thomas?" Jason asked, removing the saucepan from the stove.

Dad said, "It wasn't literal."

Lisieux sat up straighter in her chair and said, "His mom said Siena broke Thomas's heart, so he killed himself."

"Thomas didn't care a thing about Siena," Sam said, then met my eyes. "I'm sorry, sweetie, but it's true."

"Don't be sorry for the truth," I said, holding the hot mug that Sam had placed in front of me. Its heat was burning my frozen fingers.

"Brenda seemed to acknowledge that as well," Dad said, sliding into a spot at the table beside Avi.

"Problem is they got half the story," Jason said, "and without the other half, the story don't make sense. 'Course, with the other half, the story ain't believable, so either way, his death isn't an easy one to explain or accept." Jason was taking the wrapper from the stick of butter, preparing to butter the rolls that would soon be out of the oven.

"No, his death is certainly not easy to accept," Dad said, his back slouched against the back of the seat.

Jason put down the butter and gripped the side of the counter, leaning forward. "Seems to me, all this stuff with Thomas's parents and whoever else is a distraction."

"A distraction?" Lisieux said.

"A way to make you all fight with each other. If you believe in evil—which I guess by now we all do—then you gotta believe it isn't random. It's thought out. It sounds like your church is being torn apart by all of this, with people hating each other. Seems like instead of people praying for Thomas's soul people are fighting. If you ask me, that means evil's winning a second time."

Sam went to him and slid an arm around the small of his back, giving him a quick kiss on his scruffy face. "One of the many reasons I love you," she said.

"I thought you married me for my good looks," he teased.

She kissed him. "That's another of the many reasons."

"Where's Luca?" I asked.

"In his room," Sam said.

"He was cold," Jason said with a chuckle.

In a sarcastic tone, Lisieux said, "How unlike him."

Sam said, "It took me five winters before I stopped shivering."

"Yeah. She used to get the fire so hot I'd be stripped down to my underwear and still sweating," Jason said with a snort.

Lisieux groaned. "That was a mental image I didn't need."

"I'm going to find him," I said as I began to climb the stairs.

Jason said, "Dinner will be ready in about thirty minutes."

"I'm not hungry," I said from halfway up the stairs.

Sam called out, "But Luca is."

She was right, of course. Luca never missed a meal and often ate a second meal after the rest of us were done.

Five

Luca's room was at the end of the longest hallway on the second floor. My father had suggested he move into this room because it had a fireplace—at least that was the reason he'd given to Luca. The actual reason was because it was the farthest room from mine, with my dad's room safely between the two. It was not that he minded having Luca here or minded us spending most of our free time together. But the quarter of a mile between our rooms gave Dad the sort of buffer he wanted.

After all, we had other rooms with fireplaces, though Luca's was one of the nicer ones, with drywall and insulation, things Luca required to not freeze to death. I tapped at the slightly open door and stepped in.

He was sitting in a beanbag chair next to the glowing hearth, a book in his hand and a sock hat covering his curly hair. This was his typical position when he was not at work or with us in the main part of the house. I watched as he read. Unlike Lisieux, when Luca read, he had no idea what was going on around him. The rest of the world disappeared and all that existed was him and the book. No wonder he didn't hear us come home.

I went into the room. He finally noticed me when I sat on the chest that served as the bed's footboard.

"Hi," he said, closing the book.

He placed it on the area rug and came and sat beside me. He put his hands in his lap, his hip touching mine. "I'm sorry I wasn't there for you. Aunt Sam told me Gigi asked her not to let me go. I shouldn't have listened to her."

"You being there would've been worse," I said. "Thomas's mom already blames me for everything. If you'd been there, she would have been even more hateful to me. They all would've," I said, the image of Beth's stares entering my mind.

"I'm sorry," he said.

I suddenly felt cold; I stood and went to the fire. "She thinks my rejecting Thomas caused him to lose his mind and his life."

"That doesn't make any sense," he said, placing a hand on my arm.

His amber eyes were so sincere, so comforting.

"She acknowledged that, I think," I said, trying to make sense of Brenda's words. "But that didn't make it better. For some reason, that made her angrier. She hates me more than anyone has ever been hated."

"You were one of the last people her son was around before he died. She's not going to like you right now, or maybe ever."

"Thank goodness the police were there to witness him … jump. Otherwise, she'd probably think I dragged him up the cliff and threw him off. She's so vile."

He rubbed the upper part of my arm, his nails appearing white against his caramel skin. "That's not fair to her. Of course she hates you, and of course none of it makes sense to you.

Because it doesn't make sense. If you remove the spiritual side of the world, which we did when we didn't tell the police about the demons, then none of it makes any sense. Her outgoing, popular son suddenly became psychotic and jumped off a cliff without any family history of psychosis. How could she possibly accept that? And then today, you are all there, healthy … alive. How could she not hate you?"

"Your uncle said basically the same thing. But what were we supposed to do? Tell the police we thought Thomas was possessed?"

"We didn't *think* he was possessed, Siena. He *was* possessed." Luca guided me to sit in the beanbag chair, and he sat on the rug, beside me.

I watched the fire. "You've gotten good at building fires," I said, remembering some of the sloppy, smoky fires Luca made when first learning.

"Practice makes better," he said, scooting closer to the hearth.

I leaned my head against the top of the chair, the rustling of the beans inside loud as my ear pressed against the leather.

"Can't we be normal?" I said in defeat. "The inn's gone, the funeral's over. Can't we forget all the crazy demon stuff and move on?"

He rocked forward onto his knees and adjusted a piece of wood. It instantly caught, causing bright yellow flames to shoot up. He leaned back. "You can do that. You can pretend none of this ever happened. It's never been an option for me and not one

I would choose even if I could. If that's what you need to do to get through life, then go ahead."

"You think I'm a coward."

"I think you're like most people. You'd rather avoid the uncomfortable stuff."

"The uncomfortable stuff doesn't bother you?"

"Siena, I see dead people and feel demons. Trying to pretend I don't would be impossible or make me crazy, so, no, I choose to face reality, even if it's uncomfortable."

I sensed he was trying to hide his judgment of me. I lowered my eyes away from his gaze.

He draped an arm across his knee, and his voice softened. "You're dealing with a lot, and I don't blame you if you want to pretend none of it's real, but that's all it would be—pretend. Your rejecting the existence of the spiritual world doesn't change its existence, it just changes how you deal with the world, and not necessarily for the better."

"Is being normal that bad?" I said, almost begging him to let me forget the past six weeks.

"Not if that's who you were made to be," he said, with his eyes on mine—those kind, sweet, caring eyes.

There was nothing normal about him. I leaned back in the beanbag, my head resting on it as the heat of the flames caused my face to flush red.

"Maybe I was made to be normal," I said, unsure if I wanted that to be true or not.

"Is that what you want, to be like everyone else? To go through life never understanding the first bit of reality. To live a lie?"

Tears starting to form, I turned my eyes from his and focused on the darting flames. I closed my eyes a few moments, absorbing the tears.

Then I watched the flames. "Their lives are easy," I said, my tone pleading.

If Luca let me be normal, if he let me forget, maybe I could. Maybe this could all go away.

"Yes," he said, sounding disappointed. "Their lives are easy—or at least they appear easier than ours. That's why lies exist—to make lives appear easier. But behind every lie is a truth, a truth that can only go untold for so long. Don't forget that in the end, everything that's been hidden will be brought to the light."

I said, "I liked you better before you knew how to quote the Bible."

He smiled. "There's so much truth in it. It's hard not to quote it."

"If I had your gifts, it would be different," I said, thinking again of the small prayer I'd uttered during the funeral. "Maybe then, things would make more sense. As it is, I feel like nothing makes any sense."

I stood up, my face cooling as it rose away from the flames.

"Where are you going?" he asked, standing beside me.

"My room. This day needs to end." I was so tired I wondered if I could make it without passing out on the way.

"What about dinner?" Luca asked, watching me with concern.

"You can have my portion," I said.

Six

Sometime later I heard the faint tapping of someone outside my door. I tried to open my eyes or call out to them to enter or go away. I wasn't sure which I would've said, but it didn't matter. I was too tired to utter a word. In a moment I was asleep again, my dreams jumping from one scene to another. Even in my unconscious mind I wondered why this was. Why could I not stay in one place for more than a few seconds? In the deep darkness of night, when my body was most tired, my dreams turned to nightmares, or I hoped that's all they were. My body couldn't move; my eyes were open but so tired they were trying to close.

Above me, darkness swarmed … not the darkness of nighttime but another form, an evil form. There was no shape, yet it existed, something more than the nothingness that should have been above me. It plunged toward me, screeching—a furious, terrifying scream. I tried to move. My body wouldn't respond. Was this a dream? An awful, horrible dream where I was being attacked by darkness? Or was it real? Again, the shapeless form hovered above me; again it swooped inches from my body, its wide gaping mouth shrieking in fury. Fear encapsulated me … my heart beat so fast. I tried to move; I tried to turn my head away from the horrible open mouths. There were so many of them, all together in one shape. There was no good. Only evil. They dived, again and again, each time inches from my face. Some invisible barrier kept them from reaching me, enraging them as it protected me.

My body lay rigid, flat against the bed. I tried again and again to move; I could not. I could do nothing except watch these creatures come closer and closer with each pass—their cries like shrieking banshees.

My brain went blank from the terror. I could not move, I could not think. The word *pray* entered my thoughts. Yes, I wanted to pray. No words formed in my mind, until … *Our Father, who art in heaven* ... the words, so ingrained after being prayed thousands of times in my life, came quickly. My lips did not move, but the words to this simple prayer formed perfectly in my mind.

The figures disappeared immediately. The night became suddenly still. My body was alive; I could move again. I scrunched myself against the headboard, pulling into a tight ball. My heart beating frantically, I wanted to yell for help, but I was too scared. Moonlight streamed through a crack between the curtains. Next to my bed hung a delicate silver crucifix. A gift from my mother on my first birthday. I took the cross, the metal cold in my hands, and pressed it against my chest.

Was it a dream? Was it all a dream? The night was so quiet. Had there really been something in here? Something that hated me, something that wanted to hurt me but couldn't because of some invisible barrier? If so, did it leave because of the prayer? My body started to relax, my feet slipping down under the covers. My pulse slowed; my breathing was heavy, yet becoming more normal with every passing second of silence.

Nothing was there; I was alone in my room. Slowly I stretched my legs out and lowered my head to the pillow. It had been a dream, an awful nightmare. Nothing more.

With the cold metal cross in my hand, the thought of returning it to its spot at my bedside entered my mind, then quickly left. I would not release it. With my right hand I crossed myself and I prayed another Our Father, followed by the Prayer of St. Michael the Archangel. This prayer explicitly asks God to return to hell Satan and all the evil spirits who prowl about the world seeking the ruin of souls.

I pulled the covers up to my shoulders. I still grasped the cross. What a strange faith I had. A faith that in one of its most well-known prayers spoke about demons. How very strange.

It was all a nightmare. I was sure of that now. My mind was calm and my body was getting there. Within minutes I was asleep.

***

The morning was silent. I stood looking out of the snow-covered window, still wearing the dress from Thomas's funeral. One of the blankets my mother had knitted me hung from my shoulders. The rest of the night had been as quiet as this morning. A dreamless sleep had followed the nightmare. That's all it was—a nightmare.

Back in bed, I stared out the window. The treetops were covered in white and the towering cliff showed only a few bare stone edges. The spot where the inn had been appeared no different from here. There'd been no lights there since Thomas died; it was only those lights in the darkness that I could view from my room.

I fumbled through the bedsheets until I found the little silver crucifix. Reverently, I hung it back on the nail that protruded from the wall beside the bed. My gaze moved from the crucifix to the picture of my mom and me. I went to it, holding the cold pewter frame, I stared down at her sparkling eyes. What would my mom have done if the first boy she had the slightest feelings for had jumped from a cliff, into a raging ocean, and she was now blamed and despised by all who knew him?

The corner of my eye detected movement. I jumped reflexively at the snowball hitting the window. Avi was beneath my window, a pile of snowballs beside her. She threw another, and it hit right below the window.

"Come play with me," she yelled up at me.

For the first time in weeks she wasn't clinging to my father or looking horribly morose.

I stepped away from the window. I returned the heavy picture frame to the shelf. I wasn't sure what my mom would do with the rest of life, but I at least knew what she would do in that moment. She'd be outside with her youngest, throwing snowballs at my window. I smiled—this simple upward movement of my mouth brought me some peace. At the window I held up my finger to tell her "One minute."

I changed out of the wrinkled dress, hanging it in the back of my closet where I hoped it would miraculously disappear.

I dug through my drawers, finding my fleece-lined running pants and snow pants. From the shelf in front of me I grabbed a fluffy turtleneck, and quickly dressed.

My steps were light going down the stairs. I was happy to have a reason to go outside. Happy to have a reason to play.

"What are you doing?" Lisieux asked as she and Gigi sat at the kitchen table.

"Going outside to play with Avi," I said. "Want to come?"

She hesitated, and then shook her head. "Thank you for asking, though."

"Always," I said. I pulled on my snow boots and coat.

"Have fun," Gigi said. Both hands were holding her mug of tea.

"If Avi has anything to do with it, I will," I said. Opening the door with determination, I hoped it was true: that my sad little sister had turned back into the joyful one.

The cold burned my lungs, making me feel alive.

A snowball hit the side of my face. Without thinking, I bent down and retaliated as quickly as I could. Avi shrieked in delight as she dodged my snowball by falling into a snowdrift. Jackson ran between us, barking, leaping into the air, trying to catch the snowballs that flew between Avi and me. Avi was a good shot, better than I remembered.

"It's no fair. You already have your snowballs made," I yelled as she pelted me again and again while I sought cover in the corner of the house—the corner that held the burnt handprint left by a holy soul. The ashen one, made by Thomas, had washed away a week after he died.

"It is, too, fair," Avi said as she snuck toward me with an armful of hardpacked snowballs. "I woke up earlier than you and made them. It isn't my fault you were a sleepyhead."

I worked furiously to form a few snowballs before she got too close.

Suddenly she was there, laughing maniacally as she launched her attack. I returned fire, and when my arsenal was empty I fled. In my attempt to dodge two balls she threw at once, I tripped and fell headfirst into a soft snowdrift. I rolled over, laughing so hard I could barely breathe. She stood triumphantly above me.

"A perfect Siena print," she said, pointing beside me.

I followed the direction of her red glove. She was right. Beside me was a print of my gloved hands going deep into the snow—trying without success to keep my body from reaching the wetness. In the middle was my body, made wide by the snow clothes I wore, topped by the small head complete with the outline of my nose, lips, and eyes. It was, as Avi said, the perfect Siena print.

"Don't move. We need a picture!" she said, running toward the house.

It wasn't a problem not to move; I was exhausted. I sat, panting, as my dad emerged from the house, carrying his phone.

"You even have snow stuck to your hair," he said, chuckling. "This is definitely frame worthy. Say cheese."

"Cheese," I said, squinting into the sunlight.

"Perfect," he said, and showed the phone to Avi.

"Definitely framing that one," Avi said, nodding. "Want to play again?" she asked, bending to form more snowballs.

I held up my hands. "You win, game over. I'm too tired to go on." I pushed myself out of the snow.

"Here, let me help," Dad said, reaching down.

"It's nice that you're having fun," he said, releasing my arm as I brushed off the snow.

His words bothered me. It was nice to have fun, but what right did he have to comment on that? He'd been the most depressed of any of us these last six weeks.

"Yes," I said, keeping my feelings to myself.

"Want to go for a walk?" Avi asked, undoubtedly sensing my change in emotion.

"Yeah, okay." I allowed her to pull me away from our dad.

"You two have fun. I'll be inside, showing everyone this picture," he teased.

As we made our way down the hill, Avi slipped an arm through mine.

"Do you ever feel bad for the chickens?" I asked as we neared their coop. It was so cold they hadn't bothered to come out this morning.

"I feel bad sometimes that chickens are chickens. It's not such a rotten life, but it's not all that great," Avi answered.

"I meant, do you ever feel bad that they have to live outside in the cold."

Avi giggled. "You're so silly. They were made to live outside. Besides, if it's really cold, we plug in their heater."

Behind us, Jackson was sniffing the wall of the coop.

"Come on," Avi called to him as we continued down the trail.

Jackson sprang quickly ahead, clearing a path through the snow for us to follow. Together the three of us entered the trail. It was easier to walk here than in our yard. The trail was covered in snow, but without drifts. When we came to the fork in the trail, Jackson waited for us to catch up before continuing on. With all that had happened in the last two months, he no longer assumed we were going to the beach when we entered the trail. My heart sunk at this. I'd been to the beach once since Thomas died, and that was yesterday, to burn down the inn.

"To the pond," Avi commanded Jackson, pointing to the trail that Luca had taken earlier this morning to go to work. His footsteps in the fresh snow were visible.

The trail twisted its narrow way around barren, snow-laden trees. My gloved hand touched the biggest of the trees, the same one I always touched when I came this way. It was a solid beech tree, the largest on our land. Its trunk was wide enough for me and Avi to join hands and still need Lisieux to reach around and encircle it. The trail turned sharply around this tree.

Avi and I wove our way past it. After a few more steps, we left this trail for the one that led to the pond. The snow here was fresh and fluffy; no one had walked this way since at least last night and probably much longer. Jackson ran in front of us, bounding through the snow, biting it as he went.

"Do you think he does that for fun or because he's mad at it?" Avi asked as we watched our dog.

"For fun," I said. "Definitely for fun."

"That's what I think too," she said.

Jackson jumped up to the boulder that stretched out over the pond. When we reached it, I used my gloved hand to brush the snow off. The white powder fell gently onto the frozen surface of the pond. I followed Avi's lead after she sat on our favorite rock. We surveyed the mostly iced-over pond.

Avi said, "I like how the middle never freezes."

"It's because of the spring. It keeps the water warm."

"I already knew that," she said, her elbows pushing against her folded legs, her chin resting on her red gloves.

"Yes, I thought you did."

"I know more than people think I do."

It struck me that her tone sounded ominous. Or perhaps that was the tone I interpreted, sitting in the middle of the still woods. In the distance were muted sounds of construction, though those faraway noises made this place feel all the more remote.

"I'm sure you do," I answered, watching a fish swim in the center of the pond—a strange sight when there were inches of snow around it.

"There's a deer behind that tree," I said, pointing subtly in the direction where Jackson was glaring. His tail moved from side to side, clearing away the snow. Thankfully, he'd never tried to chase a deer.

Avi moved her body a little. "Yes, I already saw it," she said.

"No, you didn't."

"Yes, I did." She blinked up at me. "I told you I know lots of stuff other people don't."

"Oh yeah? Prove it," I said, teasing.

"Dad thinks all of this is his fault."

"Yes," I said somberly, "he does think that."

"But do you know why he thinks it?" she said, her face turning to me with an expression that made my skin prickle.

I hesitated. "No, not really."

"I do."

"How?"

"Because I pay attention to people. I watch them like you watch the trees and the ocean."

"How do you know I do those things?" I asked.

"I already told you, I watch people. You are people."

"Yes, I am people," I acknowledged to my baby sister, who suddenly seemed my equal. "What about Dad?"

"He was friends with Great-great-grandmother," she said sadly.

"Yes." My shoulders relaxed a little. Maybe she knew nothing more than I did—our father had, in fact, been friends with his great-grandmother. Despite his parents' warnings.

"He spent a lot of time with her inside the inn," Avi said, shaking her head in clear disappointment.

"He didn't understand what he was doing," I said, trying to defend him, not for his sake but for hers. I didn't want her to carry anger against our father.

Avi said, "He can't remember most of what happened in there. He says he remembers the fireplace, but nothing else. He can't even tell Gigi what the inside of the inn looked like."

"It was a long time ago," I said. "I forget stuff that happened yesterday. It's not a big deal that he can't remember stuff that happened before we were born."

"He knew about us," Avi remarked.

I was silent, unsure of what she was trying to say.

"He knew he'd have three daughters," she added.

"How could he?"

"I heard him whisper to Gigi that his great-grandmother told him."

"He remembers that?"

She nodded. "And I was the third girl, and after that, Mom …. After that, there were no more children."

Her face was so sad that she didn't look like Avi. Instead, I realized she looked a great deal like me.

"None of that has anything to do with Thomas," I said, refusing to be overcome by the sadness that our mom's death always evoked.

"No, it has to do with our family." She looked up at me, her green eyes so wide, so young, so wounded. "It has to do with you."

"Me?" I said, startled. "How could it have to do with me?"

"You're the oldest," she said somberly, her voice so much like mine it was unsettling.

"What difference does that make?" I inhaled slowly, calming my racing thoughts. She was eight. Yes, she was smart, but she was still only eight.

"Haven't you noticed how closely they're watching you?"

She was overreacting, reading things into innocent actions. "That's because they're worried about me. A guy I was sort of friends with jum—it's because of Thomas."

"They're worried about each of us, but there's something different about you."

"What's different?"

"You're different."

"Because I'm the oldest?"

She nodded.

I opened my mouth to speak and then closed it. There was nothing to be said. No way to prove her wrong, and I had no reason to do so. Nothing about my dad's past had anything to do with me. How could it? When Gigi's grandmother lived, my father was a boy; he hadn't even met my mother, so I wasn't born. A thought from the night Thomas died fought to enter my mind, a memory of what the demons had said. I pushed it away. It didn't matter. None of that mattered. Maybe there weren't demons—and Thomas really had become psychotic.

Memories of that night forced themselves in front of me. Thomas's black eyes, so cold, so cruel, so inhuman, staring down at me. *It is odd you attempt to keep her from us now, not before.*

Avi asked, "Are you okay?"

My consciousness rested somewhere between past and present. In the present, Avi was there; in the past, she was not.

"You weren't there," I mumbled.

"What?"

The deer in front of us jumped, spooked by something. She sprang away, deeper into the woods.

I hesitated, not wanting to tell Avi while not wanting to keep things from her. There were too many secrets, too much left unsaid.

"The night Thomas died, he said something, or the demons did. Something about how it was weird Dad was trying to protect me from them when he hadn't tried to before."

She said, "Dad has always tried to protect us. It's what he does … he protects us."

"Yes."

Dad has always done what he could to protect us. I stared down at the mostly frozen pond. A memory of another day, many years ago, played in front of me. The pond looked similar to today, covered with ice and snow so that its borders merged with the land. The only clear difference between land and water was in the very center … the center that never froze.

~~~

The day was bright, the birds calling cheerfully from the snowy tree branches above my small form. I was young, half the age Avi was now. My little legs ran faster and faster through the pristine snow. I loved the powder; it was like running through feathers. It was my favorite. I heard the giggles in my memory. I was a happy child. I had no reason not to be happy. My parents were behind me. They never thought I would get so far ahead of them.

The snow was so fluffy, so inviting. I ran faster and faster. I didn't realize I'd gone beyond the hard ground. The pond appeared the same with snow on top of it. But it was not the same.

I saw the open water in front of me and, even at four, I thought it was strange. I didn't understand that I was on the water, only that something was different. Then the bird sounds stopped when my mother screamed. Lisieux was strapped to her chest. I stood still, not daring to move.

"Siena, come this way," my father instructed, his voice calm but firm.

I did as I was told, but it was too late.

Their warning came too late.
~~~

Beneath me the ground moved. But it was not the ground—it was ice. The cracking noise, combined with the terror on my mother's face, made hot tears form in my eyes. It was the last heat I would feel that morning.

Water pooled around me, my snow boots taking in water mixed with chunks of ice. I called to them, but it was too late. My heavy clothes pulled me down. Even if I'd known how to swim, I would not have been able to fight the cold that instantly slowed my legs and arms. My heavy winter clothes soaked in ice water, dragging me quickly to the depths of the muddy pond.

My lungs filled, the cold attacking them. My mind whirled in terror, the sort that only a small child can feel. A small child that up until that moment had never known fear—yet in that moment I was certain I was going to die. I cried under the water, freezing water washing the tears away before they formed. I didn't want to leave my mother. I loved her. I wanted to be with her always. That was my last thought.

I don't remember my father jumping into the icy depths or the frantic search that ensued. It is a truth that the most important moments in a person's life are, in fact, moments … the very shortest that feel like the very longest. I'm told his hand found the hood of my coat that was floating above me. He grabbed it and threw me, like a seal, onto the ice. My frozen body slid toward my mother. I'm told that even though she carried Lisieux against her, she managed to lift me. My father tried to escape the icy trap, but the ice cracked beneath him. Again and again, this happened. My mother was stuck motionless as her daughter lay dying in her arms and her husband fought to escape death's hold.

He screamed for her to go, that he would be okay. He was close now; the ice was thicker, he yelled to her. So she did as he told her to and she ran as fast as she could, carrying both of her daughters through the heavy snow.

Hers was the first voice I heard. She was calling for Gigi, the same panic-stricken scream I'd heard when I stood on the ice. We were still in the woods, the light filtered by the snowy trees above my disoriented eyes. As she did her best to climb the slick hill, my father emerged behind us.

"Let me have her," he said.

She handed me to him. I winced in pain. I didn't want to leave her arms. Her arms were gentle. Lisieux's little hands had been touching my face. His arms were hard and cold. He ran so fast the movement hurt.

Behind us, my mother screamed again and again for Gigi. As my dad reached the kitchen door, it opened. I was barely conscious, but even in that state I could sense the terror my grandmother felt when my dad rushed past her. He didn't stop and took the stairs two at a time—the movement hurting my head, every touch felt like bruises being hit.

Water was pelting me.

I cried. What was going on? I didn't want more water. My father's arms were around me. He was trying to talk. I think he was trying to tell me it was all going to be okay, but his lips were blue and his teeth were chattering so hard I couldn't understand him. Then my mother came. She was wet too, and her arms were open. She no longer carried Lisieux. He handed me to her. My father collapsed onto the floor, breathing hard. Her eyes were on his as she held me. That was when the pain truly began, like thousands of burning needles piercing my skin. I screamed and cried. I fought against her hold, but that made the pain worse, so I stopped fighting.

"Shh, baby girl, shh, it's going to be okay. Your body got too cold, too cold to feel. Now it's heating up. Shh, once it gets back to normal, it won't hurt anymore. Shh, look at Daddy. He's feeling the same as you. It's hurting him too. I can see it in his eyes,"—her voice choked—"but he's staying calm. He's letting the water warm his body. He's letting it bring him back. Shh, shh, now be brave. You're a brave girl. Shh. Dear God, thank you."

She was crying. That was why her voice sounded so strange.

I fell asleep in the shower. The exhaustion was too much for a four-year-old.

When I woke up, both my parents lay beside me. It was dark; I was in their bed, covered in their pillowy comforter and flannel sheets. Their hands clasped as my mom's body pressed against mine, keeping me warm. Her right arm lay across my hip and my dad faced us.

I touched his cheek. It was prickly.

His eyes opened with a look of relief. He whispered, "You gave us a scare."

"I didn't know the ice was soft," I said.

"No, we didn't tell you," he whispered. "We never thought you'd run ahead of us like that. We learned a lot today. We won't make that mistake with your sister."

"I'm sorry," I said.

He moved his hand from my mom's and pushed some hair behind my ear. "It's my fault, not yours. It's my job to protect you. And I failed at my job," he said, his voice catching.

I touched his prickly face.

"You saved me," I said.

"It's my fault you needed saving."

"Yes, Daddy saved you," my mom's voice whispered from behind me. "He will always save you."

Her hand covered mine on his whiskery face. He placed his hand on top of ours and closed his eyes.

~~~

"Siena?" Avi said.

I sat up straighter. "I was thinking about the day I fell into the pond."

"The day you almost drowned?"

I nodded. "It was Dad who saved me. He risked his life to save mine."

"He would do anything to protect us," she said confidently.

I thought about her words. "If you're right about the past, then he didn't."
~~~

"He was younger than Lisieux. Of course, he didn't care about future kids."

"How could anything he did back then have anything to do with our lives?" Even as I asked the question, I knew it didn't matter—not his actions, but my question. Somehow, what he did all those years before he'd met my mom mattered to us now. It was a truth that I didn't understand, but it existed just the same.

Avi dusted some loose powder off the rock we sat on and it floated down onto the snow-covered pond. "I'm not sure, but he and Gigi think stuff back then matters."

The demons do too, I thought silently.

Seven

We heard the distant saws whir to a stop.

Avi raised her head. "Luca will be passing here soon, on his way home for lunch."

"How do you know that?" Neither one of us wore a watch, and I wasn't even sure what time I'd woken up, let alone what time it was now.

"The saws turned off and my stomach growled, two clear signs it's lunchtime," she said as she twisted herself around and began to scoot off the frozen rock.

Jackson beat Avi off the boulder, leaping into the snow. Thanks to the bare woods, we could watch Luca heading up the trail that connected our two houses. Jackson saw him too, and ran straight for him. Off the trail the snow was deeper, never compacted by humans, but Jackson didn't slow his speed.

"Hey, Jackson," Luca's voice rang out.

Avi and I were most of the way up the pond trail when Luca and Jackson appeared before us. Jackson's copper-colored fur was frosted white.

"What are you two up to?" he asked with a twinkle directed at Avi.

"We went on a walk and then stopped to watch the pond," Avi said, her voice suddenly young and happy.

Rarely was a serious tone shared between them. Something about her made him always sound happy, and something about him transformed her back into a little girl without a care in the world.

"Is it lunchtime?" Avi asked as she slipped an arm into Luca's waiting one.

"Yes, ma'am, and I'm starving," he said, patting his stomach.

She giggled. "You're always starving."

"I'm a growing boy."

"You eat enough for three growing boys," Avi teased.

"These days I do," he said, his tone slightly less carefree.

"How's construction going?" I asked, aware that food was a sensitive subject for him.

"They have it framed," Luca said.

"Roof too?" Avi asked.

"Roof too, and the exterior sheathing is supposed to be delivered later today."

Avi said, "It'll look like a house after that."

I added, "You've gotten a lot done in not much time."

"Gigi hired a good contractor. His team shows up," Luca said.

"And every day they show up, you do too," Avi said, proud of Luca. "And you work harder than any of them."

"It's right for me to do what I can," Luca said. "Uncle Jace and Aunt Sam have their jobs. I've got nothing. I should be there helping rebuild their house."

"Dad told us that Mr. Jones is going to offer you a job once your house is done," Avi said, her voice excited.

"Really?" Luca said with surprise.

"That's what Dad told us," I answered.

Luca lifted his shoulders. "I'd like that. Mr. Jones is a good guy and so are the people who work for him."

It was goodness that mattered more to Luca than anything else. Not how smart they were or how hard they worked. Were they good, honest, and kind? It said a lot about Mr. Jones and his team that Luca would want to work with them.

"I'm glad you're happy," Avi said, unlooping her arm and taking his hand as the trail widened.

"It would be nice to earn money, to pay my way," he said with a clear feeling of hope.

"Things work out in the end," Avi said, swinging their arms.

"Yes, I suppose they do. In one way or another," he said more to himself than to us.

Jackson raced into our yard ahead of us.

"Wanna see a snow print of Siena?" Avi asked with a giggle.

Luca looked puzzled.

Avi started laughing harder as she pulled Luca toward the side of the house. "It's fantastic. She was trying to dodge my snowball attack and fell into a snowbank. She made a perfect Siena print."

"Avi, you don't need to show him that," I said, sounding more embarrassed than I actually was.

"Of course I do," Avi said, stopping in front of the smooshed mound of snow.

Luca smiled broadly at the print. "You fell face first?" He chuckled.

"She had a stockpile of snowballs and she was throwing two at a time," I playfully said to defend myself.

"And you tripped," Avi said, making a goofy face.

"And then yes, I tripped."

Luca's smile deepened. "I wish I could've been here for that. It sounds like quite the epic battle."

"Oh, it was!" Avi assured him, nodding her head vehemently.

Luca bent lower, studying the print. "Aww, look at her little nose. Oh hey, there are ear prints too." He pointed, trying but failing not to laugh.

"All right, all right," I said, pulling him up. "Dad already took a picture. Avi's going to frame it. I'm sure she'll give you a copy."

Avi jumped up and down, clapping in delight. "The picture was perfect! She had snow stuck to her hair and everything."

Luca laughed harder. "I can't wait to see it. Maybe you can give me a framed copy too. It could be the first picture we put up in the new house."

"Ha-ha," I said, pretending to be irritated. But the thought of Luca wanting a picture of me, even a goofy snow print picture, made the day warmer.

"Good, you're back," Lisieux said as she appeared in front of us.

Avi asked, "Did you miss us?"

"Not particularly," Lisieux said, turning and going back into the house.

"Then why were you looking for us?" Avi asked. She followed Lisieux into the house.

"Gigi made me." Lisieux stripped off her coat and hung it up. The kitchen was warm with the fragrance of grilled bread.

"Are you sure you weren't missing them even a little?" Luca said, with a wink at Lisieux.

"Oh fine, maybe a little, but mostly I wondered what they could be doing outside for so long," Lisieux said.

It was remarkable how easily Luca was able to make her hard shell melt away.

"We went to the pond," I said, slipping off my boots by the door to keep from tracking snow all over the kitchen.

"Then we ran into Luca on his way back for lunch, so we came home with him. Plus, my stomach was growling." Avi had taken off her coat and was unknowingly flinging chunks of snow around her.

"Your timing is perfect," Gigi said, using a spatula to remove some grilled cheese sandwiches from the pan.

"Where's Dad?" Avi glanced in the direction of his office.

Gigi answered brightly, "He went to work for a few hours. He promised to be home in time for dinner. Enough about that. Who wants grilled cheese sandwiches? I put sliced apples on them, the way you three like, and I have some tomato soup to go along with them."

"He said he was taking the day off," Avi said, her depressed voice returning.

"He took yesterday off," Gigi said. She handed Avi a plate with a hot sandwich on it.

Avi whined, "But he promised." She took the plate and slumped into a chair beside Lisieux.

"It's just for a few hours," Lisieux said, putting an arm around Avi.

"He needed to go in. That's the long and short of it," Gigi said, leaving no room for discussion. "How was the pond?" she said, forcing her voice to sound carefree.

"Mostly frozen," I answered.

"Yes, it's only ever mostly frozen, no matter how frozen it may appear." Whenever it was mentioned, Gigi used the same cautionary tone regarding the pond in wintertime.

The mistake made with me was not repeated with my sisters. Before they could walk, they'd been warned over and over again of the dangers of the pond. My sisters never had to learn that deadly truth for themselves—I was grateful I was the only one.

In the briefest of moments, my mind flicked to Thomas and then back again. I wondered what other dangers I was destined to learn the hard way.

Gigi returned to the table with a sandwich for herself and two extra ones for Luca. This was what happened every Monday through Friday, the days Luca worked with Mr. Jones.

Every day one of us made lunch. Typically it was Gigi, but sometimes it was Lisieux or me, and every day we made double or triple for Luca. This was a battle Gigi fought as soon as Luca began living with us and she got a good look at him. He wasn't eating enough; that was all there was to it, she said. But he disagreed and spent the first week picking and nibbling at his food. Not because he didn't want to eat; he didn't want my dad or Gigi to have to pay for the food he was eating. After the first week, Gigi figured out how to put an end to it. She bought an obscene amount of groceries and said if he didn't eat his fill, the food would go bad, and the money and food would be wasted. Luca finally gave in and began eating more. It was as if he had years of not eating to make up for. In the month since he started eating his fill, he'd gained probably fifteen pounds of needed weight. Now the clothes Gigi bought him when he first moved in, clothes that had hung off him, fit perfectly.

He didn't like that she'd bought him clothes, either. Every time she did, he kept saying he was going to pay her back. He had even started a list of all the money he owed her. The same day she brought the groceries home, she said something to him. Neither told us what it was, but it must have been good because he threw away the list. He continued to eat plenty and gratefully wore the coat and boots she'd bought him, every day to work.

I wasn't sure what would happen when his house was done and the three of them moved out of ours, but I had a feeling Gigi would continue to make sure he had lots of food as well as clothes and shoes that fit.

Gigi crossed herself and said the blessing, the rest of us bowing our heads and praying along. Even Luca now knew the words to the simple blessing of the food.

Each of us crossed ourselves again, then lifted our heads.

"How's your house coming along?" Gigi asked, taking a bite of her sandwich.

Luca finished chewing. "Good. Exterior sheathing should be delivered when we get back from lunch."

"Already?" she said.

Luca took a drink of water. "Yeah. Mr. Jones thinks we'll have the outside walls mostly done by tomorrow. Then we can start with the siding, and electrical can get started on the inside."

"When are the electricians scheduled to be out?" Gigi asked with interest.

"Middle of next week, I think," Luca answered.

"Does Zacharia think building through the winter will be a problem?"

Luca took a drink of water. "He said unless it's so cold he can't get his truck started, he'll be here."

"There will be some of those days," Gigi said.

"That's what he said," Luca responded, shivering at the thought. "That's hard for me to imagine."

Gigi laughed and said, "I've lived here most of my adult life and it remains hard for me to imagine. On those days we enjoy our fireplaces."

Jackson stretched and went to the door leading to the garage. We listened to the sound of the metal garage door rolling up and back down again.

Jackson wagged his tail, waiting expectantly for whoever was home.

"Daddy!" Avi squealed, jumping from her seat and going to him as he came into the kitchen.

"Hi, sweetie," he said, putting an arm around her.

"You look exhausted," Lisieux said, sitting a little taller, a look of concern crossing her face.

Dad hung up his coat. "Long day."

"You were barely gone two hours," Lisieux responded.

"Long morning, then," Dad said. "You sit and finish lunch." He escorted Avi back to the table.

"Will you eat with us?" she asked.

"No." Dad's voice suggested frustration, though not with her. "I'm going into my office for a bit. Get your schoolwork done, and then maybe we can play."

He left, not waiting for us to say more. A second later we heard his door click shut. It had been an uncommon sound before Thomas's death; the door had always been open. Now it was almost always closed. None of us spoke; we had no need. A lot was going on in our dad's life and he wasn't sharing any of it with us—at least not the three of us. Perhaps he was confiding in Gigi. Though, based on her expression, she was as concerned as the rest of us.

Avi was the first to finish eating. She took her plate to the sink. "I'm going upstairs to do my reading," she said gloomily.

Dad's mood affected all of us, whether he wanted it to or not.

"I'll be up in a minute to help you," Gigi said, trying to sound cheerful.

She was doing her best to keep life normal for us, to make up for our dad's absence. She was failing, but she was trying.

Avi didn't respond. She trudged up the stairs.

Lisieux was the next to finish. "I'll go check on her," she said.

Once she was far enough up the stairs, I asked Gigi, "Is Dad okay?"

Gigi had taken a bite or two of her grilled cheese. She was staring absently past me.

"He'll be okay," she said. "Luca needs to get back to work. You should walk him back." Her eyes were transfixed on the empty hallway that led to Dad's office as she stood from the table and took her half-eaten sandwich to the counter. She left the plate and went toward the office.

I spun my body, watching her disappear into the dark hallway.

I was vaguely aware that Luca had taken both of our empty plates and placed them in the dishwasher.

"Come on," he said, "walk me back, like your grandma said."

He was in front of me, offering me his hand to help me up. I took it and allowed him to lead me toward the door.

He released my hand. I returned my attention to my dad's office. If Luca wasn't there, I would've been tempted to stand outside the door to try and overhear something, anything that would help me understand what was going on with him. Yes, he was distraught over Thomas's death; we all were. But there was more to it. Guilt pressed him down, guilt he believed was deserved—based on what Avi had told me. Perhaps he was right.

Luca brought me my coat. "Come on," he said. "Watching a hallway isn't going to answer your questions. Maybe a walk will."

The way he said that made my eyebrows rise. "Do you know something?" I asked in a hushed tone.

He shrugged on his coat, pulled on his hat, and slipped his long fingers into the glove liners that he wore inside the leather work gloves.

"Come on," he said, and opened the door for Jackson and me.

Eight

We each shivered as we stepped out into the cold. It was a little after noon, but already the sun was casting long shadows, making it seem later. Jackson didn't ponder the placement of the sun or even the chill that surrounded him. He ran at full speed and dived into a snowbank after a chickadee that flew away long before the dog got near.

"It wouldn't be all that bad to be a dog," Luca said, as if reading my mind.

I agreed.

Luca guided me forward, slowing at the snow print. "Funny. Avi has never noticed the handprint."

"What makes you think she hasn't?" The burned handprint was a few short yards from the snowbank that held my impression. It was on the side wall of my dad's office, the one without a window.

"She's never said anything to me. Has she to you?" Luca was moving away from the house.

I followed. "No, but that doesn't mean she hasn't noticed. The fact that you disappear every night could not be lost on her or Gigi or even Lisieux."

"You think they know I see souls?" he asked skeptically.

"You told Sam, right?"

He nodded.

"Then they know."

"Wouldn't they say something to me or look at me weird?"

I listened to the squishing sound my feet made on the muddy snow. "After Thomas, your seeing souls isn't all that weird."

He was silent for a moment. "It's good that Aunt Sam told them," he said as we entered the trail. "I don't like secrets."

"Me neither," I said.

Jackson had plowed into a snowbank in his attempt to catch a squirrel that was chattering at him loudly from the snow-dusted branches of a sprawling hemlock.

"What do you know about my dad?" I asked, grateful we were alone and could speak freely.

"There are rumors going around town." He hesitated. "About your family."

"What about us?" I said, concerned by the intensity of his tone.

"Stupid stuff," he said, "but I think it must be getting to your dad. It has to be."

"What sort of stupid stuff?"

He took several steps before beginning. "People don't understand how someone like Thomas could decide to jump off a cliff."

"I already knew that. His mom said the same thing. I told you that," I said, disappointed by the lack of useful information.

Luca ignored my frustration. "The interesting part is that although we took the demons out of the story, they've been put back in."

I squinted up at him. "What do you mean?"

"Some of the people in town believe evil was involved in Thomas's death. More specifically, demons."

Slowly, I asked, "Why would they think that?"

"I told you before, it doesn't make sense. None of it does. When you take the demons out of the story, all you're left with is a perfectly sane kid jumping to his death. Over what? A girl he barely cared about, or to be blunt, didn't care about?"

"Thanks," I said sarcastically.

"You know it's the truth, and so does everyone else. Thomas dated a lot, from what I've heard—a lot, a lot—and he broke up with all the others just fine. Even ones he dated intensely for months, he was never fazed. He simply moved on to the next girl. There's no reason he should respond to you breaking things off with him—when he wasn't even into you—by jumping to his death."

He was right. They all were. None of it made sense. But to leap to demons? I never would've done that. Even now, after all that had happened, there were moments when I tried and sometimes succeeded for a few hours to convince myself it was all a lie.

"Why demons?" I asked, my voice cracking slightly.

Luca was silent as we turned onto the split that led to his house. The faint smell of fresh sawdust was already in the air.

He said, "Because it's the truth, and eventually the truth comes out."

"It's a bizarre truth," I added.

"I'm not the only one who can sense things, Siena. Most people don't get sick, but they can still feel evil. The inn was evil, and all the old people that had been out here when they were younger knew it. When Thomas died, all those old stories started resurfacing."

"That was a long time ago."

"Yes, and before Thomas's death, no one except the old people paid attention to any of it. Then Thomas died and suddenly the crazy ramblings of old people don't seem so crazy."

"What do the old people say?" I asked, bracing myself for the answer.

He exhaled, his warm breath visible in the frigid air. "They said your great-great-grandparents were evil, that demons roamed these woods, and all who came here were the worse for it."

"Nothing but old stories," I said, kicking a clump of snow which disintegrated into powder.

His fingers touched my coat, causing me to stop. His eyes were kind as he gazed down at me. "Siena, those stories are true. They aren't making them up. Demons did roam these woods. I felt them. It's why I wouldn't let you walk anywhere alone."

"I thought it was the ghosts by my house that you were afraid of."

"I told you they didn't scare me, not after the first few nights. Sitting and watching them every night. … I still look forward to that. Aside from your church, it's where I feel the best. They aren't evil, but the other spirits were." He shivered at the memory.

I stepped closer; it made me feel safer. "Are those spirits still here? The evil ones, I mean."

He shook his head subtly, keeping his eyes on mine. "No, they left when Thomas threw the box into the ocean. There was still some dark energy, for lack of a better way to describe it, around the inn. But that's mostly gone, now that your dad burned it down."

"Mostly?" My eyes locked on his.

"It's like a memory. I don't think it can hurt us. It's a memory held in the trees, the stones of the fireplace, the earth where the inn stood. Memories of what that place was."

I slumped back onto a snow-covered boulder, my coat long enough to keep my pants from getting wet.

"A memory of evil," I said, more to myself than to him.

He came toward me, leaning beside me on the boulder, his hip touching mine. Ordinarily, I liked it when he was close, but in this moment it added to the confusion. Demons, ghosts, haunted inns, and then there was Luca—the opposite of all those things. How had I ever been scared of him? Now I wanted to be with him as much as I could. If evil repulsed me and good attracted me, then he was most definitely good.

"You'll get through this. The people in town will forget about it eventually, and your dad is tough. I'm sure he can handle what they're saying about him."

My shoulders pulled back, my spine straightened. "What are they saying?"

Luca rubbed the tips of his steel-toed work boots through the snow until he reached the mud beneath it.

"They say he made a pact with evil. They claim that's the reason for all of his financial success."

"My grandparents were rich before my father took things over," I said numbly.

"They believe the same about your grandmother. They say the evil has gone from generation to generation."

"What about my mom? Was she working for evil too?" I stared blankly into the barren trees.

He scratched at the earth some more. "That's the reason she died. She wouldn't join in on the pact, so evil killed her."

I arose, my shoulders slumped. "Sounds like they agree with you," I said.

"I never said or believed any of that," he said, his hand on my arm.

"You said evil was hunting my family … that my mom had been killed by it. Isn't that the same thing?"

"I never said your dad and grandmother were the cause, and I don't believe they are."

My shoulders fell in defeat. … Avi's words rang in my mind, mixing with Thomas's demon voice. "I'm not so sure," I said, with the same gloomy tone Avi so often used these days.

"What makes you say that?" he asked with concern.

I crossed my arms around my waist, and his hands gently rested on them. The sound of shouted instructions echoed through the woods.

"It's a lot, and you need to get back to work. We can talk later," I said weakly.

More shouts came from his homesite.

"Yeah, I'll find you when I get off work, okay?"

I stepped away. "Come on, Jackson."

Luca allowed his arms to fall at his side, watching me go. I turned after I'd gone a little ways. I glimpsed Luca running toward the construction site.

Nine

Jackson and I entered the quiet kitchen. I hung up my coat and pulled off my snow boots. Jackson went to his bed in the corner and began licking the ice off his paws. I started to go upstairs, but changed my mind. I went to my dad's office. I stared at the closed door. Before I could run away, I raised my hand and knocked.

There was the sound of hurriedly closing drawers.

"Come in," Dad said.

I didn't hesitate. I opened the door and went toward the far end of the room where he sat at his desk.

"What do you need?" he asked, trying not to sound irritated—though he failed.

From the window beyond my dad, I could view the gazebo.

"I came to check on you," I said, though I was not entirely sure why I was there. Part of me wanted nothing to do with him. Part of me wanted to hate him as much as those in town did, though that wasn't fair. The demons could be lying, or Avi might not be as aware as she thought she was. In short, I didn't really know if my father made a deal with the devil that resulted in a curse on our family.

"That was thoughtful of you. I'm doing well. How are you?"

That was a lie. I focused on him. How long had it been since I'd done that? His eyes were bloodshot, his expression blank, as if he was trying to hide *everything* he was feeling. What was he actually feeling?

"You don't look well. You seem exhausted and overwhelmed, like the weight of the world rests on you." I continued to study him.

He averted his eyes. "The funeral yesterday took a lot out of my week and, of course, it was emotionally draining," he said. "I'll have my work caught up in a few days. Things will be better after that." He returned his focus to the computer monitor in front of him. It was set to the home screen, with a picture of my mom in the background. This was his signal that he was done talking with me.

I started to leave … then stopped. Instead I moved closer and sat in the leather chair facing his desk.

I wasn't going to be dismissed. Not that easily.

"Nothing more is bothering you?" I asked.

He forced a puzzled expression. "Hmm, no. Should there be?"

"In a few months, I'll be an adult. Maybe now would be a good time to start telling me the truth, the way Mom would if she were here." That is, if she knew the truth, I thought, as I settled into the chair.

He leaned back in his chair, his fingertips pushing against one another. "In a few months, you'll be a legal adult. That is far from an actual adult."

"Why won't you be honest with me?"

"What have I ever lied to you about?" he asked, raising his left eyebrow.

"It's not what you've said. It's what you haven't. Sins of omission are still sins," I said, surprised by the conviction in my voice.

He turned his chair sideways and tilted his head to look out the window. "Siena, now is not the time."

"When is the time?"

"When I'm stronger," he said gruffly, in a voice I was unfamiliar with.

Still, I didn't back down. "When is that going to be? When the town stops hating you and me and our whole family? Because that might be a while."

"None of that concerns you."

"Seriously? In what world does a person's whole family being hated by practically everyone not affect them?"

He stood, towering over me. I didn't flinch. The blue of his eyes looked gray in the dim light of the room, like the color of steel, which made them appear strong. But I could sense doubt and fear behind the steel.

"I'm handling things. I'm protecting you. It's my job to protect you!"

The same words I myself had thought. They sounded different when he said them. Less convincing. He wanted to protect us; that part I didn't doubt. But was it his job? Perhaps once, but not anymore.

"Lies don't protect people, they only lead to more lies." My voice was unnaturally calm.

"Aargh," he uttered, and pushed away from the desk. He spun around to face the window, his tailored button-down dress shirt rapidly rising and falling with his breaths.

He said, "Is that what you and Luca were discussing? My lies? My past and present sins?"

I realized he might not have been working on anything. He may have been staring out his window like he was doing now.

"Were you watching us?" I asked, with an edge of distrust.

"I was watching the birds. Jackson scared them away," Dad answered. "Why did you walk with him? It's freezing out, and you and Avila already went for a walk."

"Gigi suggested it."

"Ah, of course. I should've guessed."

"Why?"

"You haven't noticed how often she puts you two together?" His tone revealed his disbelief of my lack of awareness.

"No," I said honestly.

His posture relaxed. "For what it's worth, I don't disagree with her. He's a good kid."

"He's my friend," I said, to clarify the relationship.

"He's a good friend, a good boy. I'm happy he's in your life."

"I thought fathers were supposed to hate all the boys their daughters spent time with."

He smiled, the first honest smile I'd seen from him in quite a while.

Dad said, "Luca's different."

Thinking of the various quips in movies when dads and daughters discussed boys, I asked, "Do you like him because he reminds you of yourself at that age?"

He laughed—not a happy laugh. "No, because he doesn't remind me of myself at all."

I stared at my father.

"Luca has a goodness about him that I've never had. A goodness I don't think I could possess even if I spent my life alone on a desert island—maybe especially if I was alone." He shook his head in frustration. "No, my daughter, if I were to compare myself to anyone in the story of your life, it would be Thomas, not Luca."

"Thomas!" I said with disgust.

"You said you wanted the truth"—he opened his arms, his chest unprotected—"here it is. The similarities between him and me are unsettling. Both spoiled, only children, believed to be the best around by those on the outside, loathsome creatures on the inside. Willing to do whatever we wanted, no matter who it hurt, because no one was as important as ourselves. Rules existed, but not for me. They were for the rest of the world. *I* was different—*Thomas* was different. We even shared the inn …." His voice trailed off.

I felt my pulse quicken. Blood drained from my face, my body felt numb. "The inn?"

He rubbed his dark hair as he paced up and down the length of his office. His gray slacks, the tailored shirt, and black leather belt combined to make this moment even more surreal.

I knew him as my father, the devout Catholic who never missed Sunday Mass and rarely missed praying his daily Rosary. But those things, I was starting to understand, were on the outside. Those were actions he did that others could observe. Who was he when others weren't there? Who was he on the inside?

"Yet another similarity between the poor dead Thomas and me," he said, his eyes burning with admission.

I blinked and blinked again, my back heavy against the leather chair, my body sinking, fading into it. Avi said he'd gone there; the demons said so as well. But to hear him say it—to hear him say he was like Thomas ….

I cleared my mind. No, he was not like Thomas. He was different; he was standing in front of me. He was alive.

"How …"—my mouth was so dry, my voice soft—"how did you survive?"

He stopped, his body becoming still. His gaze went to the ceiling, his mind disappeared into the past. He was remembering ….

"She wanted me to," he said, without returning to the present. "She must have."

Ten

Dad was sitting in his chair at the oversized mahogany desk, the one his parents used to share when they ran the family empire. He inherited the desk when his mom handed the company over to him. He was sitting there across from me, but his mind remained somewhere in the past, emotions playing across his face. Features changing, darkening, then brightening, then darkening again.

I summoned the strength to speak. "Who is *she*?" I asked, breaking into his thoughts.

His gaze returned to the present, to me. "My great-grandmother," he answered. His fingernails rubbed gently across the polished wood grain of the desk.

I did not speak.

His expression remained distant. "She was the one who … who was there. She was the one who was always there." He swallowed and turned his head away, his body becoming agitated again, his hands rubbing through his hair. "I-I, ah," he muttered as if fighting with himself. "I spent a lot of time with her. I helped her. … I'm part of whatever this is," he blurted out, as if forcing the words before they could recede from his lips and return to some secret place deep within.

I stared up at him, my breath so shallow I wondered if I was still breathing, if I was still real. None of this felt real. So maybe it wasn't. Was I imagining it? Maybe it was all a dream;

maybe that was it. A dream. No, a nightmare. Because it's in nightmares that good people become bad. Yes, this was a nightmare. I squeezed my eyes closed.

"Siena?"

No, I thought again, this is a nightmare, go back to sleep. If you go back to sleep, you can wake up to the happy truth.

I felt his presence near me. I reluctantly opened my eyes. He was sitting on the edge of his desk, watching me.

"You're not bad," I said, feeling like I was going to cry.

He hung his head.

He wasn't bad. He was good. He was strong and steady, never faltering.

"I thought it was a game," he said, standing, too agitated to remain seated. "She said it was a game."

He turned, facing the window. The palm of his hand pressed against the dark wood frame that encased the window. He was breathing hard, as if he'd run a long race.

Far beyond where he stood, through the trees, was the site of the inn. He could never have seen it from his office, even during the most barren of winter days. Yet, it was always there. Always behind him as he sat at this desk or prayed on the nearby couch or ate with his family in the kitchen beyond this room. He never escaped it, even when he didn't remember. It was always there, behind him.

Avi's words from earlier entered my mind. She said it wasn't about Thomas. She said it was about me.

"What sort of game?" I asked, with an odd feeling of calm. It was the sort of calm that comes in the middle of a hurricane, a quiet moment that lulls the inexperienced into a feeling of safety, when in truth the wind and waves are preparing to destroy them.

In front of me, my father's head fell as if his neck had lost the strength needed to hold it up.

"I'm not sure." His arms pulled tight across his body—hands on his shoulders. He bent his head forward as if he were trying to wrap up into a ball, trying to disappear.

I watched from somewhere outside myself, or not outside but not through the eyes with which I usually saw him. He was different, changed. Young and haggard at the same time. Not like my father at all. Or perhaps I was different.

"Your game killed Thomas." My voice was robotic, without emotion, without the innocence it normally held. I didn't know my voice used to be innocent, but I could hear the difference now.

"I didn't want that." His eyes were sorely red, but showed no tears.

"It doesn't matter what you wanted. Thomas is dead," I said, tears blurring my vision.

He didn't speak.

What could he say? I stood to leave. Passing the leather couch where I typically sat, I felt the urge to sit—to not leave my father. Not because I wanted to be near him, but because something inside me didn't want him to be alone.

I fell into the smooth leather. He watched me, expecting me to leave, but I stayed.

Eventually he stood and went to the fireplace. Soon a fire was burning. The flames allowed that something inside me to relax. Like whatever danger was lurking had passed, at least for the moment.

As I watched the orange and yellow flames dance against the darkened stones of the fireplace, he watched me.

"It was a mistake, a horrible mistake."

He was asking me to forgive him, though what I was being asked to forgive, he never told me.

I moved my head from the side of the couch; it startled him. He stood abruptly and went to the fire. His face, pants— even his gleaming white shirt looked dark compared to the bright fire.

"The demons knew you," I said, remembering that night with Thomas.

"Yes." His voice was barely audible, like it was a truth that startled him as much as me.

I sat taller. "They spoke about Mom. You told them about her?"

"*No!*" he practically shouted. "Never," he quickly added, his voice not as loud. "I've had nothing to do with the demonic since I was a kid. I didn't … didn't realize what I was doing was real. She told me it was a game."

"Imagine that—an evil old woman that your parents told you to stay away from was lying to you," I said with biting sarcasm.

He turned away and said softly, "It wasn't as clear back then."

He was lying, trying to excuse behavior that had no excuse.

"Gigi told you! She told me she did. She said that even before you lived here, she did everything she could to keep you away from her grandmother. She said she was evil. If Gigi told me, she must've told you."

"We didn't realize she was evil," he said, pleading. "They didn't like her, they told me that, but none of us understood what she was. And she was nice to me. Other kids had a grandmother. Why couldn't I?"

"Because she was living with demons."

"I didn't know that," he said, exasperated.

"It doesn't matter what you thought or why you did whatever you did. What matters is what you did! Tell me what you did," I demanded.

"I can't remember. It's not an excuse," he said. "I remember some things, but not all. I remember being in the inn with her. I remember the fireplace, the frayed carpet in front of it. I remember her handing me something."

"What?"

He shook his head again. "The memory stops there. There were other times I was with her, of course, but most times we were outside. It was only on cold days that I went inside. She'd give me this hot blueberry drink. It was good—thick. She said her mom taught her how to make it.”

I wanted to hate him for whatever unnamed sin he'd committed, but I couldn't. He wanted to be like every other kid that had a grandmother. I understood what it was like to want to be normal.

I allowed some kind words to be spoken. “It sounds nice.”

“It was nice,” he said, placing his fingers to his mouth, pinching his bottom lip in thought. “She was nice to me. That's what's so confusing. She was this awful person—and I get that—but she was nice to me.”

“Life can be confusing sometimes,” I said.

“Yes.” He was still thinking of the past. He sat on the couch across from me.

“Why haven't you told us this before?”

He watched the fire. “I didn't remember any of it, not until Thomas and the demons. Not until I heard their voice and felt their evil did I realize … that wasn't the first time.”

“How could you not remember demons?”

His body slumped against the plush leather couch and he said, “I'm not sure.”

“Do you have any idea?”

He hesitated. “Mom told me about prayers they said over me. She said after that I didn't remember hardly anything about her grandmother. Not even the little things like the hot blueberry drink.”

"What sort of prayers?" I asked. Something about the way he spoke told me to ask that question.

"Prayers of deliverance … or exorcism," he said reluctantly.

"Exorcism?" I asked, my eyebrows going up.

"Not a full one. I wasn't possessed," he said. "But I … I was obsessed."

Before Thomas, I understood nothing about demons other than I professed to believe in their existence during prayers at Mass. In truth, I did not. Now I accepted the reality of demons and that there were levels of control they had over us. Thomas, at the end, was possessed. They controlled him; they possessed his physical being. Such things were rare, but I couldn't pretend any longer that they were merely the sensational fantasies of Hollywood. Obsessions—when demons were actively wreaking havoc in a person's life—were far more common.

"You invited them into your life?" I asked, unable to hide the disgust I felt for my father.

"I don't remember. I don't remember any of it, except their voice. I'd heard it before," he said.

I had the feeling that if he was a child, his body would be trembling, but since he was a grown man, he remained outwardly calm.

"You said you played games with her. What sort of games?" I asked, certain the answer wasn't hopscotch or Monopoly.

Dad pushed the palms of his hands together, rubbing them. He was uncomfortable, more uncomfortable with this question than the others. "Games she made up, games where we talked about my children."

The word "children" made my spine straighten. "Your children?"

"She knew I would have three," he said with an edge of terror in his voice. "I thought it was a joke. I was twelve. You don't know anything when you're twelve. … She told me I should bring my children there to meet her." He shuddered violently.

"What!" My voice sounded so high-pitched I didn't think it was mine.

"I asked if she thought she'd still be there. Her face looked strange. I remember it almost changing shape. It scared me and I started to back away. She smiled—her face back to normal. She told me the inn was her home. She'd built it with her two hands and she was never going to leave it." He cringed at his own words.

"Did she expect to live forever?" I asked.

"I don't … I think maybe. From what I've read … recently, the idea of immortality is appealing to those like her. Those who—"

"Welcome evil," I said.

He nodded. A sadness in his eyes seemed to say that, even now, it was difficult for him to fully accept how awful she'd been.

"Did you ever do as she asked? Did you ever take us there?"

"No," he said, repulsed by the thought. "I told you I didn't remember any of this until … Thomas passed away."

"If you didn't remember, then why didn't you take us there? Why did you always tell us to stay away from it?"

His back relaxed a little against the couch. "After she died, I didn't have a reason to go there and I became far more interested in what was going on in town. Then I graduated, went to college, and started my life. Years later, when I brought your mom here, we walked to the beach. She immediately noticed the inn and said we shouldn't go into it."

"Did you try and take her inside?" I asked, keeping my voice as even as I could.

He leaned forward. "I remember us going toward it and her saying she didn't want to set foot in that place."

"She told me never to go into it," I said, eyes locked on my father. "It's the reason I didn't—when Thomas tried to convince me, I mean."

Dad lowered his head. "She saved both of us."

His voice sounded like he was about to cry.

"Would it have mattered?" I asked. "Could we have been hurt just by walking into the building?"

This was something Luca and my mom believed. I was not as sure.

"Yes, I think we could've. I think that's part of what my great-grandmother had done, somehow."

"What do you mean?" I felt fear tingling up my spine.

"I think she did more than welcome evil. I think she locked it there, creating a place that was so dark, so vile, that merely stepping inside would lead to an attack."

"What sort of attack?" I envisioned dark, formless shapes hovering, waiting in what had been that dilapidated building. The dark entities from my dream swooped again in my imagination.

"A spiritual attack, one that even the holiest of people would struggle to defeat," he said.

"A trap," I said.

"Yes." He rubbed his hands through his hair. His discomfort was increasing.

The palms of my hands were damp; I was sweating though it wasn't hot. "She asked you to bring your kids to visit her," I said.

"Yes," he said, his voice cracking.

I stood, towering over him, hands clenched at my side. "You helped her set a trap for us!"

His head sunk forward.

Avi told me it wasn't about all of us, it was about me. "I'm your oldest," I said, somehow aware that it mattered.

His red eyes held mine. "I remember hearing a name. I'd forgotten it. If I hadn't, I never would have …"

"What?" I asked, the muscles in my legs tight. I needed to run.

"Named you Siena," he said.

Eleven

I struggled to catch my breath. I'd run hard, away from the stranger who was in my father's office. The thought of him, of who he'd been, of who he now was … it was too much. I ran farther, pushed harder. As the dirt turned to rocks and sand, I was forced to slow down. Sprinting on rocks caused my ankles to falter. If Jackson were here, he would've flopped down in the sand out of sheer exhaustion. He wasn't with me. I'd left the house so suddenly he didn't have time to follow. I simply grabbed a coat, slammed the door, and ran. My coat hung open. I placed my hands on my hips, spreading my lungs—creating as much room as I could for air to replenish them.

I went to the water. The beach behind me was strewn with rocks. This was my favorite time: when the tide was as low as it got and I walked not on the rocks but on wet sand, far out into my cove. The waves rolled toward me, but they didn't reach me; the tide was still receding. I couldn't be still—I had to move. I walked briskly southward, to the sheer rock wall that marked the edge of our property. I must have been walking faster than I realized; I was there in minutes. My fingers reached for the stone. A smooth layer of ice clung to the rock.

I was cold. I shrugged my shoulders forward to close my coat. With icy fingers, I connected the zipper and pulled it up to my throat. I would trap the heat in.

I left the wall of ice—this was not the cliff that was calling to me. This was not the cliff I once climbed, but now never did. My feet moved with purpose toward the place that held so many memories. So very many memories, I thought again, as my resolve wavered.

A few flurries of snow fell, instantly melting when they hit the sea or the wet sand. Again, I'd moved faster than I realized. In front of me was what remained of the inn—gray and black ashes dusted with a thin layer of white. Only the stones protruded from the heap. The stones had once supported the weight of the building and the stones of the fireplace. I stood, unmoving. The air smelled of ash. I was in the forest. Another step and I would be within the boundaries of the place that had haunted my family for five generations … the place that had taken Thomas.

It was safe now; Luca and Sam both had said so. The demons were gone. Thomas had done that for us. For that, we must thank him. And for that, he was thrown from the cliff. They had wanted him to retrieve the metal box. It was their decision to use his arms as crowbars, splintering the wood, slicing his arms. They had wanted it taken—not thrown over the cliff.

Why had they wanted to take it? What had Thomas not done for them?

I stepped forward, the remains of ashen wood cracking beneath my feet. The earth was silent except for the gentle ebb and flow of the waves behind me. The birds, the squirrels, all were silent; all were watching me. I continued forward, going to the corner. The stones that marked the boundary of the back walls had been carved out of the mountain. The scars remained of where the inn had been. Beneath my feet was where Luca had been stuffed, left to die. Beneath him, the metal box had been buried. I fought the urge to kneel and touch the earth. It was gone, its secrets gone.

My father had known where it was; the demons told us so. Yet he doesn't remember. Maybe someday he'd remember not only that he helped bury the box, but what was in it. Perhaps on that day we'd have answers. The wind blew, lifting my thoughts with it. Or perhaps it didn't matter. Thomas took it, throwing it into the ocean. Whatever was in it, he destroyed it for us. For the first time since his death, I felt gratitude toward Thomas.

A gull cried in the distance. I inhaled the frigid salt air. The wind whirled around me, tousling my hair. I longed to be part of the wind. To float through the trees, unafraid.

My feet began to move. I was going uphill. Before I realized it I had abandoned the scarred remains of the inn. I was beyond it, among the trees, climbing up. The sun was beginning to fade, the day nearing its end. The earth below me was darkening, the mountain blocking the rays of the setting sun. I raised my head. Above me the sun glowed brightly on the slope, lighting my path, beckoning me to continue climbing up the slope that I hadn't climbed in eight years. The same slope Thomas had climbed in minutes. It would take me longer, but it was not taking me as long as when I was young … when my mother was beside me, guiding me.

Now I was alone with the wind. The wind was pushing me forward—begging me to become part of it. To be part of everything and nothing at the same time.

When I reached the sunlit area, the rays instantly warmed me as my feet crunched against the thin ice formed around rocks and tree roots. The wind wasn't cold—it wasn't my enemy. It was lifting me higher and higher, freeing me from the guilt of Thomas's death and the pain of my mother's. She and I had shared this place, the same place that had set him free.

The breeze died, its enchantment fading as I neared the top. One of my ankles twisted on a root and my knees slammed hard against the rocky slope. The pain grounded me, reminding me that I was bound to this earth by my body. I pushed myself up and brushed the icy pebbles from the palms of my hands and the knees of my pants. My knees ached; I could feel the bruises already forming. The pain made me happy. It was a strange feeling, one I didn't understand, yet there was gratitude in it. My gratitude was for the cold, the sun, the wind, and the pain.

The discomfort didn't stop me, though I felt every step more intensely. I reached the top of the slope; my cliff overlooking the ocean lay in front of me. The sun enfolded me like the shadows had when I stood inside the inn. The earth here was not scarred—the past didn't bind it.

I went to the edge, the part of the cliff where my mother and I used to eat our snacks. I stared down at the rounded boulder. I envisioned us there: her auburn hair pushed behind her ears, the wind playing with it and with mine. I crouched down, reaching my hand for it. A feeling of warmth and love spread over me. It was as if my mother was there, her arms embracing me. I lay down, wanting to feel her, my cheek pressed against the tiny pebbles that rested on the boulder—a boulder that must have extended deep inside the mountain.

Above me a bird soared. I raised my head and watched. Its white head and tail reflected brightly in the late afternoon sun.

"An eagle," I said to myself.

There were eagles all up and down this coast. People saw them all the time, but we didn't. Never on our property. It was always a mystery to us. Why, when we had so much land and eagles were so prevalent, did we not have at least one nesting pair?

The bird circled gracefully. It cried out. As I turned to look behind me, another eagle soared closer. The first moved to be nearer to its mate. They were united, emotionally connected—that could be sensed even from where I sat.

"Siena."

I jerked up my head, turning to see behind me.

"Luca?" I said, surprised he was coming toward me. My face felt damp. I wiped at my eyes. Had I been crying?

As he moved toward me, I called over the wind: "What are you doing here?"

"Taking a … stroll," he answered, out of breath.

"Up a mountain?"

"Can I … sit down?" he asked before collapsing beside me.

"Are you okay?" I asked with concern.

"I'll be … fine." He lay beside me, his chest rising and falling quickly. "I ran. … That's all."

"Ran from where?"

He held up a finger, asking me to wait. His thick curly hair, covered in a sock hat, lay against the damp boulder. I shifted my gaze toward the heavens, where the eagles had been. They were gone, probably to the other side of the mountain. I wondered how long that side would remain free and wild.

After his breathing slowed to a more typical rate, I asked, "Why are you here?"

"I was taking a walk," he said, still breathing heavily. "And I thought I'd come up here. The climb was more than I expected."

I watched him quizzically. "You were taking a walk after working all day, even though it was going to be dark soon and getting colder—which you hate?"

"I wasn't that tired after work," he said, pushing himself to a sitting position.

"So you were taking a walk, and you decided to sprint up a mountain."

"I decided to *climb* a mountain."

"I climbed the mountain and reached the top still breathing," I said.

"You're in better shape than me," he answered quickly.

"Do you often go for walks after work?" I asked. The shadow of the mountain appeared far behind us.

He hesitated. "Not often."

"Ever?"

"There's a first time for everything."

"Uh-huh. Did my dad tell you to come look for me?"

"Your dad? I haven't spoken with him. I told you, I left work and thought a walk would be nice."

I studied him. No one knew where I'd gone. I doubted if anyone besides my dad even realized I was gone. I was sure he'd watched me enter the trail, so if I wasn't at the jobsite or the pond, it was a relatively easy guess I'd be at the beach. But if Luca hadn't spoken with him ….

"How did you know I was up here? That's why you're here, right? You were looking for me, but if you haven't talked to my dad, then who told you I wasn't at home?"

"That's a funny story," he said, after I refused to look away from him.

"Funny ha-ha or funny strange, as in demons are hunting your family?"

He shuddered. "Somewhere in between. Somehow," he said, raising a hand, "I have no idea how, but somehow I can sense where you are."

I tilted my head, my eyebrows pulling together.

"It started after … after Thomas died. I don't try to do it or anything," he said, defending his actions against my imaginary attack. "Your presence is sort of … there." He raised his left hand and circled it above him. "It's like … maybe like a magnet or something. When I get closer to you, the sense of you gets stronger, and when I move away from you, it gets fainter."

He waited for me to react. When I didn't, he continued. "So when I got off work, I started for your house, but you got fainter. I debated what to do. Since it was going to be dark soon, I figured I could go for a walk and sort of accidentally run into you. I followed your presence to the beach and then—" His voice caught.

I sensed the fear. He'd been scared.

"I could sense you were up here, but I couldn't see you. I, ah …." He lowered his eyes.

I said, "You thought I'd jumped."

He pinched at his eyes.

I reached my hand for his. "I'm sorry I scared you," I said softly.

He nodded, trying to push the fear away. "I didn't think you did, but I couldn't understand where you were. And this place—"

"Is where I used to come with my mother," I said, taking his hand in both of mine. "She and I used to climb up here together. Ever since she died, I've been afraid to make the climb. But today it was like I had no choice. I had to be near her. I'm sorry I scared you."

He inhaled and exhaled, turning away from me to hide the emotion that was overwhelming him. "I thought—" He broke off.

"It wasn't about that," I said. "It was about my mom. I needed her."

He nodded and pushed his lips together in a slight upward movement of exhausted relief.

I touched the side of his face. "I don't want my life to end before it's really begun."

He leaned into my touch. "This place is just …. I'm sorry I followed you here. This place is special to you. I had no right to intrude." His eyes studied mine.

"It's okay," I said. The tips of my fingers grazed the thin layer of dark stubble on the side of his face. The heat from his skin warmed my hand. I reluctantly pulled my fingers away, aware that I'd left them there too long already.

I said, "I'm sure if I could somehow sense you, and knew you were on a cliff but I couldn't see you, I would probably freak out too. Though, of course, I'm completely ordinary and would never actually have any sort of gift like that to begin with."

"That's not a bad thing, Siena," Luca said, sensing my annoyance at being ordinary.

"It sort of feels like it, with you and Sam around. It's like you two have superpowers the rest of us don't."

"I'm grateful for who I am," he said, "for who God made me to be, and I trust in his wisdom. But before, when I had no sense of God and no understanding of his plan for me, these abilities seemed far more like curses than gifts."

"That's hard for me to believe," I said.

"It's the truth, and if you ask Aunt Sam, she'll tell you the same. Being different isn't easy." He zipped his coat in an attempt to keep out the wind.

"Can she feel anyone?" I asked.

"I'm not sure. I haven't told her about my newest … gift."

"It is a gift. Don't say it like it's not," I said, watching him with tender eyes. "Who else can you sense?"

He sat taller, his body becoming tense. He cleared his throat, looked away, and then back to me like he was stalling. He cleared his throat again.

"What is it?" I asked, half amused by how nervous he was acting. "Who else can you sense?"

He looked deep into my eyes. "Just you," he said softly. "I can sense only you."

Twelve

My face flushed hot despite the dropping temperature.

"Only me," I said. "Why?"

Luca shook his head. "I don't … I don't understand any of it."

I kept still.

"I'm sorry," he said. "I don't try to sense where you are. Most of the time I sort of push it away and pretend I can't feel it, I mean you … I mean *it*," he said, embarrassed. "Normally I ignore where you are, but it's going to be dark soon and the temperature will keep dropping. … I couldn't go back to the house when I knew you were out here. I'm sorry," he whispered.

"I'm not," I said, into the wind. "You and I … it makes sense in some weird way."

His shoulders relaxed, the sides of our bodies touching.

"Yeah," he said, staring at the world beyond the cliff. "In some weird way it does make sense."

We sat in silence; his breathing slowed to match mine.

I sat straighter. "We should go before it gets too cold," I said, pushing myself up off the rock.

He got up. Each of us stared at the spot where Thomas last stood. Neither spoke as the wind enveloped us. Luca shivered, reminding us that night was falling and, with it, below-freezing temperatures.

We began silently retracing our steps from earlier. Every step took us closer to the darkness. When we entered the woods, the sun's bright rays were gone. The vibrant colors of a few seconds before were replaced by the faded blues and grays of twilight.

The wind pushed strong between us, the cold making my eyes water. I ducked down into the trees, the wind calming as I did so. Luca followed, his hand briefly touching mine as we used the same tree to help maneuver down the side of the cliff.

I paused, wondering how much of myself to share with this boy who already knew more than anyone else. "Was … was anyone else up there?" I asked.

He looked at me quizzically.

"I felt such a draw to be there, to be by my mom. Was she …. I mean, was there, maybe, a presence of someone else around us?" I was both hopeful and embarrassed for asking such a question.

"No, we were alone, as far as I could tell," he said slowly.

"Can you always tell?"

After a moment of reflection, he said, "I sense what God allows me to. There could be more there. I'd never know."

I was silent for a few steps, thinking over his words.

"It was stupid of me to ask," I said, embarrassed that I'd revealed such a childish hope to Luca.

"It isn't stupid to want to know about someone you love. Lots of people do that." He'd said the last few words under his breath, making it difficult to hear.

"What?" I asked.

He raised his voice. "Nothing. A conversation for another time."

"Another time, like the next time you magically sense my presence from miles away, go out into the night, and climb a frozen mountainside to find me?"

He chuckled. "I didn't go out into the night. I simply took a detour on my way back to your house."

"A detour that extended your time in the cold, which you hate," I countered.

"I'm starting to get more used to it, but back to your original question,"—his voice changed a little—"I was hoping another time might be tomorrow night."

"Fine with me. You know where to find me." I giggled at my joke.

"That's true, I guess I do." He laughed, probably more at the corniness of the joke than the actual joke. "I was sort of hoping we could plan where you would be, and that it would be having dinner with me at a restaurant," he added hurriedly.

"A restaurant? Just you and me, or everyone?"

"I was hoping not everyone. I mean just you and me, if that's okay."

My heart beat faster as a sweet smile formed on his perfect lips.

"That would be …very nice," I said calmly while my emotions were twirling.

Luca's expression matched my own; his whole being radiated joy.

"Good," he said simply as we continued down the slope, carefully making our way in the dim blue light that remained of the day.

"And don't worry," he said, "we won't go anywhere in town. We can go a bit south of here to avoid meeting anyone who might recognize you."

His thoughtful words reminded me of what I'd momentarily forgotten.

"I hadn't thought of that," I mumbled, shoulders falling as the weight of life returned.

"It'll be fine. There's a restaurant the guys I work with told me about. They said it's a good ways from here and locals don't tend to go there."

"What's its name?"

"The BayTree."

I'd been there once when I was a kid. In general, he was right; not many people from our town drove that far for a meal, especially not in the winter when the roads could be unpredictable. That reality brought me some peace. It didn't feel right to go out with Luca, but it didn't feel right to keep hiding from life, either. My mom didn't want me to do that. Perhaps that was why I climbed the cliff. Perhaps she was telling me to return to her, to return to life.

"What time should I be ready?" I asked with determination.

"Really?"

"Yes, really."

"I get off work at four."

"I'll be ready a little after four," I answered. I was excited, but mostly nervous. Not because I'd be alone with Luca, but because I'd be away from my sanctuary.

The moon was rising, causing the water to sparkle like a million diamonds.

"It's breathtaking," he said.

Both of us stopped to watch the water twinkle in the still night air. The wind had faded, causing the night to feel warmer than the day.

"Nature is so majestic," he added as he inhaled the damp forest air.

"Yes. And then there's what people create," I said as the ruins of the inn appeared beneath us.

"A few people, not all," he said.

"Those few cause so much pain," I said, the night suddenly feeling cold again.

"It can't hurt us anymore," he said.

He led the way down, not bothering to avoid the ruins. He stepped into the footprint of where the inn had stood.

"Just memories," he said, and offered me his hand to help step down from where the mountain had been carved away.

I released his hand when we stood by the fireplace. The stones were ragged, hewn—like all the stones of our home— from the landscape around us. It's the reason the cliff was so sheer near our house. Trees and moss covered the scars, but the memory of their loss remained.

I took my hands from the pockets of my jacket; the rough stones were calling for me to touch them. I gently slid my fingertips against their ragged, frozen surfaces. I wanted to pull my hand away to warm them in my pocket, but for some reason I didn't. Instead of retreating from the cold, I welcomed it, pressing my palm against the stones.

"They feel so sad. Like the dampness isn't caused by the weather but by their tears," I said sorrowfully.

Luca moved to my side. "They're stones. They don't have feelings."

I closed my eyes. "They do feel," I said, the sadness increasing.

"Maybe it's your emotions you're feeling," Luca said, his body now close enough to touch mine.

I shook my head. "It isn't coming from me. It's from outside of me. Touch them."

He did as I instructed, his fingers beside mine.

"Do you feel the sorrow?" I asked, barely keeping myself from crying.

"There's a long-ago darkness," he said, "but it's only the hint of a memory. There's no emotion."

He watched me focus on the cold stones. I pressed my palm against their damp surfaces. I inhaled the scent of the inn's ashes. A moment flashed in my mind. A moment that was not mine. It was of a thin white arm, held high above the orange glow of a fire. Its flames felt hot against my frigid fingers. A silver knife glided across the pale arm, blood dripping from it. I pulled my hand away from the heat of the flames. The image was gone. In its place, the cold, empty stones.

I knelt, shaking, in the ashes of the inn. My fingers timidly felt along the base of the fireplace, where I saw the blood drip from the arm. The stone in the center was missing. My finger traced the slight bit of nothingness. It had been removed. The stone that would have caught the blood had been chiseled out. I studied the stones. Removing this piece would not have been difficult. It wasn't a large gap and many of the stones were loose. Though all the others remained in place.

"What is it?" Luca asked as he knelt cautiously beside me.

The emotion of a moment ago was gone. Now I felt only cold. I shivered and wrapped my arms around myself—my hands so cold, they felt numb.

My voice trembling, I asked, "Did you see that?"

"What?" he asked, placing a comforting hand on my back.

"The arm. Did you see the arm?"

"No," he said.

But his tone held meaning. He was worried about me, his hand heavy on my back like he was trying to keep me near him.

"There was an arm … and a fire. It was hot. I felt the heat."

"There's no fire," Luca said, eyes narrow with concern.

He was right, of course. There was no fire, no arm. "How did I see something that wasn't here?" I said, my voice quivering.

His thumb moved against my back. The simple movement grounded me, returning me more fully to the present.

"You've been through a lot," he said. "And this place holds too many memories." His hand fell from my back as he swirled around.

The sudden change startled me. "What is it?"

"It's not quite as safe as I thought," he said, pulling me to my feet. "We need to go."

He took my hand as I stumbled after him, tripping at the edge of the inn's boundary. His grip was tight—he didn't let me fall.

The tide was coming in, forcing us to remain among the trees. He was walking fast, so I had to run every few steps to keep up with him. Once we reached the trail, his pace slowed a little.

"I don't feel it anymore," he said, breathing heavily.

"What was it?" I asked.

Luca moved a branch out of the way for me. "An edge of evil, only for a second."

"Evil? From the inn?"

"It must've been," he said. "I thought it was gone. So did Aunt Sam, but it must … there must be a remnant. But no, that wasn't a remnant," he reasoned aloud, trying to understand what he'd felt.

"Could it have been passing through, sort of a coincidence?" I asked, doubting my own speculation.

Luca hesitated before speaking. "I felt a connection. A tie between the inn and the evil, so I don't think it was passing through. Besides, I'm not sure it works that way. Everywhere I've felt evil, I've felt it connected to something or someone."

"Could it have been hiding?" I asked. "I mean, since you didn't feel it before?"

"I—I don—I'm not sure," he answered, with no more understanding than I had.

His lack of certainty concerned me. This edge of evil, as he called it, was not what he was used to feeling or experiencing. Something about it was different.

Even with the moon lighting our way, the trail was dark—much darker than the beach had been. Though it was probably no later than six or seven, it felt like the middle of the night.

Into the darkness, Luca said, "You said you saw an arm?"

"I imagined it, like you said. That place creeps me out," I said quickly, dismissing any possibility of having seen a thin arm dripping blood onto the hearth of a forgotten fireplace.

"Are you sure?" he asked cautiously.

"Yes, of course. That place is not exactly a neutral location for me. It would be almost impossible for me not to imagine some bizarre scene at every corner of the ruins," I said, certain that was exactly what had happened.

"You're probably right," he said, his teeth chattering.

The night had gone from cool to cold in what felt like seconds. I walked faster, imagining the warmth we would soon experience as the lights of my house came into view.

"It's about time you two showed up," Jason said from the shadows of the house.

Jackson ran up to us, happy we were home.

"Gemma and Sam were about to send us all out to search for you, and tonight is too cold to go searching for anybody," Jason said, his hands stuffed in the pockets of his coat.

"Sorry," Luca said, "time got away from us."

"Uh-huh," Jason uttered, unconvinced. "Do me a favor. The next time it gets away from you, make it during the summer, or at least during the day. Come on, Jackson."

We plodded toward the kitchen door while Jackson ran from one of us to another, with chunks of frozen snow clinging to his fur.

Thirteen

When I crawled into bed, my knees reminded me I'd slammed them against a mountainside. They'd feel better in the morning, but tonight they were grateful my day was done.

Despite our arriving late, everyone had waited to eat with Luca and me. Everyone except my dad, who hadn't eaten dinner or left his office all evening. Even now I wondered if he'd come up to bed or remain locked in his dungeon. That wasn't my concern. I couldn't fix him or force him to act more like a parent, a role he'd clearly abdicated to Gigi.

My body was exhausted, but my mind was alert. I doubted I'd fall asleep. The memory of last night's nightmare suddenly returning, I shuddered and removed my hand from the bedside lamp I was about to turn off. My head leaned against the whitewashed wood of the headboard.

I was being childish, like a little kid afraid of the dark. I reached for the light and defiantly turned it off, then instantly wished I hadn't. Instead of lying down, I sat, head propped upright on the headboard.

Outside, a squirrel screeched, fallen prey to an owl. It was not a comforting sound—an innocent creature's last cries. I shuddered, pulling the blankets up to my shoulders. The house was silent. Aside from my dad, I'd been the last to go to bed. I had schoolwork I needed to finish, and I wanted to take a bath instead of a shower to soak my knees. The room next to mine contained a clawfoot tub that I used from time to time. When I emerged from the bath, all the other lights were out.

The memory of demons continued to play in my mind, made worse by the dark. I sat up and pulled open the drawer of my nightstand. I fumbled around until my fingers felt the soothing beads. I removed a rosary, one of the many I owned. I lovingly held the crucifix, then carefully wrapped the beads around my hand. I clutched the crucifix tight in my right hand … the memory of demons faded into the past. They became nothing more than the dream they'd been. I scrunched down into a lying position, my head resting gently on the down pillow. Peace came over me. Sleep followed.

In the stillness of the night, I heard my name spoken loud and clear, as if the speaker was standing beside me. My eyes opened abruptly, my body jerking awake. My room was dark, but my eyes, already adjusted to the darkness, told me I was alone. No one spoke my name. I lay back down. It must have been a dream—a vivid one, but still a dream. I closed my eyes and was soon asleep.

Again my name was called, but this time I did not wake. There was no way I woke up because beside me stood Thomas. Not the boy I saw jump from the cliff, but the boy I'd known all my life. A moment later he was gone. I opened my eyes. He was not there. He had not been … that was impossible.

***

Today would be better.

This was the first conscious thought I had on Friday morning. My dreams of the last two nights had been strange, but why wouldn't they be? My life was strange; that's how it went. Today would go fast; I had plenty to keep me busy and then tonight I would go to dinner with Luca. I slid the cuffs of the flannel pajama pants I was wearing up past my knees. My right knee was bright purple. The left was a tad sore when I touched it. My right knee hit the ground first, taking the brunt of my weight. I swung my legs to the side of the bed, wincing a little as I stood. The pain didn't bother me. In some ways it was an escape from memories and dreams.

I'd heard my name so clearly, it had woken me from sleep. Yet, it was impossible. Thomas calling out to me was impossible. It was a dream, nothing more. But my name … my name was so clear. It didn't sound like it was coming from inside my head. It sounded like it was coming from outside, like Thomas was there, not imagined. His image was not clear—it was hazy at best—but his voice … there was no mistaking his voice.

"It was a dream, nothing more than a dream," I mumbled to myself on my way to the bathroom.

I squinted at my reflection in the mirror, the light so bright. I touched my hair. It was knotted and matted. "How did that happen?" I asked my reflection.

I took a brush from the drawer and began the tedious process of brushing out the knots. After a few minutes, my hair was back to normal and I was dressed.

I went downstairs, my right knee reminding me to think of it, not of dreams.

"You're just in time," Gigi said. "I was about to put everything away. Would you like some bacon and eggs?"

"You don't need to cook for me," I said, opening the refrigerator for some orange juice.

"I would like to. Luca ate almost a whole pack of bacon by himself, so I opened a second pack and I'd rather not save an open pack."

"Okay, thanks," I said.

"Scrambled eggs?" she asked.

"Yes, please." I took my orange juice to the table where my sisters sat, finishing their meals.

"Has Luca gone to work?" I asked, sipping the orange juice.

"Of course he has," Lisieux said. "It's almost nine."

"Is Dad gone too?" I ignored my sister's unspoken complaint at my sleeping later than her.

"Everyone who leaves, has left," Lisieux said, rising from the table with her empty plate.

"Luca told Dad he asked you out," Avi said, nibbling her eggs.

I paused mid-drink of orange juice. It obviously wasn't a secret, plus there would be no way to keep it a secret even if we tried, but I hadn't thought of him as having *asked me out*, just that we were going to dinner.

"What did he say?" I asked, curious how he'd worded it.

Gigi spoke first. "He was a true old-fashioned gentleman. He very respectfully asked your father if it was okay if he took you to dinner tonight, and apologized for not asking his permission first."

"What did Dad say?" I asked.

"He choked on his coffee," Avi said with a giggle.

"He gave it some thought and his blessing," Gigi added. She handed me a plate with a few pieces of bacon and some scrambled eggs.

"I guess it's a date, then," I said, taking my fork in hand.

"You guess?" Lisieux said, irritated. "How do you keep not realizing when you're asked out on dates? Can you please assume, from this point forward, that if a boy asks you to go to dinner or on a picnic or anywhere else, it's a date! It might save us some trouble."

"Lisieux," Gigi said in an admonishing tone.

"I'm sick of her not knowing or pretending, or whatever it is, and then boys falling in love with her and then—." Her voice cut off, her expression glaring. She placed her plate loudly in the sink and stomped upstairs.

I sat motionless, watching the steam rise from the eggs. "I'm sorry," I said, feeling like I was going to cry. "I didn't mean to …."

"Oh, that girl!" Gigi said in exasperation. "You did nothing wrong. Eat your food and ignore your sister."

"She's jealous," Avi said. "She wishes Luca asked her out instead of you."

I forced a forkful of scrambled eggs to my lips. I didn't believe Avi. Lisieux was not that way. She was not jealous of others. She liked her life as it was, or how it had been.

"She's not wrong," I said, staring at the stairs my sister had taken to flee from my presence.

"This is what evil wants," Gigi said. "It wants to divide us, to turn us against each other. Thomas's death is a tragedy, but it's not your fault and neither are the repercussions."

Staring blankly, I said, "I heard him call out to me—in my dream last night, I heard him calling my name."

Gigi took a towel from the side of the sink and dried her hands. I could feel Avi watching us, but she didn't speak.

"If he came to you in a dream, you must pray for him," Gigi said decisively.

"I do pray for him," I said.

"Pray harder."

"That's all?" Avi said. "A dead boy comes to her, and you tell her to pray for him."

"What more should I say?" Gigi asked. "If it was actually Thomas, with some request or message, that means he's not eternally damned, and so prayers will assist him. If it was a dream, prayers will certainly not hurt him. So yes, she must pray. What else could she possibly do for him?"

I said, "You make it sound so ordinary."

"It was, once," Gigi said. "Only in our modern world is there such a separation between the living and the dead. It used to be common for the deceased to appear to their loved ones, and everyone knew that meant they were asking for prayers or forgiveness or something similar. But now, in our world where so few pray, few appear—what good would it do? If Thomas came to you, pray for him. If he did not … pray for him."

"I will keep praying," I said, recognizing the truth in her words.

"Then you've helped him," she stated. "Avila, let's go upstairs and work in your room. My back is hurting this morning. I'd like to sit in the chair in your room."

Avi quickly gathered her schoolbooks. "I'm sorry your back is hurting," she said with sincere concern for our grandmother.

"It's okay, sweetie. Nothing a comfortable chair won't fix."

After they left, only Jackson remained, asleep at my feet. I closed my eyes and thought of Thomas, of the boy he'd been. Of my dream. I felt hope: hope that he had not been lost, hope that Gigi was right that he was asking for prayers—that he was not beyond their reach.

Fourteen

I sat at my desk, my computer screen bright with the literature report I had mostly completed. Despite how the day began, it had been productive. At my request, Avi kindly brought a sandwich to my room for lunch. I told her I needed to get schoolwork done, which was true. I didn't tell her I was anxious about my date. She was always happy to have a job to do, especially one that was easy and still came with praise.

It was a little over four hours ago when Avi had come and taken away my empty plate. Now I was tapping my pen on the notebook as I stared past my computer screen to the window beyond, hoping any minute Luca would appear from the trail. I was already in the green sweaterdress and dark leggings I'd selected to wear tonight.

I clicked my phone: 4:03. He wouldn't be here yet. He usually didn't arrive home until four thirty at the earliest. I tried to convince myself to go back to working on the report, but my attention stayed at the edge of the forest. A second later, at least twenty minutes earlier than he'd ever been home before, he burst through the woods. He slowed to a brisk walking pace when he entered our yard. I bit my lip to keep from smiling too hard and quickly ducked out of the window's view. He'd been running! He was as excited about tonight as I was. I felt giddy as I went toward my bathroom to finish getting ready.

There was a knock at my door. I went to it in surprise.

"Come in," I said, breathlessly wondering how Luca got up here so quickly.

"Got a minute?" Dad asked from the doorway.

My excitement fell. I didn't want to be around my dad, especially not now, when Luca and I were about to escape this place—even if for a short time.

"I guess," I said, instantly feeling bad for how clear it must be that I didn't want him here.

He came in and shut the door. As he did, I heard Luca's heavy steps on the stairs. He would shower and then be ready. As much as I looked forward to being alone with Luca, I was even more excited to be out of the house. Before Thomas's death, it felt like my choice to be here—it felt safe. Now it felt like a punishment. I wanted a break from this place. I wanted to go on my first real date. I wanted my dad out of my room so all of those things could happen.

"How are you?" he asked, with seemingly no awareness of what was going on.

"Fine," I said.

"We haven't talked since yesterday. I wanted to check in."

No, he had no idea I was about to go out with Luca. How was that possible? Luca asked him this morning.

"I'm fine."

"Are you sure? Our conversation yesterday was a lot … a lot to take in."

"Completely sure," I said, tapping my phone to glimpse the time. Luca took fast showers. He'd be knocking on my door any second.

"You look nice," Dad said, starting to realize something about tonight was different.

I straightened my dress. "Luca and I are going to dinner."

He stared, puzzled.

"He asked you this morning," I said.

His expression shifted slightly. "Yes, of course," he said, though he appeared no less confused.

"Don't you remember?" How could he forget something like that? The first time a boy asked his permission to take his daughter out. That was one of those moments a dad should remember. At least for a few hours.

He rocked on his toes. "Of course I remember. It was a long day. I forgot for a second, that's all."

I wasn't sure I believed him, but it didn't matter. I needed to freshen my makeup and brush my hair. I wasn't going to be late, not tonight. To my frustration, Dad didn't leave. Instead, he sat on my desk chair and watched as I applied another layer of mascara to my otherwise invisible lashes.

"Luca will be here in a minute," I said. "You don't need to watch me."

He turned the swivel chair and pretended, as I'd done earlier, to look at the schoolwork sprawled across my desk.

"How's school going?" he asked.

He rarely asked about school. It was Gigi I went to if I had a question. She was oddly well-versed in most subjects. Only in chemistry did I have to ask for help from the online teachers.

"Fine," I answered as I went into my closet. I retrieved the boots I was going to wear and flipped off the bathroom light. Dad followed me as I took the boots to the edge of the chest at the foot of my bed. I put my boots on. They mostly covered the tall wool socks I wore.

There was a sweet knock at the door. I tried to beat my dad to it, but he got there before I could.

"Oh, hi, Paul." Luca was understandably surprised my father answered my bedroom door.

"Mr. Cameron," Dad corrected, though he'd spent the last six weeks telling Luca to call him Paul.

Luca's shoulders fell. "Sorry, I meant Mr. Cameron."

This was not helping me like my father. Luca was so sensitive to things like that, and Dad knew it. We all did.

"Tell me again where you two are going?" Dad's voice was so severe, so clearly saying he was the one in charge.

"The BayTree," Luca said, keeping his eyes lowered. "Some of the guys I work with recommended it."

"The guys you work with—on a construction site?" My dad's voice was repulsively snobby.

Earlier, I had doubted his similarity to Thomas—now I saw it.

Luca pulled his shoulders back. The movement made him look older, more confident. "They're good guys," he said, sounding like my father's equal.

Dad checked himself. "The BayTree is nice," he said after a moment. "And a nice distance from town, though the food is good enough that people do make the drive for it. Especially this time of year, when there aren't tourists at every table and the roads are still mostly clear."

"It will be okay," I said. "We'll keep a low profile. No one knows us, anyway."

Dad thought for a moment. "More people know you than you realize, and the two of … you don't exactly blend in."

Luca didn't blend in anywhere in this pale white town and my red hair had never helped me go unnoticed, either. Together … my dad was right, but what was the alternative?

I said, "We can't hide in this house forever."

Dad rocked back on his heels. "No, no, I suppose not."

"Come on," I said to Luca as I stepped past my dad.

Dad dug into his pocket. "Here, you can take my car."

I reached out my hand to take the keys.

"Thank you, sir, but that won't be necessary," Luca said. "Uncle Jace is letting me borrow his jeep."

Dad raised an eyebrow. "Your uncle's jeep is far from the safest of vehicles."

"The roads are clear, and I'm a cautious driver. It wouldn't be right to take your car, not tonight."

Dad and Luca looked at each other for a few seconds, as if they were having an unspoken debate.

"The roads are clear today," Dad said, "but in the future, any outings will be done in my car or Mom's, and that means Siena will drive. Got it?"

"Yes, sir," Luca said appreciatively.

I wasn't sure what just happened or why it mattered to Luca to be the one to drive, but apparently my dad accepted his unspoken argument. I was grateful for that small ounce of kindness he'd shown Luca, though I didn't understand it.

"Come on, we don't want to be late for our reservation," I said. I went past Luca and my father. I wasn't sure if Luca made a reservation or, if he had, what time it was for, but I wanted to leave.

Luca followed me from the room.

"Have fun and be careful," Dad called after us.

My dad was right. He and I had a lot to discuss, but tonight was not the night to think of his past or my past or even Luca's past. Tonight I'd think of the present moment. Tonight I'd think solely of Luca and me and the yummy dinner we were going to have—away from the rest of our families.

***

Sam greeted us with a broad grin when we entered the kitchen.

"You two look very nice," Gigi said as she placed her hand on Avi's shoulder, preemptively ready to stifle any inappropriate comments she may have been about to make. It wasn't necessary.

"Beautiful," was all she said in a calm voice.

It was startling to me that I used to wish for her to be more mature. It was so unnatural that it made me regret ever hoping for such a thing.

On the other side of the kitchen, Lisieux was helping Jason cook something. Since breakfast, it felt like there was a mountain between Lisieux and me. She didn't even glance in our direction. Jason at least offered us an approving wink.

"Here you go," Sam said, holding the keys out for Luca. She was trying to hurry us along, to get us out of the kitchen as quickly as possible.

"Thanks," Luca said, accepting the keys. He took his coat from the hook.

Sam held my coat. "You look lovely," she whispered as she handed it to me.

"Thank you," I whispered back.

"You two have fun," Gigi called. Avi's arms were wrapped around Gigi's waist.

"We will," Luca said, holding the door open for me to enter the frigid garage.

Luca hurried in front of me and opened the passenger side of the jeep.

"Thank you," I said, feeling very much like a princess despite the ripped seat patched with duct tape I was about to sit on.

"Wait a second," he said, pulling a mostly clean towel from the back of the jeep. "Sometimes the edge of the tape leaves a sticky mark on clothes."

Once the towel was in place, I climbed up onto the seat. The dash was cracked in places, but the car was clean, far cleaner than Dad's or Gigi's typically were. I wondered if Sam had cleaned it for us. The few times in the past when I'd glanced in the jeep, the floor mats had been covered with dirt; now they were spotless.

Luca opened the driver's door and slid in. In front of us, Sam hit the button to open the garage door and the garage began to get brighter. She waved goodbye and disappeared into the house—no need to allow arctic air into the kitchen.

"I'll get the heat going," Luca said as he turned the key, an action I'd seen in movies. Neither my dad's nor Gigi's car had an ignition switch, only a power button.

"What's that?" I said, pointing to a wide opening on the dash.

Luca laughed. "I had to ask Uncle Jace the same question. It's a tape player. It's what they had before CDs."

"Before CDs?" I said, running my finger along the opening. CDs were old enough; I hadn't thought about what existed before them. "Do they have tapes to go in it?"

"Yeah." He reached his hand to the glove box and his arm brushed my knee. "Take your pick."

The glove box was deceivingly large, overflowing with yellowed plastic rectangles. I picked up one with a picture of men with long, puffy hair and electric guitars on the cover. I turned it over. It was a box. I pulled on one side. It opened to reveal a smaller plastic rectangle with two holes. "I've never seen one of these before," I said with amazement.

"The sound's not bad. I mean, the stereo system is as old as the car, so nothing sounds great, but the tapes don't sound any worse than the radio."

"Can we listen to this one?" I said, choosing one with another group of men with long, messy hair and tight, ripped clothes pictured on the weathered insert on the inside of the scratched plastic cover.

Luca glanced over at the one I held. "That one sounds a lot like screaming. If you find the ones with handwritten labels, they're better. They came from Aunt Sam and don't have as much screaming. She calls them mixed tapes."

"What makes them mixed?" I said as I dug through the glove box, eventually finding one with Sam's handwriting on it.

"She made them herself. She said you could record songs from different bands onto one tape. That's one of her favorites. I don't love it, but I like it better than the screaming."

"Do I slide it in?"

"Line up the wider side with the wider opening," he said, his hands holding the steering wheel as we neared the gate.

"This is so weird." I inserted the tape.

It clicked into place, Luca turned the volume dial, and the music began as Luca turned out of our driveway. Music, outdated, not very good music, blared through the crackling speakers. That, combined with riding in an old rusty jeep, made the whole moment feel unreal, like a moment out of someone else's life. I closed my eyes and felt the rhythm of the tires against the road. I was grateful for the many bumps I could feel, more jarring than in my dad's or Gigi's cars; the bouncing kept me focused on the world in front of me. No memories, no dreams, merely the physical world as it *really* was.

"Are you okay?" Luca asked, turning down the music. "We can turn off the tape if you want. It's definitely not my favorite."

"I'm fine," I said, keeping my head against the headrest while at an angle to watch him. He was right; he was a cautious driver. Both hands were on the wheel and when he looked in my direction, it was for the shortest of moments. I wondered if he always drove like this or if it was because I was in the car. Either way, my father had nothing to worry about. Luca was a safer driver than he was.

"Do you want to talk about anything?" he asked.

He didn't believe I was fine.

"No, I'm good," I said, smiling to prove my point. In truth, I didn't want to talk about anything. I wanted to listen to music from tapes that were probably made before I was born. If Luca and I talked, I wanted it to be about something meaningless, but since I couldn't think of a meaningless topic, I listened to the song, envisioning a man and a woman with long, unkempt hair, singing together.

My eyes almost closed as the world of white and brown whizzed by, the edge of the scenic highway bordered on both sides by blackened snow. And usually, beyond that lay pristine snow.

"I like watching for animal prints in the snow," Luca said, his focus occasionally going to the side of the road.

"That's one of the funnest parts about fresh snow," I said with a nod.

"That must be a popular spot," Luca said, pointing toward a meadow area on my side of the road that held many tracks. He slowed for us to observe it longer.

"There's a pond farther back in the woods. Mom used to take me when I was younger," I said in happy remembrance. "Something about the ground around it or the way it was formed made the bank sandy instead of rocky. It was soft on my toes, like what I imagine Florida beaches would feel like."

"Do you go there much?" he asked. "In the summer, I mean."

"I haven't been in years. Dad took us once, after she died. I begged him to, and he gave in. But not since. He said there are too many leeches."

"Really?" he asked with concern.

"They're common up here. I'm surprised no one told you about them. And the ticks."

"I've been warned about the ticks."

Everyone who came to Maine was warned about the ticks.

"We have leeches in Florida," he said. "People don't talk about them, though, 'cause we don't swim in ponds."

He was so adamant it made me giggle. "Why don't you swim in ponds?" This was the sort of meaningless chatter I was hoping for.

He shuddered. "I seriously can't imagine anyone doing that. Maybe in the middle of the state, where they don't have oceans, but even then,"—he squirmed again—"the thought is gross. Blech!" He made a disgusted face and stuck out his tongue.

I giggled. "What's so awful about ponds in Florida?"

"They're so gross," he said, shaking his head. "Almost all of them are covered in algae and swarming with snakes that are definitely not harmless. And then there are the alligators." He squirmed. "The thought completely freaks me out."

I laughed. "Okay, got it. If I ever go to Florida, I will definitely not swim in ponds."

"Good plan," he said, nodding his head forcefully. "Do you want to go to Florida?"

"If the ocean water is warm, I'd like to go. When I watch people swimming in the ocean on TV, I'm so jealous."

"Where I'm from, during the hottest part of summer, the ocean feels almost like bathwater."

"It sounds heavenly," I said, thinking of the hot Florida beaches.

"Does the water here ever get above freezing?"

"If your definition of freezing is the technical one, then yes, it's almost always above freezing, but if you mean is it ever warm enough to comfortably submerge your entire body in without a wetsuit? Maybe a day or two a year, in a hot year."

"I was afraid of that," he said with a grimace.

"Do you like swimming in the ocean?" I asked.

"I love it. I feel most at home by the sea. Being in it is even more peaceful."

"At least when you moved up here, you didn't have to leave the ocean," I said. My head leaned against the seat, my mind and body relaxed. I was grateful to be talking about simple things like his love for the ocean and his ridiculous fear of Florida ponds.

"Yeah, that was one of Aunt Sam's selling points. Not that she needed a selling point. It's not like I had a lot of options."

"You didn't have to go with her. You were about to be eighteen."

"I love being with Aunt Sam," he said, glancing in my direction. "I would've come up here even without the private cove."

"A private cove with a haunted inn," I said wryly.

He laughed. "She waited to tell me that until I got here. It's okay, though. Now it's not haunted, and even when it was, the far end of the cove didn't bother me. Watching the waves, fishing—it's what I love to do."

"Watching the waves is my favorite thing to do too," I admitted. The rhythmic movement of the jeep was making me drowsy.

Luca's arms jerked hard to the left.

The turn had been too abrupt and we were spinning too fast. I screamed, my body instinctively pulling into a ball. Around and around went the jeep—my heart beating so fast.

Were we going to die? Was this my last moment on earth?

The jeep finally came to a stop. It started to creep forward.

I opened my eyes. We were in the middle of the road, facing the wrong direction. Luca was pulling the jeep over to the side.

"Are you okay?" he asked, breathing hard as the jeep crawled to a stop.

I didn't answer. I blinked at him, slowly moving myself out of the ball position.

"There was a … bear, I think. I don't know what else it could've been. It was too big to be a dog. I'm so sorry—it came out of nowhere. I turned to look at you and I saw it coming out of the trees. It was so fast. I had no idea bears moved that fast. Was it a bear? It must've been. I'm sorry. Say something. Are you okay?"

"We have a lot of bears around here," I said faintly. "Usually, they're hibernating by now."

Luca leaned his head against the steering wheel. "I've never seen a bear before," he mumbled.

I burst out laughing. I couldn't help it. The emotion of almost dying, coupled with the relief of not dying, and then his having never seen a bear before … something about that was beyond hilarious.

"Are you okay?" he asked as I continued to laugh uncontrollably.

He placed a hand on my back. I fell into him.

"Seriously, why is that funny?"

"You've … never … seen … a bear … before," I managed to say between fits of laughter.

"No, I never have," he repeated slowly.

The effect made me laugh even harder.

I was conscious of him gawking at me in bewilderment, but it didn't matter; I couldn't stop laughing. After several minutes my sides were hurting so much I was groaning. I breathed deeply. I wiped my eyes, hoping the black mascara hadn't smudged into raccoon eyes.

"Sorry," I managed to say with a steady voice.

He pulled his arm away from my back. "Don't be. It was nice to watch you laugh."

I sniffed, the laughter finally fading. "This helped me realize something. I've got to start living life. As much as I try to be careful, as much as you are a cautious driver, danger finds me. I could hide in my castle for the rest of my life and I'd probably end up getting struck by lightning or something."

"Danger does seem to find you," Luca admitted.

I leaned back in the seat. "I'm starving," I said, touching my stomach.

"Are you sure you don't want to go home?"

"And bring the lightning strike down on the whole family? I'm probably safer away from them."

"That could be true," he teased as he turned the ignition switch.

Fifteen

A few minutes later we were driving over the bridge that signaled we were leaving our small town and moving into an area visited by more tourists. During the summer months, traffic on this part of the scenic highway was horrific. The view of the bay was incredible, and all the tourists crawled through this area. During the winter, it was left to the locals.

The tide was low. Wooden piers jutted above a sea of mud. In another few hours the tide would reclaim this place, reaching twelve feet higher than it was now; the piers that currently stood against the middle of the sky would be only a few feet above the water.

"The ocean is so different here," Luca said, glancing out at the bay.

"I've heard that. Actually, I've heard it a lot." It was one of the things most often remarked on by the various tourists who occasionally attended Mass at our church.

"Yeah, I bet. It's hard not to be amazed by it. At home, the tide sort of drifts in and out so gradually, you don't notice until your stuff gets wet. But here, it's like the ocean is completely different at different tides."

"You should go up north," I said. "Our tides are twelve feet here, but up there they can be fifty feet."

"That's incredible. Have you been there?"

"Once, when I was Avi's age. It was the last trip we took as a family." I cleared my throat. "It was a lot of fun. We almost got soaked, though. The tide came in so fast, we had to run off the beach."

"The tide here catches me off guard all the time. The water pours in much faster than at home. The guys at work told me about people getting stuck on Potter's Island."

"Every summer, someone—sometimes, multiple someones—will wander out on the land bridge at low tide and not listen to the warning. They'll end up spending the night out there," I said, slightly amused.

"You don't feel sorry for them?"

"Are you kidding? There are signs everywhere, and people ignore them. They park where they aren't supposed to and are angry at the city when their cars are flooded with saltwater. Then they stay on the island too long and call 911 when they can't get back."

"What does 911 tell them?" Luca asked.

"That being stuck on an island for the next twelve hours does not constitute a medical emergency. There are signs posted for water taxis, but they ignore those too. It's like they expect the tides to stop flowing for them."

"People tune out signs," Luca said sympathetically.

"Potter's Island literally has a siren that goes off when it's time to go back," I said, moving my hands emphatically to prove the point.

Luca chuckled at how worked up I was getting. "People tune out sirens too, I suppose."

"You are far kinder than me," I said. I noticed the sun had dropped below the trees, causing the road to be streaked with shadows.

"I've watched people miss plenty of stuff that's obvious to me."

I thought about his words. What was obvious to him was a mystery to the rest of us. "Oh, fine, make me feel bad for thinking the tourists are stupid."

"I never said they weren't," Luca said, eyes gleaming, "but I understand how stuff that is so painfully obvious to some people is completely lost on others."

The jeep slowed. "I think we're here," he said, pulling the vehicle into a gravel parking lot. "This place must be good if there are already this many cars in the lot."

"It's beautiful," I said, noting the loosely draped white Christmas lights swaying gently in the faint ocean breeze.

"Yeah, it is," he said.

He and I both stared at the lights that somehow transformed the old two-story wooden structure into a magical place.

"I haven't been here in years," I said, wondering if the lights were a new addition.

"It's definitely a first for me," Luca said as he opened his door and I did the same. He raced around the jeep to help me out, but I was closing the door when he reached me.

"Sorry. Do you want me to get back in the jeep?" I said, grinning up at him.

"No, I guess not," he said, but in a way that told me he did.

"Oh my gosh, you do," I said, turning to open the door and climb back onto the towel covering the cracked leather seat.

"No, no," he said, holding the door shut. "My attempt at chivalry is over." He hung his head in mock failure.

"I'll let you open the door to the restaurant for me," I said.

"I mean, it's not the same thing, but I guess it'll have to do," he said in faked defeat.

"The restaurant door is far more important than the car door," I said, giggling. I was so grateful to be out with Luca and away from everyone we knew.

"You're just trying to make me feel better," he said as we neared the entrance.

For a joke, I reached for the door. He darted in front of me, blocking my way.

As Luca reached his hand out, the door swung open.

"Welcome to the BayTree," the hostess said.

I forced my mouth closed to keep from giggling too loudly. Luca cleared his throat and tried his best to keep his amusement to a minimum.

"Thank you. We have a reservation for two," Luca said as we entered the dimly lit restaurant.

This building had been here forever and had many different lives before it was a restaurant. From the appearance, I was pretty sure most of what I was seeing was original. The floor certainly was—worn and scuffed, completely unfinished. I couldn't help but think of all the splinters you would get by walking barefoot across it. Rustic chic was in, making this one of the most popular tourist restaurants in this part of Maine.

"Do you prefer to sit inside, or outside on our heated deck? It overlooks the bay," the hostess, who was maybe a few years older than us, asked in a cheery voice.

"He's not from here. We'd better stay inside, near the fireplace," I said, teasing Luca.

"No," Luca said abruptly. "Outside, under a heater, please."

"Of course. Give me a moment to get your table set up," she said, disappearing into the restaurant.

"Are you okay?" I asked him.

"Fine," Luca said, averting his eyes.

I was pretty sure he was lying.

All around us were framed newspaper articles highlighting the history of the building and the restaurant's opening. Luca studied them.

The hostess approached us and said, "Right this way, please."

She led us around tables and past a roaring fire in a large hearth. Part of me wished I hadn't teased Luca about not being able to handle sitting outside. A hot fire would've been nice. Outside, the air was cold, but it would be pleasant enough at a table under a heater.

"It's so beautiful," I said as she sat us near the edge of the deck. A full moon was reflecting in the rippling water, and the Christmas lights were twinkling above the heater which stood next to our table.

She paused for a moment, her gaze shifting out to the bay. "One of the perks of working here—great views. Chase will be your waiter," she said, before turning and going inside.

"This is really nice, Luca. Thank you for inviting me here," I said as I gazed across the table at him.

He casually rubbed his forehead. "Thank you for agreeing to go out with me," he said, his voice no longer filled with laughter.

I studied him. "Are you sure you're okay?"

He put his hand down. "Perfectly. Just a little hungry."

"You're lying."

"I have a headache, but it will go away."

I leaned forward and whispered, "Is there evil?"

He unwrapped the silverware and placed the white napkin on his dark jeans. "I'm fine. Let's look at the menu. The guys told me the Lobster Mac N Cheese is fantastic. They also suggested the Lobster Ravioli, but I'm more of a Mac N Cheese kind of guy." He rattled on until the waiter appeared at our table.

"Welcome to the BayTree. Have you two been here before, or are you joining us for the first time?" he said as he poured each of us a glass of water from a silver pitcher.

"I've been here, but it's been years."

His eyes rested on me. "Well, we're glad you're back," he said with the hint of something I didn't recognize.

"And you, sir, have you dined with us before?" the waiter asked, his eyelids drooping low as he appraised Luca.

"No, this is the first time, but I've been told to order the Lobster Mac N Cheese," Luca said cheerfully.

"Yes, it's a definite favorite of our patrons. So the Mac N Cheese for you, sir? … Miss, do you happen to know what you would like?" he said, turning to me.

"I hear the Lobster Ravioli is good."

"It is," he said with a nod. "Is that what you would like?"

"Yes," I answered, handing him the menu I hadn't bothered to open.

"Would either of you like something to drink besides water, some hot tea, perhaps?"

"No, thank you," I answered for Luca and me.

"Very well. I'll be back in a moment with some warm bread and honey butter." He looked at me one more time and abruptly turned to go into the restaurant.

"Man," Luca said after he was gone, "I'm glad I can't read people's minds."

"Why do you say that?"

"I'm pretty sure I'd end up punching him in the face," he said, and took a sip of water.

"Why?" I couldn't believe Luca would ever say something so violent.

"You didn't notice how he was staring at you?" Luca said, raising an eyebrow.

"I noticed something," I said, realizing that Luca interpreted the waiter's overfocus on me as attraction—I did not. I wasn't sure what it was, but I didn't think that.

"Something?" he said. "Siena, it was like I was a toadstool and you were a fairy princess."

I took the opportunity to change the subject. "I've always wondered if fairies are real."

He leaned back. "My mom told her clients they were."

The waiter returned, placing a basket of steaming bread and warm butter between us. "Enjoy," he said and left.

Luca took a piece of the bread and spread an inch of butter on top of it.

I took a risk. "What was your mom's job? You've never told me."

He slowly chewed the bite of bread that was in his mouth and took a drink of water.

"She was a psychic," he said. "At least, for the last eight years or so."

"A psychic?" I asked, confused. Previously, he made it sound like his mom was awful, and I assumed that meant whatever she did was illegal or mean, but being a psychic was neither illegal or mean—unless she cheated people.

"The term 'medium' is more accurate," he said, the muscles in his jaw flinching.

"Being a psychic or a medium is bad?" I asked, taking a piece of the bread.

"Few things are worse."

"Did she lie to people, tell them she could channel spirits when she couldn't, or something?" I was thinking that it might be the lies that made it such a horrible profession.

"No," he said. "She never lied." His jaw remained tight.

The hostess showed another couple to a table not far from ours. Luca took advantage of my distraction to turn his gaze out to the bay. Moonlight sparkled as the water started to spill over the oyster shells beneath the high deck.

"Have you ever been on a sailboat?" he asked, his voice subdued.

"No," I said, watching him gaze out at the bay.

"Me neither, but that's my dream."

"To go on a sailboat?" I asked.

"To live on one. To float out in the middle of the ocean, away from the rest of the world. Away from the—." He stopped mid-sentence.

"Away from the evil," I said.

He offered a weak smile. "The bread is delicious," he said, reaching for a second piece. "You should eat the piece you're holding."

I placed the bread onto the appetizer plate in front of me.

"The butter is amazing," he said as he finished spreading another inch on the piece he held.

I accepted the knife he offered me and spread butter over my bread. The smell was intoxicating, the taste even more so.

"Something about warm bread on a cold day," he said, relishing his second piece.

I said, "Wouldn't you miss fresh-baked bread if you lived on a sailboat?"

"I'm not talking about only eating fish for the rest of my life or anything. I'd still go to the store for supplies, and I'd want a boat big enough for at least a small oven."

"Freshly baked bread on a sailboat," I said, contemplating the idea.

"Nice, right?"

"Yeah." I was surprised by how good that idea felt.

A shadow crossed our table. With his attention on me, our waiter said, "May I fill your glass?"

Both Luca and I sat straighter. I didn't realize how much we were both leaning toward each other.

"No, thank you," I said. My glass remained mostly full.

"I'd like some," Luca said, holding his glass up.

"Absolutely," our waiter said. "You two picked a beautiful night. Sometimes the winds off the ocean are too strong, but tonight is perfect. The sailboats are my favorite. Your meals should be out in a few minutes."

He disappeared as abruptly as he'd appeared.

"Do you think he heard us?" I said.

"I think he was far too busy focusing on you to actually hear you," he said, raising an eyebrow.

"He's not attracted to me," I said, and took a sip of water.

"Whatever you say," Luca said, spreading butter on another piece of bread.

Luca leaned away from the table when our waiter reappeared, carrying two ceramic bowls with charred oven mitts. "These are very hot," he said as he placed the first one in front of Luca and the second carefully in front of me.

"That was fast," Luca said.

"We do our best," he said with a lazy smile. "Can I get you two anything else?"

"No, thank you," I said.

"Then I'll leave you to enjoy your meals." He went to another table to take their order.

Luca took a bite of his Lobster Mac N Cheese. Strings of hot cheese trailed to his mouth. "The guys weren't kidding. This is seriously good."

I cut a ravioli into fourths and speared one of the smaller pieces with my fork. "Very good," I said as its creamy texture indulged my mouth with happiness.

We were silent for several minutes, enjoying our food. Gulls called to one another as they swooped down into the partially filled bay. We could hear the sound of waves gently lapping against the exposed oyster shells.

In the relative silence of gulls and waves and the murmurings of other diners, I felt grateful. Grateful that I was here with Luca, away from the castle I imprisoned myself in, and away from the vindictive eyes of the people at our church and town. Here I could be free, I could be me.

"Thank you for bringing me here," I said as Luca took his last bite of food.

He placed his fork against the thick ceramic bowl. Even at home, he ate so quickly he was starting to wash the dishes before the rest of us were halfway through with our meal.

"Thank you for coming with me."

Luca ate another piece of bread as I finished my ravioli.

"Would you like dessert?" he asked.

"Maybe we could split something," I suggested, not sure I could eat any more, but not wanting our time together to end. "I'm going to find the restroom. Feel free to order while I'm gone."

"I'll get a menu. We can pick something out when you get back," he said.

"Perfect," I said as I scooted my chair back.

Inside, the restaurant was warm and cozy, with fires burning in at least two fireplaces.

"Can I help you?" our waiter said, noticing me on his way back to the kitchen.

"Where's the restroom?"

"Up the stairs—here, I'll take you," and he began leading the way toward the front of the restaurant. Next to the stairs, there was a sign that pointed up for the women's restroom.

"I'm sure I can find it," I said.

"It's an old building. The restrooms are kind of off the beaten path." He led me up the stairs.

I winced at the first step.

"Injured?" he asked.

"I hurt my knees," I said.

"That's too bad," he said dismissively.

How Luca thought this guy was into me, I had no idea. He could barely stand walking in front of me.

The second floor was as dimly lit as the main floor and equally crowded with delicious smells in the air. Every table or so, I saw a dessert that made me forget I was full. We continued toward a side hallway. He was right; this was out of the way.

"Here you go," he said, stopping in front of the women's restroom.

"Thank you," I said.

He hesitated. "You aren't what I expected."

"What you expected?" I asked, puzzled.

"You're the one who was with Thomas when he died. Siena's your name."

Heat rushed through me.

"Are you paying your servant boy to date you, like you paid Thomas? You going to kill him too?"

I reached for the restroom door—my escape. He moved out of my way, not trying to block my path.

"Beth was right about you," he said as I slammed the door and slid the lock into place.

I stood with my back against the door, breathing rapidly. My head spun. My body shook. I thought I was safe here, that no one knew me or Luca. I was foolish to have believed I could ever escape. Stupid to have left my house.

I felt dizzy. Tears stung my eyes. Beth was right? What did that mean? I wanted to turn and run from the building, but what if he was still outside the door when I left? I looked around; there was a sink and a door. I went toward the door—maybe there was another entrance, one less out of the way. One he wouldn't be waiting at. I opened the door. There was a toilet, and there was another door. The room was oddly large for a simple water closet. The second door was not as tall as the door leading into the water closet, the top of it angled with the ceiling.

My pulse quickened. Maybe it was a way out.

I stepped into the water closet, leaving its door open. I turned the knob of the angled door, assuming it would be locked if it didn't lead out of the restroom. The knob turned. I pulled open the door, excited at the prospect of eluding Beth's horrible waiter friend. The cold was overwhelming, the space dark, subtly illuminated by the bright lights of the room behind me. This was not an exit. It was … I studied it … part of the attic.

The bottom of the roof tilted upward, wooden trusses shoring up the roof. There was plenty of space for me, or anyone else, to enter. The floor felt stable, finished with thick planks of wood—not like the simple plywood used in modern attics. This wood was made to support the weight of many people and heavy furniture, not merely to keep you from accidentally falling through the beams of the attic. This space, despite the beams crossing along the edges, was another room. I shivered, my breath coming out in a cloud. Above me was the strong wood supporting the roof; there was no insulation. This could never have been used as a room, at least not during the winter. Its inhabitants would've frozen. It was merely attic access. I tried to relax … and calm my swirling emotions. What were the emotions? All that made sense was to feel anger at the waiter, but I felt more. Much more. What was it?

I stepped forward into the darkness. My trembling hand automatically went to a beam of wood beside me—anything to bring stability to my racing body. I felt the rough splintered wood, the corners with jagged edges. In the wood I felt … fear. I pushed my hand flat against the uneven grain. The fear was not mine. This was an empty attic, the waiter was not here— there was nothing for me to fear, and yet I felt fear so deeply I wanted to cry, to cower in a corner until someone found me and saved me. In front of me, children appeared—dark faces stared up at me. Their eyes were hollow and burning with pain. They huddled together, bodies covered in rags. It was their fear I felt. I was seeing what was not there. I tilted my head, my eyes narrowing. They were not there, I told myself, but they looked so real. I reached with my right hand toward one of them. She ran from my movement, inches from my touch.

They saw me.

I was real to them, just as they were real to me. They tried to hide; they were terrified of me. Not the me I was, but the me I represented. It was as if they knew who I was, but of course they didn't. They clutched one another. The rags that covered them were not created to be rags; they were once beautiful clothes lovingly selected for each child. These children had been loved once. They were still loved, but not in this place.

The smell of human waste wafted in the warm, humid air.

They were so … so afraid. I wanted to help them, to tell them I wouldn't hurt them. I moved forward, bending toward them, sliding my hand down the beam. The children pulled back. I was a threat to them, someone who was going to hurt them.

"Siena!" I heard my name called from a great distance.

My hand instinctively pulled away from the wooden beam. The children were gone; their haggard faces disappeared. An empty attic remained.

My breath caught in the frozen air. My fingers went toward the beam. I didn't want to witness the pain of the children, but I needed to understand.

"Siena, let me in," Luca's weak voice called behind me.

I reluctantly stepped back, out of the darkness. My mind cleared. I ran from the water closet and unlatched the door.

Luca believed I was in danger; I could read it in his expression. He wrapped his fingers around my arm.

"We need to leave," he said, pulling me down the hallway.

He didn't give me the chance to speak, though I didn't think I could, even if he'd asked me to. My mind whirled so fast that nothing made sense. Other diners stared at us; I didn't care. I wanted out of this place as badly as Luca did. How did he know I needed him? How did he know to come to me?

He raced down the stairs. I winced in gratitude at the pain in my knees. It reminded me of reality, that I was flesh and bones. That Luca was real, that we all were. All who were alive … were the children alive? No, they couldn't have appeared and disappeared if they were alive.

Luca pulled cash from his pocket and thrust it at the hostess. "This is for our bill," he said to her without slowing down. His hand was on my back, guiding me forward.

"Is everything all right?" she asked with feigned interest.

"No," he said as we hurried toward the door.

"Have a nice evening," the hostess called as the door swung shut behind us.

The cold clung to the sweat that covered my body. The cold didn't matter—nothing mattered except the haunted expressions that floated in my mind.

Luca guided me steadily across the parking lot. One hand on my back, the other on his forehead. Part of me wanted to speak to him, to tell him what I'd seen or ask him why he'd come to me, but still, no words came.

We reached the jeep. He fumbled with the key. His hand was shaking.

Had he seen them too?

He unlocked the door. I climbed in. He slammed the door and ran to the driver's side.

I cast a glance at the roofline of the restaurant. A dim light shone from the ladies' restroom … beside the attic.

Sixteen

Luca turned the key in the ignition. The jeep followed his commands as we quickly spun out of the gravel parking lot.

Luca held his forehead, his breathing shallow. He was in pain. After a mile or two his breathing relaxed and he removed his hand from his head, placing it carefully on the steering wheel.

"Are you okay?" he asked, his voice frail from the headache that was leaving him.

Was I okay? "Yes," I answered meekly.

"You didn't ask me what I was doing when I forced us to leave," he said, trying to steady his breathing.

"No," I said—the thought of remaining for even a moment longer in that place engulfed me in a blanket of darkness.

"Why not?" he asked, as if afraid of my answer. As if my awareness of all that had been in that place was even more dangerous than the place.

"You were right," I said, clearing my throat, my voice becoming stronger. "We needed to leave."

"How did you know?" he said, his voice trembling.

Yes, he was more afraid of my awareness of the danger than the danger itself.

I turned my head away from him, watching the trees blur past as the jeep's headlights illuminated them. "I saw something. When I touched a beam of wood I saw ...." I couldn't go on with the truth. "I saw something."

He was silent for a moment, his expression still as stone, and then he said, "Like what happened at the inn?"

Was it like the inn? That seemed so long ago, though it was yesterday when I saw the blood dripping from Thomas's arm, down his thin fingers.

"Yes," I said. If the question came from anyone else, I would have left it at that or, in truth, never mentioned any of it, but he wasn't anyone else—he was Luca. Luca, who felt evil and saw holy souls. Luca, who for some reason, knew to find me.

I continued. "But it was ... more intense. Like it was happening now."

I watched him. Even in the darkness of the jeep, I could tell his dark face had turned pale.

"You're afraid," I said, voice trembling. If he was afraid, how much more afraid should I be?

His eyes flitted to mine and then back to the road. "Yes."

My voice shaking, I said, "Why?"

Why was he afraid of the haunted children? He hadn't seen them—he hadn't felt their fear. Yet his voice trembled. My body shivered. The cold was seeping into the very essence of my soul. I doubted I'd ever be warm again.

The trees blurred past us. Luca held the steering wheel tight, unwilling or unable to take his eyes from the road.

"You aren't the first person I've known who saw the memories of places." His voice sounded timid and young, nothing like his normal voice.

Even in the darkness I could sense he was near tears. His world, the world he created for himself, was collapsing in front of me. Why should the images of the past two days matter so much to him? The metallic taste of fear rose to the back of my throat.

"Who else?" I whispered.

He shook his head. He could not or would not answer. His face was so pale I was afraid he'd faint. He was driving twice as fast as he had on our way to the restaurant. He pulled the jeep onto a side road. Thank God the roads were clear. If he'd taken the turn that fast with even the thinnest layer of ice, the jeep would've been wrapped around a tree.

My dad was right; from now on I would drive. That assumed Luca would ever venture out of the house with me again. Something about the death grip he had on the steering wheel told me that was unlikely. He guided the jeep up the hill that led to our church. He didn't need to explain where he was going or why. He went to church often, as often as Sam would lend him the jeep. It's where he felt the best. It made sense that he'd go there now, when he felt his world crumbling. He didn't tell me that was how he felt, but I was right. My hands trembled. I pushed them together in my lap to try and steady them.

Of the houses near the church, some had lights on, some didn't. The parking lot was well lit. There were no other cars around. The church would be locked, but it didn't matter. Father Luke had given Luca the code to the lockbox that held the key. It had been at Gigi's request; Father Luke never said no to Gigi.

Luca didn't bother to pull into a parking spot. He stopped in front of the steps and turned off the jeep.

"I need to go inside. Will you come with me?" Luca asked, trying to keep his voice calm.

"Yes," I said. I could never deny him such a simple request. Nor was I brave enough to sit alone in the jeep, not after the waiter … the children ….

He jumped from the jeep. I undid my seat belt, but was still sitting when he came around and opened the door. He offered a faint smile. He thought I was allowing him to open the door for me. In truth, my mind had moved too slowly to open the door myself.

He took my hand and gently guided me from the car. I stood, facing him, my eyes on his. I touched the side of his face. His skin was soft; he'd shaved for our date.

"It will be okay," I said. Why I said this or where the understanding came from, I didn't know, but my words were true. Somehow it would be okay.

He leaned into my touch. His eyes closed. I caressed his cheek and a tear wet my thumb. He sniffed and straightened. He opened his hand, inviting me to take it. I did so. He squeezed my hand as if determined not to let me slip away. I read too much into it—I was sure—but in his grip … I felt him holding on to me as if he was refusing to allow the darkness to steal me away.

He started up the stairs with me by his side. When he reached the lockbox protruding from the wall of the church, he had no choice but to release my hand. Still, he kept his body close to mine.

He entered the combination, a slot opened, and a key slid into his open hand. He took a few steps and inserted the key into the lock, pulling the door open. The foyer was illuminated by the faint blinking glow of a smoke detector. There were no windows in this part of the church. After a few seconds, our eyes began to adjust.

Luca slipped the church key into the pocket of his jeans. Behind us, he clicked the deadbolt, locking the double doors. I felt relief when the door was locked; no one could enter behind us.

The foyer was far from warm, but it was not nearly as cold as the outside air. Most of the time, the heat was turned off, programmed to turn on when the sanctuary was in use during Mass times. Today was Friday; the last Mass had been at noon and the church had begun cooling soon after.

When the smoke detector blinked, I was reminded that I had not used the restroom at the restaurant. "I'm going to the restroom," I said quietly. Even at night, with no one around, speaking in a regular voice at church felt wrong.

"I'll go with you."

"I'd rather you not," I said with a wry smile.

"I'll stand outside the door." He was going toward the hallway where the restrooms were.

I placed a hand on his chest, blocking his way. "It's okay. The church restroom isn't haunted." I meant it as a joke, but he took it seriously.

"If it is, it will be with holy souls," he said thoughtfully, "so you should be okay. They might startle you, but they won't hurt you."

His words added to my fatigue. Two months ago I would've thought he was joking; now I knew better. Luca never joked about the holy souls. Instead he prayed for them continuously, honoring them as much as others honored saints.

"I'll be right back," I said.

In the hallway I turned on the light. I was far too jittery to walk around in the dark, even if there were only holy souls around. The restroom light turned on by itself when I entered— a recent upgrade to the electrical system.

I was right. There were no ghosts, no memories in this restroom, only those replaying in my mind. As I washed my hands with frigid water, I stared at my expression in the mirror. My eyes were fearful, but nothing like the eyes of the children in the attic. What had to happen to a person … a child, to create such haunted expressions?

The foyer was empty. I went toward the sanctuary. I didn't have to wonder where he'd be.

My boots echoed off the worn pine floors. Hints of moonlight filtered in through the stained-glass windows on the east side of the church. The moonlight was the only light other than the candle burning inside the red glass holder. That candle remained lit as long as Jesus was in the tabernacle.

Luca was there.

This was where he'd spend all of his time if he were allowed to. I thought of the prophet Samuel, how much Luca would have loved to live in the temple as Samuel had done. Perhaps the prophets were the same. Perhaps they, too, felt God's presence in a tangible way. Having Luca as an example of this brought a new understanding of what these men and women may have been like. Outside, they would've appeared like the rest of us. Inside, they were very different.

Luca was kneeling, head bent low, almost touching the base of the tabernacle. There was a rug on the altar in front of where the tabernacle stood, which meant Luca could stay in that position for hours without much pain. But he never remained kneeling for hours. He knelt for minutes and then switched to a sitting position. This was at Father Luke's request, and Luca always did as Father Luke requested.

I genuflected, knees throbbing as I bent them, and slipped into the first pew. Luca looked up at the tabernacle and bowed again. He stood and reached out his hand, touching the gold box, a replica of an ancient temple with its carvings on the sides. He kept his fingers against it for a few seconds, head bowed. Then he removed his fingers, crossed himself, and came toward me. He knelt with both knees going down to the pine floor, an action the rest of us only did when the Eucharist was exposed in the monstrance. He bowed his head low again, then rose, and sat beside me.

We sat in silence for several minutes. When he finally spoke, his voice was stronger, back to how it was earlier in the evening. "Will you tell me what happened?"

I picked at a snag on my dress. "Will you tell me who else has had … who else is like me?"

"I asked you first," he said calmly.

I could have argued this point since I'd asked him first, in the car, but I let it pass. It wasn't him—that much I was sure of—nor did I think it was Sam. Who else could it be? Part of me didn't want him to answer.

"You were wrong about the waiter," I said, quietly beginning. "He was not attracted to me. He recognized me … he recognized us. He's friends with Beth. He said I was exactly as she described me."

"He recognized us?" Luca said, leaning toward me in concern.

I nodded.

"What did he do?" His eyes were wild.

He hadn't expected danger on the human level, only the spiritual. I wondered at this moment which one he thought to be more dangerous.

"He led me to the restroom and said some awful things, so I went inside, locking the door behind me. I didn't want to run into him when I left, and it was a strange room, so I figured there might be another way out."

"How was it strange?"

"There was a sink and another door."

"I'm sure the other door opened to the toilet," Luca said.

"It did, and that room was larger than the first room and it had another door. I thought it must go to another entrance, so I opened the door."

Luca's hand went to the back of the pew as he leaned in closer to me.

He sensed danger. He felt in this moment what I had not. If I had, would I have entered the attic? Would I have seen those children?

I swallowed down the fear. "It … it wasn't a way out."

Seventeen

Beside me, Luca's body became rigid.

"Where did it go?" he asked through gritted teeth.

"The attic," I answered. "The ceiling sloped down and wooden beams were crisscrossing all over it."

"What was in it?"

"Nothing … at first."

"At first?" His voice cracked.

"I felt something. I didn't understand it, but it was so strong. My fingers went to a wooden beam for stability. Being in there, feeling whatever it was I was feeling—it made me uneasy. I needed stability," I said, defending my actions even though he wasn't accusing me of any wrongdoing.

"When I touched the beam, they were there." The memory of the roughly hewn oak against my fingertips transported me back to the dark space where children huddled in terror. Their eyes so hollow, their faces so thin. They were together, trying … to keep me from them.

"Siena," he said with concern.

I shivered violently. I was in my church, Luca beside me. "I didn't want to see them. I didn't want them to be there," I said, choking back tears.

"Who?" he said, his arm going around me, offering me safety—something the children never had—not in that place.

Safety did not exist there.

I inhaled, trying to catch my breath. "There were children, little children, younger than Lisieux." I swallowed. "Some were younger than Avi. They were terrified, absolutely terrified," I said, tears falling at the image of the haunted expressions.

He held me protectively. "It's okay," he said. "They're gone now."

I wiped my nose on the back of my hand. "I'm not crying because I was scared, though I was," I admitted. "I'm crying because of their pain."

He was silent a moment. "You believe they were real?"

"What else could they be? I mean, I don't think they were there now, but … it was… it was like I was seeing the memory of the attic."

"Tricks can be played on people," he said, his arm still around me though he sat up straighter.

"You think it was like a projection or something?" I asked, realizing that Luca was studying me as I had studied him when I thought he was crazy. Did he think I was crazy? Maybe he did. Maybe I was. With all that I'd been through in the last two months, would anyone blame me if my mind broke?

"Did it look like a projection? Were the images flat, only visible against a wall?"

I thought back. There were children in the middle of the room, children that fled from my appearance. "No."

"Then I don't think it was a projection," he said.

"Do you think I hallucinated?"

"It's possible," he said, "though unlikely."

"What do you think it was? Where did they come from?" I said.

"Evil can plant things in your mind—thoughts, images, words."

Suddenly the defense of my sanity was no longer relevant, not when Luca said something like that.

He offered a muted laugh. "Now you think I'm the crazy one."

I was silent.

"We're at war, Siena. Never underestimate your enemy, especially when he's smarter than us."

Luca often spoke like this, comparing life to war—a spiritual war for each soul.

"You think evil planted that image?" I asked, my eyebrows pulled together.

"It's possible," he said.

"Does evil plant things in your mind?"

"It tries, it always tries." His voice sounded tired. "I'm fortunate, I guess. I can sense when demons try to invade my mind. I can tell that those thoughts, those desires aren't mine, and most of the time I can shut them out."

"Only most of the time?"

"Sometimes I'm too tired, sometimes I'm too weak. Sometimes they enter so subtly that they gain a foothold before I realize what's happening. Most of the time I recognize the attack and fight it off. I don't believe most people are like that.

They can't feel when darkness descends on them. Instead, they believe the lies their minds tell them."

"I've had enough talk of demons for tonight," I said, and thought, for my lifetime, as I leaned against the pew, no longer allowing Luca to hold me.

"Angels are far smarter than us. The fallen ones are no exception," he said.

I wished he hadn't said that.

The red light beside the tabernacle flickered in the darkness. There were times in my life when thoughts that led to anger, envy, and division entered. Never before did I doubt where these thoughts came from. They were in my mind, they were mine. Now ….

"Demons can invade our minds?" I asked, afraid of what might be lurking beside me.

"I'm not sure if they can read our thoughts, but they can trigger thoughts in us. That much I can sense. Demons exist to keep us from God, which is what sin is—separation from God. There's no quicker way to do that than by creating evil inside the hearts and minds of humans."

"The children were so real. I could feel their terror."

Luca rubbed his hands together. My words terrified him, far more than the discussion of demons.

"If the image was not an illusion of some form, then it was from God, which is possible. You weren't seeking them, you weren't trying to bring them to you." He was speaking, now, more to himself than to me. "So it could be, but if they were from God, there would be a reason. Some good could come of it—his allowing you to see what you saw."

I thought back to when Luca had taken my hand: the relief I'd felt, the peace he offered even though he was in pain.

"You were sick, so it can't be from God," I said, my shoulders trembling.

He shook his head. "I was sick, but it doesn't mean the vision was evil. It means there was evil lurking nearby."

"Is that why you called to me?"

If he hadn't called my name, I would've touched the wood again. I would've been surrounded by the children again. I leaned forward against my aching knees. I felt safer that way, with more of my body covered.

The memories of Thomas's pictures all over our little church mixed with the terrified children. I pushed my hands against my skull. It was too much. Too much pain, too many memories.

"The darkness was growing," Luca said. "That's why I came to you. I felt it when we were first in the restaurant, but didn't realize what it was. I thought it was attached to the people there. There's always a certain amount of evil whenever people are gathered. So I did my best to ignore it. It's why I asked for us to sit outside. When you got up from the table, I realized it was more than the normal amount. Your goodness was blocking it. I came to you as soon as I realized what was happening." His tone was apologetic. "But ...."

"What?"

"I didn't call your name."

"You didn't?" I asked, sitting up.

He shook his head. "The first time I said your name was when I was at the door. A second later, the door opened."

I leaned back. "If it wasn't you … who was it?"

His silence made me wonder. I said, "Did you feel anything else, any … any goodness? Whoever called kept me from going back to that place."

"I always feel goodness when I'm near you."

"Nothing more than that?"

"You make it sound like what I feel around you is no big deal—it is a big deal. Though I guess extra goodness could've been there. I wouldn't have been able to tell. It's like there's a scale and when the scale tips one way or the other, I can feel it. Good or evil."

"I wonder," I said, only partially listening to him, "if the voice was my mom's."

"Your mom?" he said with concern.

"Maybe she was the one who called to me. I mean, if it wasn't you, who else could it have been?"

"Your mind playing tricks, your guardian angel, the creepy waiter dude, a whole bunch of possibilities that would be more likely than your mom," he said, oddly upset by the mention of her.

He was wrong; her voice was the most likely. The waiter wouldn't have called to me. Why would he? The guardian angel theory was just as unlikely. I'd been hearing about my guardian angel since I was a young child. The effect of so many stories made it seem like nothing more than a fairy tale, to go along with all the other fairy tales I'd heard growing up.

"I don't believe in guardian angels," I said.

"You didn't believe in demons before," Luca stated.

I didn't answer him; I didn't need to. This was not something he could convince me of. Guardian angels couldn't exist. If they did, my mom wouldn't have died. My mother may not have recognized evil coming for her, but an angel warrior would have.

We sat in silence for a long time. The air around us, which initially felt warm compared to outside, was so cold it made my breath visible. This night had been too much. I wanted to be home, to be warm, to be safe. I lowered my eyes. Luca's hand was on the pew beside mine. His hand was so dark, it blended in with the night—my hand ghostly white beside it. The pit in my stomach grew.

"There's something else," I said weakly. How could I say this? How could I tell him … especially him?

"What is it?"

"The children," I said, as cold sweat began to build on my skin. "They were … I mean, they weren't … they weren't white."

Luca's hand tightened against the pew. "None of them?" he asked, his voice quiet.

I shook my head. I wanted to cry. Luca stood out in our white family and our white parish. Even the paintings and statues in the church were white. He was the one person of any color anywhere near us.

It made me uncomfortable—not the color of his skin, or mine—but the hurt those two colors represented. It was not our hurt, not what we brought to our lives. It was the pain of the past, the pain others long before us brought to our lives. The pain that still resonated through our country—and now, to have seen an image of horror in the eyes of Black children from the past ….

"I'm sorry," I said, though I'd done nothing wrong. I was sincerely sorry for whatever those children and all the other men and women like them, like Luca, had experienced.

"Evil preys most clearly on the most vulnerable. Little children of color … long ago. It doesn't get more vulnerable than that."

I could barely choke out, "N-no."

I prayed Luca was right, that the children had never been real. That I was not witnessing the torment of children who once lived, only made-up images from a mind that lost hold of reality.

Eighteen

I shivered; even though the church had been cold, I wasn't prepared for the arctic temperatures outside. It was rare for me to be out this late, when the sun was so long gone. My face burned as ice tried to form anywhere near moisture. I pulled the collar of my coat up and snugged it around me. Luca quickly locked the building and returned the key to its spot. I didn't wait for him as I hurried to the jeep. I climbed in, grateful he'd left it unlocked. Luca ran to the driver's side and cranked the engine.

"It's so cold," he said, teeth chattering as he tried to warm his hands with his breath. The steering wheel in this old car wasn't heated. Yet another reason to take my dad's car.

"Why was it so important to you to drive tonight?" I asked, the frozen leather of the seat making me even colder. This car also lacked heated seats.

He rubbed his arms to try and warm them as he pulled the jeep away from the front of the church and we crawled through the church parking lot toward the exit.

"It's our first … umm … time out together. The guy should be the one to drive."

"Even if the girl has a warmer car?" I said, holding my arms tight across my body. The heater tried, unsuccessfully, to keep the cold air from pouring in.

"To be fair, if we were in Florida, this wouldn't be an issue," he joked.

"If this were Florida, we never would've met," I said.

"I wouldn't be too sure about that."

"Why not?"

He was facing forward, purposely not looking in my direction. "My mom," he mumbled. "She told me one day I would have a good friend with red hair."

"Did Sam tell her about the family of redheads she lived next door to?" I asked.

He gazed into the night as the jeep pulled out of the parking lot. "No, it was before Aunt Sam came up here."

"Oh well, there are lots of people with red hair," I said, my hands cupped around the air vent, trying to capture every ounce of heat I could.

"There are," he said, with half a smile. "But not that many who live in a giant house, near a cliff."

"Red-haired girl who lived …." My voice trailed off. "How could she have guessed that?"

"She didn't guess. She was a psychic. I told you that."

"Psychics are real? I mean, I didn't think they could actually tell the future. I thought they were either smart con artists or sort of silly people who made things up without realizing it."

He leaned back in his seat. The air was beginning to warm slightly. "Most are exactly that, but my mom was different. She was not a con artist and she didn't make stuff up."

"She could tell the future?" I asked, staring at him, his face subtly illuminated by the lights on the dash.

"She could not," he said. "The spirits who spoke to her could."

"Spirits?"

"She believed they were angels." His jaw clenched in the fading glow of a streetlight. "Maybe some were." His body visibly relaxed a little.

"What were the others?" I asked, anxiety building in my chest.

"You know the answer to that question," he said without emotion.

"Demons?" I whispered into the darkness.

"Yes."

"Demons told your mom about me?" My voice quivered.

"No," he said, his head leaning to the side. This memory didn't bother him; this memory was not associated with pain. "She told me about the red-haired girl when I was very young. I was sitting on her lap when she did." The fingers of his right hand gently rubbed the steering wheel. "There was no darkness around her then. Sam was with us. We were happy, we were at peace. It was good back then."

"What happened?" I asked. "Why did things change?"

Luca's expression fell. "She flew too close to the sun."

"Her pride was her downfall?" I leaned my body sideways against the seat, facing him.

He glanced at me. "At first it may have been ignorance, but it turned into pride. She believed she was the one in control. She was wrong. When demons are involved, humans are never in control."

The sound of the tires running along the road was the only sound for several miles. My mind retreated into itself, wondering how this was my life. How were demons and psychics and a haunted inn and, now, a restaurant, so much a part of it?

Luca finally broke the silence. "I understand more now, more than I did before I moved up here. It isn't fair for me to blame her like I have." He tilted his head as if working through these thoughts as he was speaking them. "Pride was there, but that stemmed from ignorance. She didn't understand what she was involved with. She didn't understand the demons were not her friends, that they could never wish her anything but death. Their entire purpose is to destroy. She believed them. … She should never have believed them," he added quietly into the darkness.

"They spoke to her?" I said, facing him.

A truck passed us, briefly illuminating his features.

"Yes," he said. Such a simple word, with so much meaning.

"Why did she …?" How could I ask this question?

Luca shifted his body.

I swallowed hard and said, "Why did she speak to demons?"

"She believed they were angels, beautiful and bright, or sometimes souls of the dead, good souls coming to help their loved ones."

"What makes you think she was wrong?"

His face contorted in revulsion. "I could feel them. There was nothing beautiful about them."

"Maybe you were wrong. If she believed they were angels, maybe they were. Angels do appear to people in the Bible."

"Have you ever thought about after you die?" he asked.

"I've thought about my mom, about her being dead," I said, wondering if he was purposely ignoring my question.

"What have you thought about her? Have you thought of her bored, wishing she had something to do, waiting to do people's bidding on earth?" He glanced at me as the jeep went around a curve.

"No," I said, thinking of my mom, of how much I missed her and wished for any form of communication from her. If she were waiting to do someone's bidding, as Luca phrased it, she would've come to me.

"And what about the souls of those who have died far from God, those who chose hell? Do you think of them hanging out around people?"

The thought made me cringe. "No," I said. "They're in hell. They can't leave."

I was taught there's an uncrossable chasm that keeps the damned from leaving hell. Otherwise, the world would be overrun with the souls of the damned, and there would be no question of the existence of good and evil. The truth would be clear and people would be terrified into choosing God. This would not allow for free will.

"So you agree it's not likely that people see the souls of those who have passed on," he said.

My forehead wrinkled. "You see them every night?"

He tilted his head. An oncoming car brightened the jeep. "I do, but they're not there because I summoned them. They're there because of your prayers. They're there because God is allowing them to be there and allowing me to see them. God allows the holy souls in purgatory to interact with living people when he chooses, not when living people choose or even when the souls choose. It's because of his mercy that he allows them to be seen or felt at all, so that those living may pray for that soul or gain awareness of things they need to gain awareness of—not for their entertainment and certainly not at their command."

"Did Father Luke explain that to you?"

"He gave me the words to understand what I felt."

"So that's why you think your mom wasn't talking to angels?" I asked.

"Angels can't be summoned, holy souls can't be summoned, the damned can't be summoned …." His voice trailed off.

"But demons can?"

"They want to confuse, to draw people away from good. They will do whatever they need to do to make that happen. It's their one reason for existing. So yes, in that way, they can be summoned."

The wind whistled through the fabric of the jeep, the cold air continuously pushing itself in.

"I could sense the evil. I told my mom. Aunt Sam told her. She didn't care. She told us they were angels. I want to believe that she believed they were angels … good angels, but it's impossible for her to be that unaware."

I detected the disappointment in his voice.

"That isn't fair," I said. "Most people can't feel things the way you do."

His grip on the steering wheel tightened, though his voice became soft. "She wasn't 'most people.' Her gifts were stronger than mine and Sam's put together. How could she not have known?"

He was pleading with me, hoping I had an answer to a question I barely understood.

"You told me demons are smarter than us. If all of this,"— I swallowed—"if it's all true, she would've been easy to trick. We all would."

An image of my dad as a scrawny teenage kid entered my mind, and my anger at him cooled. "It wasn't her fault, Luca. It wasn't my dad's, either. If you haven't experienced evil, how would you know to be afraid of it, especially if it presents as beautiful angels or a … a loving great-grandmother."

"Even if everyone around you tells you you're wrong?" he said, wanting to agree with me that his mother was not completely to blame.

I inhaled the barely warm air as Luca neared our property. Once we entered my home we would be surrounded by family, by people who loved us. "You and I are lucky."

He raised an eyebrow in doubt.

"I never would've thought so either, but it's true. We're surrounded by people who love us, people who have learned hard lessons and are trying to protect us."

He silently reached a hand to the visor and pushed the button, causing the wrought iron gate to swing slowly open.

"And still evil finds us," he said as he inched the jeep forward.

"At least we aren't alone," I said.

He clicked the button for the garage. "No, we're not alone," he said stoically.

Nineteen

My room was dark. I tapped my phone—1:05. Had I slept at all? If I had, it hadn't been for long or very deeply. The children haunted me with their terrified eyes. I pulled my blanket around me and pushed my face against the pillow. I wanted their images gone from my mind. I wanted them to disappear. No, I wanted to go back in time, to have never entered the attic at that restaurant. I wanted to have never set foot in that place. Then I would've never witnessed the fake torment of fake children.

I sat up, pushing the hair away from my face. Why? Of all the restaurants we could've gone to, why did it have to be that one? Why did Luca have to choose that one? He hadn't seen their hollow expressions and yet he was more frightened by them than I was. Why was that? I wasn't the only one who saw images of the made-up past. Who was the other person? Why was it so awful? He saw dead people and they didn't scare him, but for some reason, this did. Part of me wanted to call him a hypocrite, but that wasn't Luca. He was truthful in all he did and thought, perhaps to a fault. But he had changed the subject, instead telling me of how his mother was a psychic visited by demons. This had nothing to do with me. I was not a psychic and I did not mistakenly believe I was being visited by angels.

I pushed hard against my head. I couldn't get them out. Couldn't escape. Is this how Luca felt? No, the visions he saw

… the ghosts didn't scare him. This was not the same. The children, the bloody arm, these images were not happening now; what he saw was. Somehow that made a difference.

I couldn't lie in bed any longer. I got up, wrapped my robe around me, and shivered.

"It's freezing," I said to myself as I stepped into my slippers and shuffled to the radiator. The air didn't feel warmer when I neared it. I reached out my fingers, tapping it quickly so I wouldn't be burned. I didn't need to worry. The metal was cold. I stooped to adjust the dial on the side of the undulating metal tubing.

I expected to hear a sound or feel warmth … nothing happened. I hesitated, unsure of what to do. The radiator had always worked.

I could start a fire, but what if the problem wasn't my radiator? What if it was our boiler? If that was the issue, my sisters' rooms would be ice-cold.

I went to my door and opened it. I hoped the hall would be warmer. Nope. A faint light seeped from my dad's room. I went toward it, stopping at his open door.

"Dad," I whispered.

There was no answer. I took a few steps into his room. The paisley duvet cover my mom had picked out was pulled back and the bed was empty. I glanced around. She no longer occupied the room, but he'd left her things hanging in the closet and stored in the drawers. On her nightstand lay the book she'd been reading. He dusted around her things, but otherwise left them as they were.

"Dad," I called quietly toward the bathroom.

I went to the radiator in his room. It was as cold as mine.

It wasn't the radiators—it was the boiler. The boiler that had worked perfectly every day since my grandparents first installed it.

I left his room and went soundlessly toward the dark stairs. I'd wait to turn a light on once I was downstairs; I didn't want to risk waking up the others.

My name was whispered as a hand touched my shoulder from behind.

I jumped partially out of fright, mostly out of reflex.

"What're you doing?" Luca whispered.

"You scared me," I said, my hand clasping the collar of my robe.

"I didn't mean to."

"The heat isn't working. I was trying to find my dad to tell him. He's probably already in the basement, working on the boiler. Did the cold wake you?"

"Not exactly," he said as he followed me downstairs.

Of course the cold didn't wake him. He kept his room at sauna temperature. Even after hours of sleep, there were probably still hot coals in his fireplace. There always were. Plus, Gigi got him an electric space heater a week or so after he moved in.

"I was looking for you," he said.

"Why?"

I clicked the kitchen light on, dimming it as low as it would go so it wouldn't light up the second-floor through the stairwell.

"I ah, I felt you move from your room. I decided to check on you," he said in an apologetic tone.

I wanted to be mad at him, but it was impossible. Even in the dim light, I could see the kindness in his eyes. It wasn't his fault he could sense me, any more than seeing the terror-stricken children was my fault.

"Come on, let's find Dad. Maybe we can help him get the heat working so we don't freeze."

His expression changed to one of relief when I didn't chastise him for following me.

We went down the hallway that led to the basement stairs as well as my dad's office. To my surprise, the basement door was closed. Firelight was flickering from the office door that had been left ajar.

I stopped. I hadn't expected this.

"I thought he'd be in the basement working on the boiler."

"Maybe he doesn't realize it's out."

I sidled to the door and peered through the opening. I straightened my body and cocked my head, then pushed the door open. It swung open with a squeak. My dad was there, asleep on the couch. The fire was burning brightly. On the end table was a bottle of brown liquid, half empty.

I went in, not trying to be quiet, internal heat burning my cheeks. He was asleep. Our house was freezing, and he was asleep.

"Bourbon," Luca said, reading the bottle's label.

"He doesn't drink," I stated.

Luca bent toward him. My dad's sleeves were pushed up, his left hand resting on his chest, wedding ring in the same place it had been for the last nineteen years. His right hand hung loosely, grazing the floor.

Luca stood up with a startled expression. He blinked rapidly and said, "He reeks of it. Either he poured it all over himself or he drank a ton of it."

I stormed away, not bothering to go quietly from the room. In the hallway I flung open the basement door and pounded down the stairs, flipping the light on as I went.

"Are you mad?" Luca asked as we reached the dusty wood floor of the basement.

"He's passed out! My sisters and grandmother are upstairs freezing and he's passed out. He doesn't even drink," I said, my voice loud. It didn't matter; no one on the second floor could hear me and neither would my father.

"This hasn't been an easy time for him," Luca said.

I rounded on him. "Don't! Don't make excuses for him. We've all had to figure out how to live with the guilt—and being hated. He doesn't get a pass because his life is hard. All our lives are hard."

"His guilt is greater," Luca said calmly, hands in his pockets.

I stormed toward the ancient boiler that was making loud noises every few seconds.

"Thomas was my friend. He was here because of me," I said, staring at the thick iron cylinder with multiple protruding pipes.

Luca said, "I saw something when we were in your dad's office, something on his arm."

"What, a fresh tattoo or track marks from all the drugs he's been shooting up?" I said, eyes burning.

"He's hurting, more than you realize."

I turned away, staring at the hunk of iron in front of me. An orange glow escaped. The fire was still burning.

"How long has he had that scar?"

"What scar?" I fumed as I kept my focus on the boiler.

"The one that crosses the width of his arm," Luca responded. He edged to the back of the boiler and examined it.

"He fell into a thorn bush or against a rock or something. I don't remember exactly." Though I did remember the scar. As a young kid, I would trace it when he held me. The memory softened the anger.

Luca glanced at me doubtfully.

"Have you got that thing working yet? It's freezing," Jason called from the stairs.

I slumped onto a wooden chair that used to be part of our kitchen set.

"At least it's warm down here," Sam said, trudging along behind Jason, her naturally wavy blonde hair sticking out in a variety of angles.

"Is it supposed to be making that thumping noise?" Luca said. "We don't have things like this in Florida."

Jason teased, "I don't suppose ya do. Let me have a go."

Luca stepped away as Jason carefully edged around the hot metal.

"This must be as old as the house," Sam said, appraising the impenetrable iron.

Luca sat on a chair next to mine. He never even glanced at me. Instead, he watched every move his aunt and uncle made.

He was trying not to look at me, not to talk to me.

"You don't think that's how he got that scar?" I said, forcing him to pay attention to me.

Luca's shoulders slumped slightly before he pulled them back. "I didn't say that."

"But that's what you think."

"How could a thorn bush or a rock do that?" he said in a low tone.

"I don't know. Thorns are sharp. So are some rocks. They can cut you like any other sharp thing."

"They don't usually go from one end of your arm to the other unless you make them. Seems like a weird thing for a kid to do—if that's how it happened," Luca said matter-of-factly.

"What're you two talking about?" Sam asked.

"The scar on Paul's arm," Luca answered.

"Aah," Jason said as he tinkered with the boiler.

Sam tilted her head at him. "Do you know something about it?" she asked her husband.

"He was picking blueberries. Fell against a rock. There, I think I got it working," he said, wiping a greasy hand on the bottom of his shirt. "Time for bed. Your rooms'll be gettin' warmer as we speak."

Jason didn't wait for us to follow. As he went toward the stairs, Sam glanced at Luca and me. It was a telling glance; she knew her husband wasn't being wholly truthful, but tonight wasn't the time to find out more.

Luca and I were alone in the basement. The boiler was quiet compared to the thudding it had been making.

"We should go up," he said.

I rose from the chair. My legs felt heavy. I followed Luca, the two of us moving in silence. When I reached the top of the basement stairs, I turned off the lights and shut the door—the faint glow from my dad's open office door falling onto the floor in front of us.

"Come on," Luca said, placing the tips of his fingers against the small of my back. "There's nothing you can do for him tonight."

"How long has he been like this?" I asked, eyes beginning to sting as I blinked away tears.

"Not tonight," Luca whispered. "You need to rest. You've had a long day."

He was right. I was exhausted. No clear thoughts came in the middle of the night, especially when that night followed the type of day I'd had.

I allowed Luca to guide me up the stairs, turning off the lights as we went.

Twenty

The remainder of my night was restless; I dreamt of my father, intermixed with the children. The morning was cold, though warmer than the night had been. After all, it took time to heat our giant castle.

I pulled a sweatshirt on over the long-sleeved shirt I'd slept in. The cuffs of the long flannel pajama bottoms covered the tops of the fuzzy slippers, that protected my feet from the cold bathroom floor. I brushed my hair, the ends flying up from the dry static. I wanted to check on the rest of my family, so I went downstairs. The smell of cooking food met me in the stairwell.

From halfway down the stairs, I could hear my dad's cheerful whistling.

"Good morning," he said as I entered the kitchen.

He was acting like nothing was wrong, as if he hadn't drunk himself to the point of passing out the night before. Gigi and my sisters were at the table. Avi was eating French toast while Gigi drank tea. Lisieux held her fork containing a piece of French toast and a book in front of her face. How many times had she been told not to read at the table? None, in the last several weeks, I realized. Not because she hadn't been reading at the table, but because no one cared about it.

"Were you aware the heat went out last night?" I asked, eyeing my father while wondering if any of them realized it.

"The heat went out?" Gigi said with disbelief.

Dad held a spatula in his hand. "The heat has never gone out," he said with equal doubt.

"There's a first time for everything," Lisieux said, lowering her book and taking a bite of the French toast.

Gigi said, "How did it go out?"

"I don't know how, only that it did." I took a mug from the cabinet and filled it with water.

"Did you fix it?" Gigi asked.

"Jason did," I answered, putting the mug of water into the microwave.

"How did I sleep through that?" Gigi asked in wonder. "Why didn't you wake us?"

"I didn't think you'd be able to fix it," I said to her. "And Dad was sleeping so *soundly* in his office, I didn't want to disturb him," I said, mildly attempting to hide the anger I felt.

He turned away and flipped a piece of French toast in the pan.

"You slept in your office?" Gigi asked with a hint of concern.

"I didn't mean to," Dad said in a cheery tone. "I was trying to get some work done, but must've passed out on the couch. I had a fire going in the office. That must be why I didn't wake up from the cold."

I literally bit my tongue to keep from speaking. How easily he lied. I plopped a tea bag into the steaming water while glancing toward the table. Lisieux and Avi were watching me. I turned away, holding the hot mug.

"Did you wake up Jason and Sam?" Gigi asked with concern.

I shook my head. "They found us in the basement."

"Us?" Lisieux said.

"Luca met me on the stairs," I answered.

"Poor boy must have been a popsicle," Gigi said. "How did Jason fix it?"

"I'm not sure. The boiler was making an awful thudding noise. He did something, the sound stopped, and heat started to go up to the radiators again," I said.

"Sounds like air in the lines," Gigi said.

Dad said, "I'll talk with him today and ask if I need to get someone out here to do some maintenance. Want some French toast?" He held a plate out for me.

"No, thanks," I said, and sipped the tea.

Gigi placed her mug on the table and said, "Avila and I would like some more, and yes, we need to be sure and speak to Jason today. I was wondering why he and Samantha hadn't come down yet. They must be sleeping in after being awake in the middle of the night. Thank goodness they were here, or we might have some missing toes this morning."

"It wasn't that cold last night," Dad said. He set the rest of the French toast on the table.

"Cold enough for an old woman," Gigi said, cutting a slice in half for her and Avi.

Lisieux had stopped watching the interactions, her book held up in front of her again.

Dad took her empty plate to the sink and started the dishes.

The scar on his left arm was visible with his sleeves rolled up. Why hadn't Jason wanted to talk about it?

Gigi and Avi ate quickly.

"Come on, Avila. You and I need to attend to the chickens," Gigi said, standing and taking the rest of the empty plates to the sink.

"You're going to help me?" Avi asked with relief.

"Yes, I feel like getting outside a bit. Might as well be productive while I do. Besides, today is a nice day. Cold, but sunny with no wind. The best we can ask for this time of year."

The two of them started layering on their snow clothes.

Lisieux closed her book, though she hadn't finished it, and rose from the table. "I'm going back to bed," she said as she started toward the stairs.

"Oh, to be fourteen again and be able to sleep the day away," Dad mused aloud.

I wanted to tell him she was depressed. That was why she was sleeping more and interacting with us even less than usual. But I kept it to myself.

"It used to drive your father crazy when you did that," Gigi said to Dad before she, Avi, and Jackson left the house.

"I remember," Dad called to her lightheartedly, a broad smile plastered across his face.

Only the two of us were left in the kitchen. He turned to the dishes. He appeared so normal, like he had every morning of my life. Did he drink himself to sleep every night? Did he take something every morning to wake up? No, not when I was young. When I was young, it was rare for there to be a night when one of us didn't go to him with a nightmare in the middle of the night. He was never drunk. I never even saw him drink a glass of wine. Until last night I would've sworn there was no alcohol in our house. Until last night I would have acknowledged that my father was seriously struggling, but not struggling like that. Drinking to pass out, using something in the morning. Was there ever a time of day he was not on something? How had he become that person? These thoughts were too much for me.

Leaving my tea on the counter, I quickly turned to make my way toward the stairs. At the first step, I stopped.

"How long?" I said, my voice shaking with too many emotions to feel any of them clearly.

The silence was so long I thought he hadn't heard me. It was for the best, I decided, as I took a step. Best not to ask a question when you didn't really want the answer.

"Too long," he said, his hands resting on the edge of the white sink. He didn't turn to face me—it was better that way. I fled up the stairs, away from the stranger in my kitchen.

I hesitated when I reached the second-floor landing. I could go to my room. I could hide there, alone and protected. I could focus on schoolwork. I'd become good at pretending I was okay. I could continue to do that.

Instead, I went in the other direction. I passed my sisters' rooms. Their doors were open. Lisieux was in her bed. I wondered if she was asleep. The next room, Avi's, was empty. I stepped inside. It was clean … it was never clean. Dad was always telling her to clean it, but she never did. Not really. She'd stuff things under the bed, into the back of her closet, and behind the bookcase. But now …. I lifted the bedspread. It was clean, actually clean. I should have been pleased by this. Her room usually was atrocious, but this … it was unnatural. This wasn't my baby sister's room. She wasn't the sullen, withdrawn neat freak. I was.

My eyes burned from the transformation Avi had gone through. It wasn't fair to her. None of this was fair to her. She deserved better. Better from me and way better from our father. I left the room; I could stand the pristine organization no longer.

I entered Luca's room without bothering to knock. He was sitting by the fireplace, a laptop in front of him. Technically it was Gigi's laptop, but she rarely used it. She'd asked him to use it to keep the updates fresh. He knew it was an excuse and appreciated having a way to get online.

When he saw my face, he immediately came to me.

"What is it? What's happened?" he asked with trepidation.

I shook my head, biting my lip in a futile attempt not to cry. I hated that I cried so easily. "Nothing. Just the same from last night."

"Which part?" he asked.

I allowed my head to fall forward. Last night had been so long. "The last part," I mumbled.

"Your dad?"

I nodded, staring at the fire, trying hard not to think of anything else … only the flames, the flames that rose and fell and did not die.

"Did you tell him you saw him passed out?" he asked, his hand on my arm. He led me toward the flames.

"Not with those words. After the others were gone, I asked, 'How long?' "

"What did he say?"

"He was silent for a long time, so long I started to wonder if I'd spoken the words or imagined them. Then he said 'Too long.' " Fresh tears of disgust escaped.

Luca lowered his head. "I'm sorry," he said. "Maybe one night is too long, in his opinion, which it is. To drink like that, I mean."

"You should've seen him in the kitchen, cooking French toast for everyone. He acted as if nothing was wrong. He seemed to be in a great mood, yet last night he was passed out drunk on his couch. He lied so easily."

Luca guided me to his beanbag and sat on the floor beside me. The fire's warmth helped me keep from crying.

"He's lost," Luca said, his voice soft.

"We're all lost."

Luca was silent for a moment. "Do you think he knows he's lost?"

I considered his question; he was right. There was a difference between someone who accepted their brokenness and someone who didn't. Everyone was broken, to different degrees. Was my dad able to accept the extent of his brokenness? Not in a way that caused crippling shame, but in a way that allowed him to face the truth.

A knock on the door frame drew our attention.

"You two are awfully cozy," Sam said as she and Jason entered the room.

"Paul isn't going to be okay with that," Jason added. "Not in his house, or anywhere, but definitely not in his house."

"We were talking," Luca said, each of us sitting straighter, creating space between us where there'd been none before.

"Of course you were." Jason chuckled and sat on the cedar box at the foot of Luca's bed. "That's what all eighteen-year-old boys and girls do when they're alone in front of a fire."

Sam squeezed between us and sat on the hearth. "Oh, that feels so good on my back," she said, wiggling with joy. "Our room is still trying to get warm."

Luca and I didn't respond.

"I guess you were just talking. You both look so serious," Sam said. "Clearly, you two don't understand the typical boy, girl, teenage thing."

"You and I both know," Jason said to his wife, "there isn't a typical thing about either of them."

Sam raised her arms, stretching in front of the fire. "I don't suppose there is," she said with the slightest hint of sorrow.

I put my head in my hands and stared at the pale blue rug Gigi had bought for Luca's room. It arrived the same day as the beanbag chair and the plaid blue-and-gray comforter, all things she thought a boy simply must have.

Jason said, "Does it have to do with your dad?"

I didn't lift my head. I had the feeling that Luca gave them a "not now" signal, because the room remained silent.

After several long moments, Sam spoke again, her voice upbeat. "Never mind about that. Tell us about your dinner last night. I've been dying to hear all about it."

Jason said, "She's been nearly killing me talking about it. Wondering what you ate, what you talked about, if you're going to go out again. The list continues."

My head slumped even further toward the carpet.

"It wasn't good!" Sam said with a gasp.

"Parts of it were," Luca answered quickly.

I moaned softly to myself.

"It couldn't have been that bad since you two are still sitting here next to each other," Jason said with a surprising amount of concern.

It hadn't occurred to me until that moment that they cared if Luca and I had a nice time together, not just because they wanted us to have a nice evening, but they wanted us to have a nice evening *together*. They saw something in the two of us that made them believe we could be more than friends.

"It was nice being with Luca," I said.

Sam asked, "Did something happen? Was the food bad?"

"Everything okay with the jeep?" Jason asked, beginning to stand, I supposed to go check on the jeep.

"The food was good, the jeep is fine," Luca answered.

"Then what happened?" Sam asked.

Sam's expression was growing more worried with each passing second.

"I have an active imagination, that's all," I said.

"What do you mean?" Jason said.

Luca said to me, "I spent the night researching the restaurant. Nothing's there."

"Or there could have been a trick," I added. "The waiter was awful."

"What about the restaurant and Siena's imagination?" Sam asked, with a catch in her voice.

"Nothing. I must've imagined it, or the waiter … he's friends with Beth. He could've done something that made me think I was seeing something when I wasn't. Maybe I hallucinated. Food poisoning can cause that sometimes."

Jason said, "Did you get food poisoning?"

I wished I could say yes. "Not in the traditional sense. Maybe my imagination getting weird was the symptom."

"Tell us what you imagined," Sam said forcefully.

"Kids. In the attic, there were terrified kids." I wished I could believe it was merely my imagination.

"You left them there?" Jason asked, his body activated like he was ready to fight someone in order to rescue the children.

"They weren't really there," Luca said calmly.

Jason's posture relaxed, but his face showed increased confusion.

I said, "I saw them when I touched a piece of wood in the attic. When I moved my hand away, they were gone."

Sam put her hand to her open mouth. She stood up, turning her back to us.

"Why were you in the attic?" Jason asked.

"I didn't know it was an attic. I thought it was another way out of the restroom."

"She was trying to avoid the waiter," Luca added. "It was a trick of her mind, or the waiter, or something. It must've been. I spent the whole night—or at least when I wasn't in the basement—researching the restaurant. Nothing happened there."

"It's an old building," Jason said. "Not that I'm believing Siena now sees ghosts. I'm just saying it's not like that place was built to look old. It was built, and over the next hundred years or so it became old."

"I dug through every possible source," Luca said with certainty. "Old newspaper articles, the property appraiser's website, I researched each of the owners. When it was a business, I researched the people who worked there. I'm not sure what Siena saw, but it wasn't the history of that place."

Sam turned to face us, her fingers against her lips. Despair had washed over her. Luca's hope faded as he studied her expression.

"Last night, after you left," she said, her voice weak, "Gemma told me she never liked going to that restaurant. She said the food was good, but the place itself, she couldn't get past it."

"What does that mean, Sam?" Jason asked.

She rubbed her hands together, her right thumb pushing into the palm of her left hand. She wasn't trying to hide her anxiety. "Gemma said it was a long time ago, long before she was born, but her mom told her and she couldn't forget."

Luca went to his aunt. They looked at each other, and then she turned away. His expression became more worried.

"Gemma said her grandparents were friends with the people who built it … just as evil." Sam crossed her arms in front of her. "She said she could never go to the BayTree because of what happened there."

Luca took hold of her arms, forcing her to focus on him. "What happened?"

"I don't know. Gemma didn't say."

Luca released her.

"You don't know anything?" Jason asked.

Sam shook her head slowly.

"Then why are you worrying us all?" he said, frustrated with his wife.

"Gemma didn't tell me because she said it was too awful to speak about."

Luca turned to me. "Come on," he said, taking hold of my right arm and drawing me up to my feet.

"Oww," I cried. My knees were stiff after sitting a while. "Where are we going?"

"To find your grandmother," Luca said, pulling me from his room.

Twenty-One

"What happened in the restaurant?" Luca blurted out as we entered Avi's room, where Gigi was sitting in the upholstered rocking chair in the corner. Jackson, curled up on the rug at her feet, had raised his head when we entered.

"What restaurant?" Avi asked. She was placing a little porcelain doll onto a bed in the dollhouse.

Gigi's expression changed from one of calm contentment to concern.

"The restaurant from last night, the BayTree," Luca said, his words so rushed it was difficult for me to understand him.

Gigi's face darkened—she understood his meaning. Sam and Jason were right behind us.

"What's going on?" Lisieux asked from the doorway. Jackson stood and went to her. She petted his ears. Together they went to Avi's bed. Lisieux sat on the bed, Jackson on the rug near it.

"Tell me what happened there." Luca's voice was shaking. He paid no attention to anyone else in the room—only Gigi.

"Did you sense something last night? Why didn't you tell us?" Gigi asked. She was equally focused on Luca; she was concerned for him, afraid he was the one who had discovered the restaurant's secret.

"Tell me what happened, please," he said, kneeling beside her, begging for an answer.

"I'm sorry that happened to you," she said, reaching her wrinkled hand for his.

He didn't correct her. "Tell me," he said, holding her hand.

She sunk back into the chair, appearing smaller than she was, or smaller than I believed she was.

"It was a long time ago. It happened when my mom was young," she said, gliding back in the chair. "Before she left this place, long before my time." Gigi paused, as if hoping her second-hand knowledge excused her and she wouldn't have to tell us more.

"Go on, please," Luca begged, still kneeling beside her.

The rest of us stood, except for my sisters, sitting on Avi's bed. Jackson was on his feet, and Lisieux absently rubbed one of his silky ears.

Gigi said, "She told me she never liked the man who lived there, or his wife. But her parents were friends with them, so they went there often. It took longer to get there, back then. It took longer to get everywhere. When they went, they spent the day, but never the night. She was grateful for that. She said occasionally that couple came to visit her parents at the inn. They had one small boy. My mother would take him out to the trails to try and give him something normal," she said, her expression becoming sadder, her body shrinking even more into the upholstered chair.

"The BayTree was originally someone's house?" Luca said with fear.

That information must have been missing from his research.

"Yes, but I don't think it's been one since their time," Gigi said.

"How did I miss that?" Luca said, blaming himself for some unknown crime. "I searched everywhere."

"It was built so long ago, I can't imagine records go that far back. They built it themselves. The land had been in her family long before that. Once they were … once they were no longer occupying it, it sat abandoned for quite a while. Long enough for people to forget, I suppose," she said, her voice drifting off. "By the time my husband and I moved to the area, a store was using the building. I'm not sure who they bought it from."

"Johnson's Market was listed as the first owner," Luca said under his breath.

"Yes, that was the name," Gigi said, rocking in the chair and smoothing one of Avi's blankets on her lap.

"They were nice people. I felt bad I never was able to bring myself to go in there. I would have liked to support them. Oh, well. They ended up leaving town after five years or so. The grocery business is hard in such a small area. They sold it to a doctor, who lived on the second floor and saw patients on the first. His family was there for a while, ten or fifteen years, I think."

"Sixteen," Luca said.

He'd done his homework … but not well enough.

"After that, it was a restaurant, I believe," Gigi said, trying to remember.

"Then a bed-and-breakfast, then one restaurant after another," Luca said, his back slumping against the foot of Avi's bed.

"Yes," Gigi said. "One after another."

Jason said, "I've never heard anything weird about that building."

"No, no, you wouldn't have," Gigi said. "People have forgotten. Even by the time I moved back to town with George, people had already forgotten. But I hadn't." She rocked a moment and said, "How could I?" Her gaze extended to the past.

"What happened?" Avi whispered, her hand clasped in Lisieux's.

Gigi blinked, returning to her granddaughter's room. She straightened her shoulders a little. "I was never told the details, thank God. The generalities were enough. Though even if I did know specifics, I wouldn't share them with you. But since I don't know, it's better for all of us."

Gigi's eyes fell on Luca. "I'm sorry you felt them. I should have warned you. I was foolish to think that what happened a hundred years ago didn't matter. I can tell by your expression it does … a great deal. I'm sorry for not warning you."

"Please," Luca begged, "tell us what happened."

"There were children," she said sadly. "Children who were taken, children who … I'm not sure anyone knows how many there were."

"Children like me?" Avi gasped in horror, Lisieux holding on to her.

Jason turned to the wall. He was not a man who liked to show his emotions, though he was a man who felt a great many of them.

"Like I said, I don't know the details, I don't know their ages, only that …."

"Their skin was dark," I said meekly.

"How did you … ?" she asked, staring at me and then Luca.

He faded onto the floor, his expression blank, unreadable.

"Were you able to feel them?" Gigi asked Luca. "I'm so sorry. I should have thought it through. I should have realized it would be a problem for you." Her fingers reached out, touching his dark face and his even darker hair.

He took a long breath. "It wasn't me," he managed to say.

"Then who?" she said kindly.

I wondered if I should answer. Luca didn't have the strength. But my voice didn't come. Until Thomas died, I thought Luca was insane. Now I was seeing things that happened a hundred years ago. Thomas's pale arm dripping blood flashed in my mind. I closed my eyes, trying to force out the image.

Sam's voice broke the silence. "It wasn't Luca. It was Siena."

"Siena?" Lisieux said as Avi clung to her.

Jackson's body tensed, the hairs on his back rising as if he expected an imminent attack.

I held my arms tight across my body. I felt so cold, so alone. "I saw them," I said in a whisper, the only voice that would come.

"How is that possible?" Gigi asked, doing what she could to make her voice calm.

"I-I touched the wood in the attic, and I saw them," I said.

"The attic? Why were you in the attic?" Lisieux said with an accusing tone, like this was my fault.

She was right. It was my fault.

"I didn't know it was the attic. There was a door off the restroom. I was trying to find a different way out," I stated.

Gigi's hand fell from Luca's face and hung limply over the chair arm. "The attic is where he kept the children," Gigi said, her voice shaking, along with her body. "How could you have known that?"

No one spoke. My sisters were staring at me like I was a freak. I focused on the dollhouse, half expecting the pieces in it to come to life. That could not be any stranger than my visions of the gruesome past.

"It's a gift," Sam said, breaking the silence. "Some people are given that gift." However, her tone did not give the impression it was a gift you wanted to receive.

"Excuse me," Luca said abruptly, standing and leaving the room.

Jackson whined and followed him out.

"Where did he go?" Lisieux asked.

"This is difficult for him," Sam said. "Siena is not the first person he has known … and loved,"—her voice cracked—"who could see the memories of a place."

Jason remained steady beside her.

"Who else could do that?" Avi asked.

Sam's hand held Jason's arm that was wrapped around her waist. "His mom had the same gift," she said reluctantly.

My mind whirled. That was the reason he was terrified. It wasn't that I could see the past, it was that his mom could too, and his mom was dead.

I could tell by Sam's expression she was afraid it would be my fate. Luca's running from the room told me he feared the same thing.

Even Gigi and my sisters would not meet my eyes. Only Jason offered me a faint smile before he followed Sam from the room.

Twenty-Two

Nobody argued when I told them I was going for a walk. Without me around, they could talk more freely about the oddity I now was, or maybe always had been. That didn't matter; I didn't need their thoughts. I needed answers. Answers only Luca and Sam could provide.

After Sam fled, with Jason following her, we heard their bedroom door close. A minute later her sobs could be heard through the closed door.

My sisters searched for Luca. When they said he wasn't in the house but that Jackson was whining by the back door, I excused myself. I needed answers. I needed to find Luca. I drew on my coat, boots, and hat, and escaped the echoing sound of Sam's sobs. Jackson followed me out. He was the only one who was not, on some level, scared of me.

As we entered the trail, my feet automatically began to move faster, to run, to free me from the binding earth. For once, I didn't argue as Jackson sprinted down the trail that led to the beach. The sea was calling to me, as it called to Luca. We were different in so many ways, but not in this one. I didn't have to wonder where he was.

As the trail widened, the bright morning sun hovering just above the sea caused my eyes to narrow as they adjusted to the blinding rays. Farther in front of me, white froth spread across the beach, making it appear like snow was floating on top of the churning water. When the trail gave way to the sand, my eyes fell on Luca. It was as if he'd been waiting for me. The tide was high; there was not much room for us on the beach, so Jackson and I stuck to the edge of the forest—where the dead winter grasses met the waves. Jackson was trotting in front of me, cautiously avoiding the splattering of the waves. He was smart enough not to get wet on cold days. Together we made our way to the center of our cove. Luca sat on the edge of the forest, his feet resting on rocks with icy water lapping gently around them.

As I approached, he said, "I'm sorry I ran." The sound of the waves muffled his childlike voice. "I needed the sea."

"Me too." I sat beside him, my coat long enough to keep the snow from wetting my pants.

"Have you and your grandmother ever talked about that restaurant? I mean, when you were younger or anything?" he said eagerly, as if he'd been waiting for years to ask that question.

"No," I said, wishing I could answer differently. "I would've remembered something like that, even if I was young when she told me."

Luca stared out at the sea. Jackson went to him and placed his head on Luca's lap. Luca placed a hand on the dog's head, hungrily accepting the support and warmth Jackson offered.

"I was hoping you had imagined those things last night. I thought you had. There was nothing I could find out about it. But after what Gigi said … there's no way …." He lowered his head against his bent arm.

"No way I could have randomly imagined the right details," I said as a wave rolled toward us, bringing a heap of brownish-yellow foam with it.

His body slumped forward, his head going onto his hands. His elbows rested on his knees. He looked beaten; life had beaten him.

"What am I?" I asked, keeping my voice steady.

"You're a woman who's been given a great gift," he said solemnly.

"Then why is your aunt crying uncontrollably, and why did you run from our house, and why … why does it feel like I've been given a death sentence?" I said, my voice far from steady.

He put his hand on top of mine.

"It is a gift," he said. "But gifts can be dangerous."

"You have a gift … and so does Sam. Maybe I'm like you," I said with forced hopefulness.

"Your gift is not like mine. It's like …." He didn't have the strength to form the words.

"Your mom's," I said, raising my voice above the sound of the waves. "Sam told me. She told us right before she ran out of the room and started sobbing."

"It's a lot for her. And for me, if I'm being honest."

"You told me last night your mom was a psychic, a medium. That's not what this is. I can't tell the future or talk to spirits."

Luca offered a sad grimace that he meant to be a smile. "That's how it started for her. That's what lured her in."

I tilted my head, asking for an explanation.

He poked at a rock with his boot, and the water rushed into the space. "She could always sense evil. That was something she was born with, the same as Aunt Sam … the same as me. But she was different. Evil didn't make her sick like it does me and Aunt Sam. She could sense it, but it didn't bother her. Whenever we were where evil had existed, I felt it, but it was distant—faded like an old forgotten memory. She would try to sense it, to understand it. She saw its past."

My mouth became dry. Some part of me was the same. When I saw Thomas's bloody arm or the children in the attic, I didn't pull away. I wanted to see more, to understand what was in front of me.

"Did your mom want to be near evil?" I asked, hoping the answer would clearly distinguish her from me. After all, I didn't seek evil, as Thomas had done.

"No," he said, his shoulders dropping a little. "I don't think it was that. I think she could sense something and she wanted to know what it was. Like a mystery to solve. Like, if there was a tiny piece of something sticking out of the sand, you'd dig deeper to try and uncover it."

My back straightened. We were the same.

Beside us, Jackson whined. Could he sense my discomfort, the fear I felt?

Luca spoke. "Interacting with the spiritual world is like a muscle. The more you do it, the better you are at it—for better or for worse. For many, that leads to better. For her, it did not."

"Why …"—my voice cracked—"why not?" I had to understand what led to the destruction of this woman Luca loved, this woman … like me.

"She began to call on the spirits to help her understand what happened in these places," he said, using his fingers as quotation marks for the word *spirit*. "They were not good spirits, as she believed."

"Demons," I said, his words from last night fresh in my mind.

He nodded slowly, painfully—these were not pleasant memories. These memories ultimately led to his mother's death.

"It was Aunt Sam that told her how dangerous it was. This is what they fought over. It's why Aunt Sam moved up here. She'd already met Uncle Jace online, but I doubt she ever would've come up here to him if she didn't have to leave."

"Your mom kicked her out?" I said, surprised that anyone could ever be mean to Sam.

"No, Mom loved her. Aunt Sam was the only family she had, the only family *we* had. She wanted her to stay. *I* wanted her to stay," he said, the heartache of the past evident on his face. "But Aunt Sam's like me. She could feel the evil beginning to invade our house. She had no choice. She couldn't stay. She begged my mom to let me come with her."

"Sam left you there?" I pictured Luca as a young boy, left alone, surrounded by evil.

"It wasn't her fault," Luca said. "Aunt Sam was more sensitive to it, more aware of it than I was—at least back then. She was sick whenever she was near Mom, and Uncle Jace offered her a good life up here. What choice did she have? She loved my mom and me. I never doubted that. I understood why she had to go," he said. "Plus, I was a kid. I loved my mom and didn't want to leave her."

"If Sam was so sick around your mom, why weren't you?" I was grateful for the bright morning sun and calm ocean. They kept me steady in a world that was anything but.

"I wasn't as sensitive back then. So things weren't that bad for a long time. Only toward the end did it become too much for me. Then, I did my best to stay away from the house. I went to school, did my homework outside, anything I could to stay out of the house or at least out of the sunroom, where Mom saw clients. That's where it was the worst." His body shook in a spasm at the recollection.

He rubbed the back of his neck. "It was manageable for a long time. She still had her other job. She did this on the side. The evil was not … all-consuming. It didn't start to get really bad until my dad stopped sending child support. Then she felt she had no choice."

"He couldn't afford to help you anymore?" I asked.

"It's not *help* when it's your child. I was his responsibility. But no, he had plenty of money. He simply didn't want to pay anymore, or maybe his wife didn't want him to." Luca shrugged. "Either way, he stopped."

"Your mom didn't make him pay?"

Luca scoffed. "You make it sound like she could order him around. He didn't care what she said. She didn't have the money for an attorney, and he could afford the best. She would've lost in court, same as she did when I was a baby. Thank God he didn't want me, or I'm sure he would've gotten full custody. As it was, he got away with paying pennies, compared to what he should've paid. But the truth was my mom hated taking money from him. The things he said to her, the things he called her." Luca rubbed his hair as he lowered his head into his arms. "We're each responsible for the decisions we make in life, but so much of the darkness she experienced was because of him."

"I thought you said he wasn't possessed."

Luca sat up straighter. "There were no demons around him, no more than the ordinary amount. They didn't need to be there. He was creating enough evil on his own."

I was sorry for all that Luca had been through and for what his mom had experienced in this life. Sorry, too, for the pain his father had caused, all on his own.

"His checks were never much, but with Aunt Sam gone and no money from him, it was hard for Mom to make rent. That's when she quit her other job and became a psychic full-time. Things went from bearable to unbearable pretty quick at that point."

"What did you do?"

"I went to the beach," he said sadly. "If I wasn't in school, I was at the beach."

"What about friends?"

"I didn't have many. None, really. No one was ever mean to me or anything. To be honest, I felt invisible, which I guess is better than being actively disliked. The truth is, I didn't fit in. Never had. The beach was my friend and my family. I could walk to it from our house, so that's where I went when the school bus dropped me off. It's where I was as the sun was rising and setting on Saturdays and Sundays.

"Eventually, I sort of made friends with the guys who fished in the waves. We never talked about anything other than fishing, but they taught me how to fish. Aunt Sam sent me a little bit of money for birthdays and Christmases. Eventually, I had enough for a pole. Then I could at least start providing some food for the two of us. But it was too little too late," he said, staring out at the fluffy clouds gliding toward us, low above the ocean.

With them came warmer air than that of the forest at our backs. The slight warmth felt like a gentle caress against my cold, reddened face.

"What happened to her?" I asked, with a steadier voice than I thought possible. She killed herself. This I knew; we all did. But why? How could a mother leave her child, especially a child as good and kind as Luca?

He picked up a stick that floated toward him. The icy water dripped onto his hands as he held it. "The darkness that Aunt Sam felt, that I felt—it went from being outside of her to being within her."

"She was possessed?" I gasped, remembering Thomas. Had Luca experienced that level of evil twice in his life?

He shook his head. "No, it wasn't that it owned her like it did Thomas. Her body wasn't theirs to control. It was more like … she was a glass filled with darkness. It was destroying her. I tried, but I couldn't get within fifty feet of her without my head pounding and my stomach lurching. Except for one night." He grimaced with a mixture of sorrow and gratitude. "The night before she died—I'm not sure what happened—it was a gift … from God, I guess. A gift to her or me, I'm not sure."

"It was a gift to both of you," I said, tears beginning to burn my eyes. Somehow I knew part of the story he was about to tell. The part where the darkness faded and she was able to love her son.

He clasped his hand over mine. "She returned that night. I had my mom back, her true, good being—for the first time in years I wasn't alone."

Tears ran down my face. Luca sniffed.

He'd already lived this story—but I was living it for the first time, with him. My heart was breaking for the man who sat beside me. The man I once thought was a creep. Now I questioned what life would be like without him.

"We talked all night. I hugged her. I was almost eighteen, and I was hugging her and crying like a little kid, begging her not to return to the darkness. Begging her to stay with me as she was in that moment. Begging her to be my mom."

I clasped his hand with both of mine. "She didn't stay?" I said, tears dripping into the ocean that surrounded our feet.

"We were up all night. She believed the spirits who spoke to her were what they told her—angels. She believed she was helping people and the angels. But she agreed to stop if it meant that much to me."

"What happened?" I asked, feeling the tension build in his body.

He squinted away the tears. "She didn't … she didn't have a choice. When the sun rose, it all came back. The evil, all the horrible things around her were back, and even stronger than before. I had to leave. It was like a magnet pushing me away. But it was different. This time she recognized what it did to me. She saw how much pain I was in. I tried to hide it from her but I couldn't. I vomited as I ran out the front door. She tried to come to me to comfort me, but every step she took made me sicker. Finally, she stopped trying.

"In that moment I had the sense that the full weight of her actions became clear to her—all she'd done to me, to herself … to us. As sick as I was, the most pain came as I watched her struggle with the knowledge of her actions."

"What did you do?" I whispered over the murmur of the ocean.

"The same thing I did today. I fled to the only consistent home I've ever had, the beach."

I squeezed his hand.

"She died that day."

I turned my head away in anguish.

"I came back to check on her before sunset. There was a police car in my driveway. My entire body started to shake."

"You knew?" I asked, tears streaking my face.

Luca was silent, watching the waves. Then he said, "There was a live oak not far from our house. She loved that tree. Its limbs canopied the road."

He stared at the waves, unseeing. "Every year for my birthday, she made me stand in front of that tree and she'd take a picture. Not the last couple of years." He inhaled and exhaled. "In the end, maybe its beauty called to her, or maybe it was too much for her to be reminded of what she'd lost—of what she threw away without realizing it."

After a deep breath he said, "Her car was found smashed against the tree. She wasn't wearing a seat belt."

Sobs rocked my body. She and I were the same—the thought swirled in my grief. No, I thought defiantly, never would I leave him like she had done. Never would I allow the darkness to invade my being so completely that I'd abandon him to go through this world alone.

"A note was in the kitchen. One of the officers found it when she went to get me a drink of water. Mom's writing was barely legible, like she was fighting against herself to write it. The paper was stained with tears. She begged me to forgive her. She said Sam would come for me, that I'd be better off with her."

My salty tears seeped between my lips.

"I slept under that live oak," Luca said. "I didn't leave it for a day or two, or maybe three, I'm not sure. I was in shock, I guess. I didn't eat or … or think clearly. I just sat under the tree. Aunt Sam found me there. When I saw her, I lost it. She hugged me and I fell apart—I guess, because I could. I finally had someone to hold me. She walked me back to my house. It was a few blocks away, but I never could've found my way without her. When I stepped through the door of our house, I collapsed. All I could think about was my last night with my mom."

He looked toward the heavens. "I wanted her back. I prayed it was a dream, a horrible nightmare. It wasn't fair."

My tears for his loss mixed with the tears I cried for my own loss. None of it was fair, not to him or me or our moms. They loved us and evil took them from us.

"No," I said, "it isn't fair."

He put an arm around me. "I'm sorry you know how unfair it is."

I wrapped my arms around his chest. He kissed the top of my head. His chest rose with the slow inhalation of breath.

"Aunt Sam forced me to eat something, crackers, I think, while she packed my stuff in garbage bags. I sat at the kitchen table, the spot where my mother always sat, until Sam came and got me. She didn't take much, which was good, I guess, since what she did take was burned up a few months later. She left a check for the landlord, both our keys on the kitchen table, and led me to the car.

"At the cemetery, the urn was waiting for us next to a tiny grave marker. Aunt Sam placed it in the ground. She pushed the little pile of dirt around the urn, covering it. Her hands turned brown—she didn't wash them. I remember that, even as she drove and I fell in and out of sleep, I remember how dirty her hands were."

"She loved her sister," I said, thinking of my own sisters, of how much they annoyed me, yet how difficult it would be to live in this world without them.

"They were best friends until everything changed. The awful thing, the thing I feel most guilty about, is my mom was right. That first morning, as I woke up somewhere in South Carolina, in a cramped rental car, I realized she was right. I was next to someone who loved me, and there was no evil, only goodness. I wasn't sick. I wasn't terrified about what was going to happen to her. I could simply be still and watch as the world flew by the windows. I was loved by someone who could truly love me back. I felt peace and I hated myself for it." He lowered his head.

There was a long, awful silence.

After a few minutes, I summoned the strength to speak. "You told me a long time ago that evil killed both of our moms—I thought you were crazy. I hated you for a few hours, but I couldn't hate you for longer than that. You and I are the same in the best … and worst of ways."

"It's eerie," he said softly.

"It's meant to be," I said, suddenly sure of myself. "None of this is a coincidence. You and me. Our gifts, our losses."

"Your gift is not like mine," he said fearfully. "It's like hers."

Again, silence fell upon us. He was terrified I'd become his mother, terrified I'd fall to the evil that constantly surrounded us.

"It's not the gift," I said, "it's what we do with the gift." I breathed in the salt air and with it a sense of hope, not the foreboding that had existed a second earlier. "It's like the Witch of Endor."

He cocked his head at me. "From the Bible?"

"Yes."

"That story didn't end well. Saul and his kids were dead the next day."

"Exactly. The Bible doesn't say that people with gifts aren't real or are inherently evil. They existed before Jesus and they exist now."

"Yes," he said, trying to understand my point.

"The same people with the same gifts, used very differently, wouldn't have been called witches. They would've been prophets or some other thing that wasn't bad."

"You think my mom was a prophet?"

"She could've been, or maybe she could've helped holy souls. That's the point. The Bible doesn't say these things can't happen or that the people they happen to are evil. It says, don't call on spirits, don't try and know the future. These things are bad—deadly. But at the same time, the Bible has many prophets. People who can hear God, who know parts of the future, the part he wants them to know, or they see angels. And then there are all the saints. A lot of them could do some completely bizarre stuff—read souls, be two places at once, levitate, see the dead. These aren't evil demoniacs. These are named saints in heaven. It's not the gift. It's what you do with the gift. I'm not doomed because I can … do whatever it is I can do. That's not what led your mom to—." I caught my words, realizing what I was about to say.

"To death," Luca said.

"Her death came because she summoned spirits, which the Bible very clearly says never to do. That's the problem. That's when evil enters. The good spirits can't be summoned."

"They never were," Luca said. "Every single time, I felt evil. She said they were good, they were beautiful, always gazing toward their home in heaven. But they weren't from heaven. I told her they weren't. She didn't believe me."

"She believed they were good?" I asked.

"She wanted to." He paused. "That's not true. She believed it. She put up pictures and statues of angels everywhere, trying to invite them. She always had welcoming music playing— whatever that meant—and incense burning in the house."

"Did she have pictures of God or Jesus or saints or anything like that?" I asked.

"No," he said. "She believed in God, but she believed in angels more, and she didn't believe in Jesus. Not as God's son, though she called herself a Christian psychic."

"Those two words don't go together," I said quietly.

"She didn't understand that, and neither did the people who came to her. For the most part, her clients were sincere, seeking nice things."

"What sorts of things?"

Gigi's mom went to a psychic once, to find out if she'd ever meet the *right man*. The psychic told her there would not be time for that. Gigi's mom died less than a year later. The psychic was right.

"A lot of the clients were missing someone they loved and wanted to make sure they were okay. Some wanted peace about difficult choices or the future. Those were the most common reasons."

I thought back to the night Thomas died. I hesitated. Luca hadn't heard what the demons told me. I didn't want to be the one to tell him.

"What is it?" he asked, watching me as I tried to clear my expression.

I couldn't lie to him. I couldn't pretend I didn't know what they told me.

"On the night Thomas died, the demons spoke to me—to me and my dad," I said. "It's how I know …. Never mind, that's not important right now." I didn't want to discuss how they had chastised my father for trying to protect me, but that he hadn't earlier—how shortsighted he'd been, how far-reaching his actions were.

I said, "Thomas told us—I mean, the demons told us they knew your mom."

Luca's body shivered violently. "Wh-what … did … they … say?" he asked, barely able to form the words.

"That she brought them many souls, but that they couldn't be themselves around her, not like they could with Gigi's grandmother."

"They couldn't be themselves?" he said, staring beyond where I sat, his gaze falling on the ruins of the inn.

"That would fit, don't you think? With what she told you. She must've been seeing the lie they wanted her to see. They must have appeared as angels or maybe souls of loved ones. Demons can do that. I've read about it in the writings of different saints. They can even appear as Jesus or Mary."

"Yes," he said slowly, "that would fit."

We watched air gurgle from beneath a rock that was partially submerged a few feet in front of us.

"How did she bring them souls?" he asked.

I had hoped he'd forgotten that part of the demons' words. I wanted him to focus on how they deceived her, not how she had deceived others. To accept his mom's fate was one thing; to accept that she led others to hell was another.

"Sin separates us from God. Going to psychics is a sin," I said. "Maybe it was that simple."

He was still. "It was more than that," Luca said. "I think they liked to mess with people. Almost like some disgusting form of entertainment for them." His face looked as if he smelled something rotting.

"How could they mess with people?"

"Mom held a lot of power. I hadn't thought of that before now, but it was true. People believed what she told them. She was right so much of the time, how could they not? And she completely believed what she was saying, which made her all the more convincing. So if the demons fed her enough accurate information about the past or immediate future, then why would she not become someone they believed above all others? She didn't follow the teachings of any major religion. She was simply making up the rules of life as she went, going along with whatever the demons said. The advice she gave—if that's what you want to call it—it was dark. Even as a kid, I understood there were certain lines you don't cross, and yet the *angels* said God always made exceptions. That life was never black-and-white and people must allow their desires to dictate their actions. I get how she was leading them to hell. It was like lambs to the slaughter. How many did she hand them on silver platters? Her clients went away believing, coming back often, thanking her, and all the while she was leading them to eternal agony and they had no clue."

"Neither did she," I said, placing a hand on his. "They hid their true nature from her. She didn't know what she was doing was evil."

"I told her. Sam told her."

"And the demons showed up as angels," I said. "They made her believe that's what they were. After all, that's what they are, fallen angels. So they could easily appear as what they had once been." I realized that anyone who didn't feel the repulsion Luca or Sam did, or didn't believe the Bible when it said not to engage in divination, would be easy prey. Especially if that same person did have a spiritual gift and could reach out to the spiritual world. It made me wonder how many others were the same as Luca's mom. I'd been raised to stay away from psychics, tarot cards, Ouija boards. Gigi had made that clear. I never thought of psychics as evil people, but I certainly never thought of them as trying to do God's will. Now I wondered how many falsely believed they were listening to angels, when they were listening to demons?

Luca replied, "I want to believe she was innocent, but by the end she couldn't deny what was happening."

"By then, her mind was warped," I said.

"She knew, somehow," he said. "She wouldn't have … have done what she did in the end if she didn't realize how messed up she was."

"Luca, when Thomas died, even though I was down here and he was up on that cliff, I sensed something. He was sorry. I'm sure of it. And he threw that box with whatever it was inside it, into the ocean, despite the demons wanting him to keep it. They screamed out when he did that and threw him off the cliff."

"Even if that's true, Siena, it wasn't the same for my mom. She wrote a note. She planned to end her life and she did."

"You said she wasn't as bad off as Thomas, not as intertwined, and yet Thomas repented. He tried to make things right."

"And he died," Luca said, unimpressed with my logic.

"He died in this life. We're all going to die in this life. That doesn't matter. I mean, it's awful for those of us left behind," I said, never forgetting the loss of my mom or the horror of Thomas falling from the cliff. "In the end, this life matters because the next life matters. Don't you get it? If Thomas could repent, if he could have a chance at choosing God, then so could your mom."

Luca picked up a stick washed up by the waves and tried to dislodge a rock with it. The weathered stick snapped at his attempt. "Maybe," he said, watching the broken portion of the stick float away with the outgoing wave.

I said, "When I asked you why you were staring at my house every night, you said you were watching for your mom. You wouldn't have done that—you wouldn't still be doing that if you didn't have hope."

"It's been weeks and I haven't seen her," he said, sounding lost.

"There are millions or maybe billions of souls in purgatory. You aren't going to see everyone."

"I don't want to see everyone. I just want to see her."

"Then you're no better than she was," I said.

He stared at me. The words sounded more cruel than I'd intended, but I didn't take them back. "It's the truth. She was trying to control things, to know more than God wanted her to know. That's exactly what you're trying to do. I get it. I wished and prayed that my mom would visit me and tell me she's okay, but that has never happened, and I understand now why it hasn't. It's not God's will, and I need to accept that."

"Your mom was a saint," he said stoically.

"Hopefully, she is," I said, "but I still pray for her. We all do. That's what helps her—not going to a psychic and trying to talk to her. How does that help the dead?" I realized that was something Luca and I had not thought of.

"Maybe," I said, "that was another reason the demons told your mom the right information. If the clients were there talking to your mom, they weren't praying for the dead or offering their sorrow for the soul's purification. They were not helping them get to heaven, only dragging themselves down. If their loved ones were holy souls, they were hurting them by going to a psychic instead of praying for them."

"It sounds so thought out," Luca said, rubbing his hair. "I told you, after Thomas died, that evil underestimated me. I was wrong—I've underestimated it."

"It is thought out. There's a reason we on earth are called the Church Militant. We're in a battle. A battle for souls, but we aren't fighting alone."

"We're not alone," Luca said with exhaustion, "but it feels that way."

"Of course it does to you. You feel the evil. But remember, you feel it when it outweighs the good. Angels, real angels, surround us."

"I thought you didn't believe in guardian angels," Luca said.

I hesitated. "I think I do now," I said, starting to grasp the wisdom of the Church.

"I wish I could feel our guardian angels," he said, squinting off to the side as if trying to see the invisible. "I wouldn't feel so beaten if the good was as obvious to me as the evil."

"The person who could do that would be way more gifted than you or I," I said. "It has happened, though. Some saints have reported seeing their guardian angels."

"That would be a nice gift," he said, his body relaxing a little. "There are moments, like right now, when I'm alone with you, the ocean at our feet, when I believe the world is good—or, at least, mostly good. Then there are all the other times, when darkness seems to be enveloping every inch, stifling the air, making it difficult to breathe."

"That's what evil wants you to think. That you're in this alone, that evil is winning."

"It seems like it is most of the time," he said.

"God won the war. The outcome is known. It's unchanging. We're not fighting to defeat evil in the world, merely in ourselves."

He inhaled and exhaled, his posture relaxing further—our bodies leaning against each other.

Luca said, "It doesn't seem fair that most people make choices in life without knowing they are choosing their eternity."

"Would it matter?" I asked.

He gave me a questioning glance.

"It's like that Bible story, when the rich man dies and goes to hell, and then begs Abraham to send Lazarus to warn his brothers to live differently. But Abraham says no because if they aren't going to listen to Moses and the prophets, they aren't going to listen to Lazarus. I guess people are going to do what they're going to do. Besides, I might feel sorry for the person who was completely aware of the angelic world. The little bit you and I are aware of is difficult to comprehend. To be aware of more? It wouldn't be easy."

"That would be difficult," Luca said, his face concerned.

"What is it?" I asked.

He blinked. "Nothing."

"It's something."

"It's nothing that matters right now," he said as he stood, holding a hand out for me.

I took his hand as he led me away from the gentle waves. "Why doesn't it matter?"

He squeezed my hand. "We shouldn't spend our time in the future … or the past. We should do our best to be here in this moment, together."

We walked on in silence, my hand in his. Jackson was running in front of us. As much as Luca may have wanted to be focused on the present, he was not. He was lost in thought.

Not of the past, but of the future. A future that did not bring him peace.

An image flashed in my mind: a beautiful little girl, her hair long, with loose brown curls. Her eyes, green with golden flecks of amber, stared back at me. They glowed with an intensity that startled me. Her skin was tan with a few freckles across her nose, her mind knowing; she understood more than I did. She was gifted in all the ways Luca and I were … and much more.

Startled by the image, I loosened my hand from his.

"What is it?" Luca asked, his amber eyes bright in the speckled morning sun that shone onto the trail.

I stared up at him. "Did you see her?"

"Who?" he asked, in such a way that told me he hoped I would not ask him more.

I didn't answer, watching him.

He held his hand open for mine. "We should get back," he said.

I placed my hand gingerly in his. Was that how the child appeared? Did she come from his mind? Not his past but his future.

He wrapped his fingers around the palm of my hand.

"You help ground me," he said. "You help me focus on the here and now, not the past, and not the—"

"Future," I said, before he could finish his thought.

He squeezed my hand. "It's good to focus on the present. God wants us to focus on the present and allow him to be in control of the future."

"Yes," I said, "that's what God wants." I wouldn't ask him more or ask him to answer questions about a future that might never be.

We walked along in silence, a silence brimming with more questions than could ever be answered.

Jackson broke the silence. He barked as we neared my house. Luca squeezed my hand one last time before releasing it and allowing me to go first up the hill of my yard.

Twenty-Three

"You're back!" Avi shouted when we entered the kitchen.

The smell of garlic bread reminded me I hadn't eaten breakfast and my dinner last night was best forgotten—though it never would be.

"I'm glad you're here," Dad said, his tone buoyant. "Your sisters were getting worried."

"We weren't the only ones," Lisieux said, nodding her head toward our grandmother.

"Yes, I was equally concerned," Gigi said with a meaningful glance at each of us.

I hung my coat on the hook. "We were at the beach," I said as Jackson trotted through the kitchen to his bed near the oven, the warmest spot in the room.

"Where's Aunt Sam and Uncle Jace?" Luca asked, hanging up his coat.

"They haven't come down yet. Will you go tell them lunch is ready?" Gigi said, placing her wrinkled hands on Luca's chilled face.

He leaned into her touch. He was safe here; this was his home.

"Okay," he said, and went up the stairs.

I sat beside my sisters at the table. Dad was humming while removing the baking pan of garlic bread from the oven.

"Does he know?" I whispered to them.

Each shook their head.

"Why didn't Gigi tell him?" I asked.

Lisieux shrugged. Avi didn't respond.

"I hope you girls are hungry! Your Gigi and I have made quite the feast," he said with far too much enthusiasm.

I whispered, "What's wrong with him?"

"Nothing," Avi replied. "He's just happy."

"Too happy," Lisieux countered.

"Especially for our life," I mumbled, and then left the table.

I wasn't going to hide the truth from my father, not when he knew so much of it already. Why was Gigi keeping this from him? Secrets did not bring peace—only a fragile shell of true peace.

"Why didn't you tell him?" I asked Gigi as I stood at the counter watching her slice olives for the salad.

"Now isn't the time," she mumbled. "We'll talk about this later."

"Later? Later, when? When I suddenly become normal again?"

"What?" Dad said with a smile that reminded me of an eerie clown.

"What's wrong with him? Why is he acting like everything's perfect? Things haven't been perfect for … things have never been perfect." Perfect did not exist in this life.

"It isn't an act," Dad said, his expression the same. "I'm very happy this morning."

I stared at him. In place of my father was a man with a plastered-on smile, a man who was a total stranger to me. I saw the image of my father from last night, passed out on the couch—also a stranger.

"Everyone grab your plate," Gigi called, and within seconds I was surrounded by my sisters, Luca, and his family.

It was time to eat. It was time for me to drop my concerns of the past and the present.

"Here you go," Dad said. He handed me a plate of lasagna. His sleeves were rolled up, the scar visible.

Luca's question rang so loudly in my mind that I spoke it. "Where did you get that scar?"

The thick raised line was still pink after all these years. Why was it still discolored? I had a few scars from my childhood; they were thin and ghostly white. He was older, so the scars from his childhood should be more faded than any scar of mine, and yet it wasn't.

"What scar?" Dad said, serving plates, humming to himself.

"The one on your arm," I said.

"Oh." He glanced at his left arm. "I tripped and fell against a rock. I've told you that."

"It's still so discolored," I said, focusing on the raised line that spanned the diagonal width of his arm.

"We all heal differently, I suppose," Dad said, continuing to dish up plates.

He continued to pretend there was nothing strange about his behavior or his scar.

"It bled pretty bad," Jason stated as he took his plate to the end of the counter.

"Do you remember that?" Gigi asked him. "You would've been so young."

"A boy doesn't forget something like that, no matter how small he is," Jason said, avoiding her eyes.

"I didn't realize you saw me," Dad said lightheartedly to Jason.

Jason poked at the food on his plate, then looked at Dad. "I was picking blueberries. You came up the trail, your arm hanging straight, blood streaming off your fingers. Your eyes were …. Naw, that don't matter. Point is, a kid don't forget that, even if he tries," Jason said, refocusing on his food but not taking a bite.

Sam brought her plate beside her husband. As she sat, she squeezed his shoulder, a silent offer of support. They'd discussed this before. It was clear since she asked him no more questions. She knew this story better than the rest of us.

"You don't remember passing Jason?" Gigi asked Dad, with more interest than I expected.

Dad shook his head. "I don't remember much about that day, just slipping on a rock."

"I suppose the fever took away your memory," Gigi said.

"Fever?" Luca said.

"The cut got infected. He was fighting for his life for close to a month. It took three different types of antibiotics and lots of prayers before he was finally out of danger. Those were scary times," Gigi said, taking off the tomato-splattered apron.

"Is that why the scar is so big?" Lisieux asked. "I've always wondered."

"That's what your grandfather and I assumed."

"What sort of rock did you cut it on?" Luca asked.

It was a strange question. None of us were particularly interested in geology.

"Uh, I don't know. A rock," Dad said in a mocking tone.

"I mean, was it jutting out from the side of a slope, or could it have been an oyster shell on the beach? Where was it, what shape was it?"

"Luca, I don't remember those kinds of details about last year, let alone forty-something years ago. I don't even remember how old I was. Umm, younger than Lisieux, I think." He rubbed the back of his neck.

Avi asked Jason, "Where was he coming from?"

Jason spun in the barstool to face her. "The beach," he answered. "He was twelve," he added. "I was four."

"How do you remember that?" Dad asked in amazement.

"I remember how old I was when *she* died. So I remember how old I was when you come screaming along the trail."

"When who died?" Gigi asked.

"Your grandmother," Jason said with an edge of contempt.

"Was it that close in time, her death and his cut? How did I not remember that?"

Jason laid his fork down on his plate. "She didn't want you to," he said, this time not hiding his eyes.

"She?" Gigi said. "You believe my grandmother had something to do with the cut on Paul's arm?"

"Don't you?" Jason said, staring at her.

"I never … I never thought of the two as being related," Gigi said. "She wasn't part of our lives. Paul getting a cut on his arm never made me think about her."

Sam stared noticeably at the food on her plate.

"What is it?" I asked. "What are you not telling us?"

"Nothin'. Lasagna's good. Thanks," Jason answered, stuffing a forkful into his mouth.

"Jason, if you have something you want to say, please do so," Gigi said.

"No, nothin'," Jason said, glancing at Gigi before returning his gaze to his food.

Dad handed me a fork. His scar gleamed at me.

I was in the past, seeing the arm at the inn. Pale, thin, dripping with blood. The knife cut diagonally from one side to the other. Blood spilled. I watched drips splatter onto the center stone of the fireplace. It was not a large stone. The top was smooth, with a mild indentation. The blood spilled into the indentation; it acted as a basin, the stone absorbing the blood.

I blinked back to the present—Luca's eyes stared at mine.

I asked Dad, "What did you ...." It was hard to speak. "What did you look like as a child? I mean, as a twelve-year-old."

Gigi and Dad gave each other confused looks.

"Umm, like this, but shorter and skinnier," Dad said dismissively.

"Twelve-year-old boys are usually pretty skinny," Luca said, paying close attention to every movement I made.

"May I ..."—I lost my voice for a second as everyone in the room stared at me—"may I see your scar?"

"Siena, you've seen it a thousand times," my father said, his voice rising in irritation.

I got up and grasped his hand. He attempted to pull it away. Luca held it in place.

"Just for a moment?" I asked.

He stopped resisting us. My thumb was tracing the scar, my eyes seeing the past and present all in one moment. The edge of the blade went in at the top—my thumb repeating the action. The blade pulled slowly across the skin, like the hand that held the blade was not aware of the pain it was causing, but the hand matched the other. The person holding the blade was the same one being cut by it. The blade was dull. I could feel it tearing the skin apart more than cutting it. Finally, it released.

"The scar is the same," I said.

Luca and I let go of my dad's arm.

"Of course it's the same. Did you think it changed?" My dad's voice sounded belligerent.

I felt Luca's hand on my shoulder. The rest of my family stared at me. Sam held a napkin to her face, catching tears that seeped from the corners of her blue eyes.

Jason said, "What did you see?"

"See? She saw my scar," Dad said in a derisive tone. He stepped away, pulling the sleeves of his dress shirt down, fastening the buttons around his wrists.

I said, "That scar was made by a knife, not a rock."

"What!" Gigi exclaimed. She looked at me as if trying to see what I had seen.

"It was a rock," Dad said.

"No," I stated flatly, my mouth dry, my stomach twisting. "It was a knife. You were in front of the fireplace at the inn. Your blood dripped onto the middle stone, the stone that is no longer there."

"The inn?" Gigi stepped away from all of us. "That cut happened at the inn?" Her eyes wide, she clutched the collar of her blouse.

"She's confused," Dad said. "How could a knife at the inn have cut my arm?"

I swallowed, my voice becoming stronger. There was no doubt. I was sure of what I'd witnessed. "You did it yourself. The hand that held the blade belonged to the same person whose hand was clenched in pain."

"You have no idea what you're talking about," Dad said.

His fake clown smile was long gone.

"She can sense the memory of a place," Sam said, her voice shaky.

Dad shouted, "That's ridiculous."

"It's the truth," Luca said from my left side. His fingers were laced through mine.

"This is your fault," Dad said, rounding on Luca.

Luca stood taller. Jason, too, was standing. Avi started to cry.

"I'm not the one to blame," Luca said, stepping in front of me.

"You're crazy," Dad said, his chest broad, shoulders back. "And now you've gone and made her crazy with all of your insane talk of demons and spirits. I knew you didn't belong here. I knew you'd be trouble."

"Watch it, Paul," Jason said as he stepped beside his nephew. "Don't say something you're going to regret."

"Regret? What I regret is not kicking you off my land years ago!" Dad's eyes blazed.

"That's enough!" Gigi shouted. "I have allowed a lot from you through the years, but I will not allow you to speak that way to Jason or Luca or Siena."

Dad turned away in anger, veins bulging in his neck. "Why on earth would I have cut my arm on purpose?" Dad said, barely keeping his voice below a yell.

Behind the anger, it was clear he was not pretending. He didn't remember, and he was faced with a part of his memory that was, in so many ways, best forgotten. But it had not been forgotten—by the inn. The stones of that burned-down building remembered the evil done there. That was what I'd been faced with at the inn and the BayTree … the memory of evil.

"It was her, your great-grandmother," Jason said with quiet force.

Gigi's hand clutched at her neckline more tightly. "Why do you think that?" she asked.

She wasn't scared of my father, as she had not been scared of Thomas. But she had been scared of her grandmother. Gigi was right to fear her—even the memory of her.

"Because of the way he acted that day," Jason said. "That old woman … I hated her. I never went near the beach. My parents didn't care where I went, but I did. I wouldn't go near her. But Paul went down there all the time, and when he'd come back, he was just like her—mean. Nothing like you and his daddy. You two were always nice to me, and Paul was too, after he'd been with you. But after he was at the beach, he was like that evil old woman. That day was no different. He come up with an awful expression on his face. I was afraid of him. I tried to hide from him, but I was a clumsy little kid. As soon as he saw me, it's like he woke up and started screaming his head off. Scared me to death."

Dad rubbed his arm. His voice subtly calmer, he said, "I remember falling and cutting it on a stone."

"That's what she wanted you to remember," Jason said abrasively. "I ain't kiddin' when I say you were in a daze or fog or something. Like you were walking in a trance."

Gigi studied Dad. "Your father thought it was strange," she said. " 'How could Paul fall directly against a stone like that and not have cut up his hands or knees?' he asked me. All I could tell him was young boys get hurt in strange ways. We had no reason not to believe you. And so we did. We were wrong." Her voice held remorse.

"It was a rock," Dad bellowed, throwing a plate of food into the sink.

Lisieux screamed. I ran to my sisters and held them, protecting them from him. Luca and Jason and even Sam formed a wall around us.

Dad yelled, "Do you think I would hurt them?"

Gigi stood tall in front of all of us. The frail old woman remained unphased by the darkness in her son.

"You *have* hurt them, Paul, more than you understand, more than we will ever understand in this life. It's my fault, mine and your father's. We gave you too much freedom. We shouldn't have. I believed you when you told me you weren't going near her." Gigi's shoulders fell a little. "I wanted to believe you, so I convinced myself you were telling the truth when you were not. Just like now. I convince myself that you are sober, though you are not!" She stared at him, daring him to deny the truth.

For a moment he looked as though he'd strike her: his eyes bulged, his fists clenched. Jason abruptly angled his body in front of hers. He was small compared to my father, though far stronger, the result of a life harder than my father had known.

Luca's movement was not as obvious, a subtle step in Gigi's direction. He would not stand a chance against my father, but he could at least protect Gigi.

She did not back down. "We did not realize—that is the sole defense I can offer for my actions. The truth was not known to us at that time. It was not until after she died … after you cut your arm," she said with growing sadness.

Dad stomped to the sink in a show that he could not be bothered by his mother or the rest of us. His face was red and his body was drenched in sweat, but the veins in his neck were smaller.

Avi was shaking.

"It's okay," I whispered to her as Lisieux and I held her, protecting her, keeping her from watching our father.

Gigi went to the kitchen island. Moving closer to Dad, she slumped onto a counter stool. "How did I not realize how close in time those two events were? It must have been because after your fever broke, life turned upside down," she said.

"What happened?" Luca asked, too curious to remain silent.

For a moment Gigi was still. "How did I not put it together before?" she said, shaking her head.

Sam sat beside her and placed her hand on Gigi's back, offering support, silently telling Gigi she was loved even if mistakes had been made.

Gigi said, "We realized then that it had something to do with Paul … why didn't we make the connection with the cut?"

"What happened here, Ms. Gemma?" Jason asked with a hint of dread.

Gigi's shoulders slouched forward, causing her to look so much older—to look her age, I supposed. She was turning eighty this year. She should look old—though she never had before.

"Strange things," she said. Her voice sounded as tired as her body appeared.

"What sorts of things?" Sam asked, still holding Gigi.

Gigi's clear blue eyes misted and her fingers laced together on the counter. "Things that made us call our priest."

"I don't know why we didn't associate his cut with all that happened," Gigi said, her face contorted in a way that made me understand she doubted her mind—her memory. Two pieces that should've fit easily together did not, and she did not understand why.

"Because I cut it on a rock," Dad argued. "I can remember the rock. It was on the beach. I fell, it sliced my arm. I was a clumsy kid." His tone was harsh, though his breathing was slightly more rhythmic. He was calming down.

"That's why we didn't realize the truth," Gigi said, sitting taller, her voice matching the harshness of her son's. "You were so good at making us believe you. You still are!"

Dad groaned.

Jason interjected, remaining calm. "What were you doing before you fell?"

Dad inhaled and exhaled as if trying to decide if he would allow the anger to slip away long enough to answer the question. "I don't remember," he said sharply.

"What about after?" Jason asked.

"Probably running home."

"You don't remember, do you?" Jason said, staring at Dad and challenging him to dispute his words.

"This is ridiculous," Dad growled, though behind the anger there was doubt.

"How did we not put it together?" Gigi leaned against Sam. "It started in his room, all of it. The broken light bulbs, the pictures that fell off the wall, the pockets of cold air that never warmed—all of them started in his room before moving into the rest of the house."

Dad shook his head, disgust showing in his face.

Did he think she was making it all up? Did he want to pretend none of it was true, as badly as I did?

"Do you remember the scratches?" Gigi asked Dad, not allowing him to tune her out.

He stared at her. She stood her ground.

He fell backward, his back hitting the countertop, which kept him upright. His eyes widened. "Those were real? I thought they were part of a nightmare lodged in my memory."

"They were the stuff of nightmares," she said wryly, "but they were horribly real. More than a few scars remain."

"You think I did that?" he asked in horror.

"You did not do the scratching," she answered, the normally soft skin of her jaw set hard. "The demons used my own hands for that."

Dad stared at his mom, struggling to understand the reality he was being shown. "You looked like something out of a horror movie."

"I felt worse than I looked," she said flatly.

Avi went to Gigi and pressed herself against her, prodding a hug from Gigi. Avi said, "Did you get scratched?"

Gigi looked at her youngest granddaughter. She pushed the vibrant red hair back behind her ears. "You've asked me before why I always keep my nails so short—this is the reason." She held onto Avi, breathing in the scent of her rose shampoo.

Avi asked, "You scratched yourself?"

"In a way, I suppose I did, though in truth it was not me. There's no way it could have been me. I slept through the whole thing."

Now Lisieux came to Gigi. "How bad could the scratches have been if you slept through getting them?"

Dad cringed at the memory.

Gigi sat straight, her fingertips going to the bottom of the blouse she wore. She lifted its edge to reveal a stark white, wrinkled stomach with broad diagonal lines running across it.

"The scratches were the worst where both hands could easily reach," she said.

Avi gasped, impulsively touching one of the scars. "It's wider than my finger," she said with tears brimming.

"My finger is wider than yours," Gigi said, allowing her blouse to drop.

Gigi squeezed Avi. "I'm okay now. No need to cry," she said, wiping Avi's cheeks with her thumbs.

"How did it happen?" Lisieux asked, her voice shaking.

Gigi straightened her back. "It happened while we slept. I'd gone to bed beside your grandfather, same as every other night. Odd things had been happening in the house. We figured it was our imaginations, though we imagined the same things, which seemed a bit unlikely. Or perhaps Paul, who was finally feeling better, was playing tricks on us. After this night, we realized none of it was imagined … all of it was real.

"Your grandfather woke up first. The poor man almost had a heart attack when he saw me covered in blood. He spoke my name. I'll never forget the sound of his voice as he repeated my name over and over again. He was so scared. When I woke, I moved slightly. The sheets ripping away the dried blood caused me to become immediately alert.

" 'Don't move,' he said. 'The blood has dried against the sheets. Every movement will tear the wounds open.'

" 'Why is there blood?' I asked, petrified from the terror in his eyes.

" 'I don't know,' he said, looking first at his own hands.

"There was no blood on him. Not the first drop. Under each of my fingers, there was a dried circle of blood. At first, he thought I was cut badly there. Then he realized chunks of skin were under my fingernails."

"Skin?" Lisieux said, gagging.

"I'd done it to myself, or rather, the demons used my own hands to mutilate my body. After your grandfather carried me to the shower, still draped in our sheets, he called Father Joseph. I'm glad I couldn't hear what he told him. His voice that whole morning was so panic-stricken. Why would it not be! He was my husband, his job was to protect me, and as he slept peacefully beside me, my body was shredded. Understandably, he had a difficult time with that. It was Father Joseph who helped us understand how *real* demons are. After that, we had no doubt. We were blessed to have a priest who understood spiritual warfare so clearly."

"Don't all priests?" Luca asked.

Gigi laughed. "There's a reason I have not shared the truth of Thomas's last moments on earth with Father Luke. How often these last few weeks I've wished that Father Joseph was still with us. He would've brought so much illumination to this dark situation." She lowered her head.

I said, "How did Father Joseph help you?"

She sniffed and raised her head. "He didn't doubt our sanity, not for even the briefest of moments. That gave us peace. He accepted what we were saying and provided answers when we had none. The world of spiritual warfare was completely unknown to us. It was a gift to have someone who could be our guide and our friend. The pain he felt on our behalf … he was a true shepherd. Willing to lay down his life for one of his flock, without hesitation. The courage he showed when ours failed. I cannot thank God enough for giving us a strong shepherd when we needed him most. He died a few years after George. Do you remember that, Paul?"

Dad's posture softened as his mother's sorrow fought against the internal anguish he was trying to suppress. "I could never forget that," Dad said, sounding choked up.

"He loved you," Gigi said. "He loved all of his flock. Losing him so soon after losing George …." She sniffed.

"It was difficult," Dad said.

"Yes," Gigi said, "very difficult."

Luca placed an arm around my shoulders, and I leaned against him.

"What did the priest do?" Jason asked after a hanging silence. "How did he help? I mean, with the … with what she did to you?"

"You understand it all so clearly," Gigi said, gazing at him. "You realized the true danger she was, when we didn't."

"Children are more in tune," Sam said, one hand on Gigi's back, the other holding her husband's hand.

Dad lowered his head. He, as a child, had been far less aware than the adults.

"Father Joseph wept. That was the first thing he did," Gigi said, staring at the dripping faucet. "After that, he celebrated the holy sacrifice of the Mass in Paul's room."

"Mass?" Jason said.

"It's the strongest of prayers, so he began there. Based on Paul's reaction to it, it was the correct place to begin."

Dad didn't speak, but based on his questioning expression, he didn't recall this moment of his past, either.

"Your father had to hold you down during the consecration." Gigi slumped forward, shrinking into herself. "I'd never seen him cry like he did as he held you, pinned to the floor. Doing all he could to dodge your attempts at spitting on him."

Dad's hand covered his mouth. He turned away, leaning over the sink, his body beginning to rock. He loved his father more than he loved his own life—to be faced with the reality of all he'd done to him ….

"You were not yourself," Gigi said kindly. "Your father and I understood that."

The room was silent until Sam spoke. "What did Father Joseph do after that?"

"He blessed every inch of Paul's room and then every inch of the house with holy water. He went outside and poured blessed salt around the perimeter of the house, the entire time praying and blessing us. He blessed all the salt I had in the house so that, for months, almost every bit of food we consumed was blessed. And then he heard Paul's confession. Paul was calm by that point and, after the confession, remained calm. It was a gift to have him back," Gigi said, sitting up.

Dad said, "I remember going to confession."

"Yes," Gigi answered. "It was a powerful experience for you. After that, we had no issues with manifestations of evil in our home again. Not like that, anyway."

"Is that the same day Mr. George and Father Joseph found her?" Jason asked, with contempt for Gigi's grandmother.

"Yes," Gigi answered, "George and I were sure the evil we experienced in our home came from her. Father Joseph wanted to try and cut it off at its source, if you will. Both he and George also believed they might be able to help my grandmother. They were both such good-hearted men."

Luca said, "You didn't think they could help her?"

Gigi placed her folded hands on the countertop. "I did not. I hoped I was wrong, but in the end I wasn't. They found her on the porch. She'd been dead a few days. Rats had already found her."

I shuddered at the image. Luca flinched, yet kept his arm around me. I listened to his heartbeat, steady and strong.

Gigi continued. "After they recovered from the shock of finding her, Father Joseph blessed her body and started to go inside the inn to bless it, but he couldn't."

"Was the door locked?" Sam asked.

Gigi shook her head. "The door was open. Something was blocking his entrance, something they couldn't see and only he could feel. Your grandfather took a small step past Father Joseph to determine if he, too, was blocked from entering. When he had no trouble, they realized the inn would not allow certain people to enter it. Or perhaps that's wrong. Perhaps it was Father Joseph's guardian angel that would not allow him to pass.

"Father Joseph did all he could to try and rid the inn of evil. But never was he able to take a step past the threshold. The next day he returned with the mortician, a fellow member of our church. He, too, could take a step into the building. Father Joseph remained blocked. Again, he performed every rite of exorcism he'd been trained to perform. He even considered calling in additional priests who specialized in exorcism, but after speaking with a few on the phone, he told us instead to never go near the inn. He told us he was concerned that the evil contained in the inn might go into another nearby home or family. So the inn remained as it was—untouched, until Thomas decided to enter it."

Dad began to pace the length of the kitchen. Each of us watched him take one quick step after the other. The guilt rested on him and his great-grandmother. He'd brought whatever it was into this house. As a result, Gigi's body had been scarred. And Thomas had died.

When my mom died, we were young, my sister only a baby. He had no choice but to hold it together, and her love was so fresh in his mind. When Thomas died … we each went our own way. Mom had been gone for so long. Dad reverted to who he was before her, before us. Gigi did the same. She became the overindulgent mother she'd been when he was young. She allowed him to fall and turned a blind eye—in the false belief that she was helping him.

Jackson whined to go outside; the snow was calling him. My father barely noticed Jason dodge his pacing to let Jackson out. Dad's hands alternated from his pockets to his left arm held across him and his right fingertips resting on his lips. He was in thought, unaware of the rest of us. Aside from Jackson, no one made a sound.

I wondered what my sisters thought. Had they ever seen Dad like this, pacing furiously across a room? I had, in his office, on the day he confessed his similarities to Thomas. I cringed at the memory. But my sisters hadn't been there in his office with me. I wondered if they knew that this was an improvement because, unlike every other day, he wasn't hiding in his office. He was allowing us to see him as he was, far from perfect.

"Why me?" Dad finally said. "Why did she involve me? Why did she care about me?"

Gigi rubbed her hands together. "I doubt she cared anything for you," she said simply, but with a longing sadness. Like she wished things were different while accepting that they weren't.

"Why was she nice to me, then?" Dad said, still pacing, though his strides were less severe. "She was always so nice to me, always welcoming. If I was on the beach, she'd come out to me, friendly as she could be, offering me blueberry candies she'd made."

"You've never been around someone who's nice to your face, but mean as a badger when you turn your back?" Jason asked, raising an eyebrow at my dad.

Dad's expression shifted. He hadn't considered this.

Why would he? He was a child when he knew his great-grandmother, and a boy, at that. How many boys are tuned in to the duplicity of the people around them? It was not an easy concept to grasp, not if you were raised by kindhearted parents. Jason had learned this lesson from the earliest of ages. In some ways, his parents had prepared him better for life than my dad's parents or even mine.

"She was my great-grandmother," Dad responded. "She was supposed to love me."

"That's not the hand you got dealt," Jason said. "Maybe it's good my parents were always mean to me. I never got fooled—never thought they actually cared. I suppose there's a reason they were drawn to this land, and it wasn't 'cause of the goodness, that's for sure."

"No, but good came of it," Gigi said, determined to point out the positive aspect. "My grandmother's hatred had little to do with you, Paul. You were merely the best way to hurt me."

"Why did she want to hurt you?" Avi asked. She was enfolded in Lisieux's arms.

"Oh, I must have been the most odious of all creatures to her. In her mind, I stole her land and her future hotel," Gigi said, gesturing to indicate our home. "Money was everything to her and my grandfather. They were happy to have me when I was young. I was free labor," she said, her tone harsh. "That is, once my mother was gone and I was no longer taking care of her. They didn't care a thing about my mom or me, but they welcomed the slave labor that I afforded. They did everything they could to keep me subservient, reminding me often how worthless they believed me to be."

Gigi paused and took a sip of her cold tea.

"Thankfully, my mother raised me not to listen to the voices of others. If she hadn't, my life would've been entirely different and I doubt any of you would exist. As it was, I was strong enough to run away. Years later, I returned and bought this place from the bank when she could no longer afford to keep it. Could she hate anyone more? How could I not deserve as much suffering as she could cause? But to cause me the sort of pain she very likely wanted to cause me would have meant the end of her line. Her offspring would be dead and so she was at an impasse. When she was able to befriend my son, the world of possibilities likely opened in her evil heart."

"What sort of possibilities?" Dad asked, sounding unsure.

"I'm afraid only you can answer that," Gigi said.

"I've told you what I remember," Dad said emphatically. "You don't believe me."

She responded, "You've told us what she wanted you to remember. You're correct. I don't believe that version of the past."

Dad groaned. "I remember what I remember."

The room was silent. Jason put a hand on Sam's shoulder. She looked at him. He nodded subtly.

"There's something," Sam said timidly, "something I've always felt here."

We turned to face her, all except Dad, who had resumed pacing.

I wondered if he hoped the jarring movements would unearth a hidden memory.

As Dad's hand moved from one position to another, the memory of the scar flashed. How had anyone believed a rock made that cut? Had Gigi truly believed that? Had my grandfather?

I thought then of Thomas, of how his parents saw him as an innocent lamb, incapable of error. Was this how Gigi saw my father, at least when he was young? Now her perception of him as an adult might be different, but as a child, was he as perfect in her eyes as Thomas was in Brenda's? "So much alike." These were my father's words. He was so much like Thomas. Perhaps his parents were similar as well. I felt sadness for both Thomas and my father, and their parents.

"What've you felt?" Dad asked Sam.

He startled me by the abruptness of his tone. He didn't bother slowing his stride as he made his way from one end of the room to the other.

My father intimidated Sam. Typically, he did his best to put her at ease, but not today.

Sam sucked in air before speaking. "There's a blanket of darkness pressing down on this family, held back by something … but always there in the distance, waiting, lurking."

Jason's hand rested on her arm, giving warmth and support.

From beside me, Luca said, "I've felt the same since I moved here."

"Is it always held back?" Dad asked, surprising me by not dismissing the spiritual truth laid before him.

Sam rubbed her hands together. "No. Not always."

Dad stopped pacing.

Sam said, "The blanket of darkness has been here as long as I've lived here. At first, I was afraid. I told Jason we needed to move. He explained the history of this land of his parents and Gigi's grandmother. He told me there was no present evil. I gave it time and realized, in some respects, he was right. It was not in the past, as he believed, but it remained at a distance … most of the time."

Sam's eyes brimmed with tears. Whatever she was about to say, she didn't want to.

"The day Rebecca died," Sam said, pushing her hands nervously against her jeans, "that morning was different. It was pressing hard against her. She wasn't aware of it, I don't think. Probably because there was a barrier of goodness around her, protecting her. But it was there. I didn't understand what it was or how to tell her. What do you tell a person when evil is pressing against them? That doesn't matter. I should've told her something. She would've understood as much as anyone can understand." Sam laid her head in her hands.

Jason placed his hand against her back.

Sam continued, her blue eyes shimmering. "The crazy thing is Rebecca may not have felt the evil, but she could tell something was wrong with me. She asked if I was okay. I lied and said I was fine. She was so kind. She hugged me and said she'd be back in a few hours and asked if we could go for a walk to talk about whatever might be bothering me. She said it would be Avi's naptime anyway—and you loved napping in your carrier," Sam said, offering a tearful smile to Avi.

Lisieux was still holding Avi. Gigi reached out to her youngest granddaughter.

Sam dabbed her eyes and wiped her nose with a napkin. "Rebecca was always doing stuff like that. Always putting everybody else first."

My father's head hung low, the veins in his neck pulsing. Finally, he spoke. "Is it gone? The blanket of darkness."

Sam and Luca exchanged a look.

Luca answered, his hand now clasping mine. "It's far less than it was, but no. It's not gone."

My father looked as if the world was crushing him. His breaths came ragged and quick, like his body was struggling to keep working.

He turned, fleeing from our presence, escaping toward his dungeon. Abruptly he stopped. His hands grasped the narrow wall that separated the stairs from the hallway.

I squeezed Luca's hand as my father fought with himself. His grip was so tight on the wall his back muscles bulged against his shirt. I prayed for God to allow my mother to help him. He needed her. He needed to be reminded of who he was when he was with her. That was who God created him to be— not the lie who stood before us.

He groaned and practically pushed himself into the stairwell. From there, he sprinted up the stairs, taking them two at a time. He was running, not from us, but from whatever was hidden in his office: the lies that offered false promises.

Upstairs, in his room, the room he had shared with my mother, there was a chance to remove the darkness—a chance for peace.

Twenty-Five

My sisters, Luca, and I retreated to my father's office, where we lit a warming fire and Lisieux read some of Avi's favorite stories aloud. Happy, silly stories about a pig and an elephant or a dog and a bear. In spite of herself, Avi giggled and so did Lisieux.

While they were doing that, I was casually yet systematically searching through drawers and behind books to find all that my dad had hidden in this room. Whenever I found something, Luca expertly slipped it out of the room and threw it in the kitchen trash or down the kitchen drain. On one of his trips, Luca returned with a bag of marshmallows, graham crackers, and chocolate.

"I don't want a s'more," Avi said gloomily, suddenly remembering that she was upset.

"Awesome, more for me." Luca winked at her and quickly began making a s'more.

He wasn't kidding. He could easily eat the entire bag of marshmallows and all that remained of the graham crackers and chocolate.

After about his third s'more, my sisters each ate one and after that, I did too. Dad was right. There are few things that the combination of gooey marshmallows, melted chocolate, and crunchy graham crackers could not at least temporarily alleviate. In the back of my mind, I wondered how my father would react when he learned that his stashes of alcohol and pills were gone … or at least all that I could find. It didn't matter, I told myself as I escaped into sugary goodness, someday this would be my house. Mine and my sisters', if they wanted it, and I would not have those things in my home. Not now, not ever. I would not enable him in that way. If he wanted more, he'd have to buy more, and I'd search his office and dump it again. I'd do this as many times as I needed, until they didn't return.

After we ate a few more s'mores, Sam called us for dinner. Luca spread the logs and watched until only glowing embers remained. Then he joined us for whatever leftovers were in the house.

Soon after dinner, Lisieux and I tucked Avi into bed. My father's bedroom door was closed. None of us wanted to disturb him—or maybe none of us wanted to face him. Gigi, too, remained absent. As much as we loved each of them, we wanted nothing to do with either. Not tonight.

After we said our short prayers and kissed Avi goodnight, Lisieux and I left her room. Lisieux gave me a quick side hug before she slipped into her room. I showered, the heat of the water washing the day away. But it couldn't wash away the memories. I didn't want it to. Washing away memories was what my father was trying to do with the various chemicals he put into his body. Pretending the past hadn't happened was not the way to deal with life. Allowing it to overtake your every thought was also not the way to do it, I told myself as I exhaled the weight of the day. Somewhere there was a balance.

After my shower, I put on pajamas, grabbed my robe and slippers, and left my room. My damp hair made me cold as I trod down the hallway. I pulled the collar of my robe snug around my neck. My father's door was cracked open. No more secrets—that's what he was saying by not latching it shut. I pushed on it; it moved easily, swinging open enough for me to peer inside.

He was on his knees, rosary in hand, a single candle burning in front of a picture of my mom. The crucifix they'd received as a wedding gift hung on the wall above the picture. It was the last picture taken of her ... the morning she died. He'd been in a silly mood and clicked a candid picture of her cooking breakfast. After she died, he printed it. It was the most beautiful picture of her we had. The morning sunlight caught the soft waves of her auburn hair, her emerald-green eyes glowing with love for each of us. Her smile ... so warm, peaceful.

The sight of him on his knees in front of her and our crucified Lord, begging each of them for forgiveness, caused emotion to catch in my throat and tears to brim.

He didn't notice me. How could he, when he was focused on the love of his life?

I crept away, closing the door softly behind me.

Next to his room was Avi's. I stepped inside. Jackson's head jerked up from the rug he slept on, his eyes glowing with the reflection of the hall light.

I listened to her slow, heavy breaths. We were so different, she and I, and yet … I wondered what gifts she had. Gifts she didn't even realize were gifts. Her ability to walk into a room and understand all that was going on almost immediately was not typical. She realized Dad was falling apart. She hadn't known how. How could a young child have any understanding of the evils of the chemicals he was using to numb everything he felt, everything he remembered? Still, she'd sensed it when the rest of us hadn't.

I petted Jackson, and he put his head down. I was grateful he kept watch over the littlest in the family.

Next door, Lisieux's light was off. I didn't enter. She was not a young child who needed her big sister to check on her. She too was gifted in her own nerdy way.

Luca was afraid of gifts. I couldn't blame him. But all gifts were from God. Why we had them, I didn't understand. Was there something God wanted me to understand, something he wanted me to do? If not, why show me glimpses of evil? Why swamp my mind with horrors of the long-ago past?

You asked to see the world as it was, the small voice inside me answered.

Yes, I thought, recalling my prayer at Thomas's funeral. I did ask for this gift. I leaned against the railing that led downstairs. Never did I expect to receive an answer to that prayer when so many others went unanswered.

You cannot fight what you don't believe in. Now you believe. Now you can fight.

The voice caused me to slide to the floor.

It was right. Even after Thomas, I tried to pretend the demons didn't exist. I wanted the world to consist only of what I could see and touch—that world was dangerous enough. I sighed as I pulled my knees toward my chest. I guess I got what I wanted. Now I could see evil; my very touch brought it to me.

I couldn't fight when there was nothing, in my awareness, to fight. But now I understood. I realized every ounce of life was a battle—a battle that mattered more than any military battle ever could. This was a battle not for territory or even worldly freedom. This was a battle for eternal freedom.

Twenty-Six

In the morning I woke rested. The night had been peaceful, more than I had expected, given the last few nights. I was grateful. I dressed quickly, wondering if my family was going to church. We never missed Mass, but nothing about the previous few days or weeks had been typical. Luca would go, of this I was sure, and I'd go with him. He'd help protect me from the stares. As I left my room I realized I was up earlier than I typically was on a Sunday, the effect of actually sleeping the entire night for the first time in several days.

The kitchen was quiet; my father sat at the table. I hesitated. Should I slip quietly back up the stairs? I decided not to be a coward. Gone was the chipper father who had greeted me with freshly made French toast the day before. In his place was a haggard man with swollen eyes and an unshaven face. He was holding his coffee mug, his hair a mess.

I wondered, based on how red and puffy his eyes appeared, if he'd be able to cry even if he tried to. If I ever had a child, I'd tell them of this day—the day and night when their grandfather faced the truth of his life. The full weight of his choices had fallen on him and he had not run from it.

"Thank you … for cleaning out my office." His voice was hoarse.

I sat cautiously across from him. "How did you know it was me?"

"I'm not sure," he said, rubbing his thumb against his coffee mug, one my mom made for him with pictures of Lisieux and me as little kids. "I guess because you were the one who saw me passed out on the couch."

"I'm glad it was me and not Lisieux or Avi," I said.

He grimaced at the thought. "It's bad enough having one daughter realize the extent of your sins."

"How did you know the stuff was gone?" I asked, wanting to believe the change I felt in him was real. But if he was looking for what I'd taken, he was no different.

"I was going to do it myself, or at least try," he said, his voice tired. I doubted he'd slept. "You were very thorough. I found a lone bottle of pills. They're in the trash—it's okay if you want to check." He rubbed his hands together.

I went to the trash and slid it open. On top, under a single paper towel, was a plastic prescription bottle full of tablets.

"I'm glad you did it for me. I couldn't have handled all the others," he said.

I noticed his legs bouncing beneath the table. "Are you okay?" I asked.

"I will be," he said, though his skin was pale and sweaty.

"I don't want you to be in pain, but that's not the way," I said, feeling bad for him.

He sniffed, holding on to his arms. "You're right. This will pass. Your mom will help me."

"Did she help you before?"

"No. That's not how it works—not at the beginning of a relationship. She could never have fixed me, and she was too smart to try. I was sober for several years before we met. If I hadn't been, she would've had nothing to do with me."

"How do you know?"

"She told me. I told her on our first date. It's why we went to that pottery studio instead of a bar."

"She loved that you took her there."

"God knew what he was doing," Dad said, his body rocking slightly. "She told me if I wasn't sober and going to remain sober, she wanted nothing to do with me. I never let her down, even after she died, never. … Until now."

"His death wasn't your fault," I said.

"It was," he said, nodding subtly. "This scar, your memory, it all points to my helping my great-grandmother. It explains so much of my life, of the nightmares," he said, rubbing his neck.

"Can you tell me about them?" I asked, wondering if the shrieking demons had tried to attack him too.

"So many. Many of the inn, of the fireplace, of her. Of the center stone going into a metal box. I thought it was all a dream. I didn't realize it was memories breaking free gradually, over the last forty years. They used to haunt me." He shook his head. "They continue to haunt me."

"Is that what was in the box?" I asked, nerves tingling, making me feel like an electric current was running through my body.

He traced some scratches on the kitchen table, the result of Avi using it for her homeschooling desk. "I believe so. My blood must've been what she wanted, what tied her to me … to us. I gave something so precious, with so little thought, or none, I suppose," he said sadly.

"She tricked you," I said, only partially believing I shouldn't hold him fully accountable for all that had happened.

"I was a fool," he said bitterly. "Even after her death … the foolishness didn't stop. Hence the items you removed from my office. The nightmares,"—he pushed against his skull—"they're the reasons I began using when I was a kid."

"You can't hide from the past. It will find you," I said, thinking of how it had found me.

He stared at the pictures of Lisieux and me that encircled his mug. "I can't … figure out how to fix it, how to correct what I've done," he said, shifting his gaze out to the yard.

The sun was making the earth come to life and with it the rumblings of waking people above us.

I said, "Some things can't be fixed."

He sat taller, his eyes losing their lack of focus. "There must be a way to fix this. Thomas is gone, I understand that. Your mom,"—his voice faltered—"is gone. I understand that too, but there can't be more deaths from this. It can't continue."

Avi and Gigi came downstairs. Avi at first appeared afraid of our dad, but when he rose and went to her, she opened her arms and allowed him to scoop her up. She trusted that he was different. Gigi noticed a spot of spilled coffee on the counter.

She wiped it and then opened the trashcan. She hesitated, taking a long, deep breath before throwing her paper towel on top of the one my father had placed there.

While I could tell she was grateful the pills were gone, she would've done nothing to remove them. Why? Why would she put up with something she so clearly hated? Why would someone who was so often outspoken, not speak her mind about the awful things her son was doing to himself?

"I'm glad you're dressed," Dad said to Avi, who, out of habit on Sunday mornings, had put on a sweaterdress and leggings. "I'm going to run up and shower. First, I'll make sure Lisieux is awake."

"I wasn't planning on our family attending Mass this morning," Gigi said dryly.

"Why not?" Avi asked as Dad put her back on the floor.

"I believe Brenda and Phil will be at this service," Gigi said. "What happened at the funeral doesn't need to be repeated."

Dad hesitated, but then said, "There's no point in trying to avoid them. It would be impossible. We live in the same town, worship at the same church. It is what it is."

It was unusual for Dad to disagree with Gigi about something like this, and definitely in the last two months. It was a small decision, but one that meant he was making a decision, actually being our parent.

"Come on, Avi, you and I will check on Lisieux," I said, deciding it best we leave the kitchen.

"Luca wants to go too. I'll make sure he's awake," Avi said, racing up the stairs ahead of me.

I knocked on Lisieux's door and Avi went to Luca's. Both were already mostly awake.

Within the hour we were pulling up to our church. My father held Avi's hand. Lisieux, Luca, and I walked beside one another. Gigi trailed us. She'd made it clear she thought it best we attend a different service or possibly drive the hour to the next closest Catholic church. Dad disagreed.

Gigi wasn't wrong. There would be whispers, or worse. But Dad was also right: it was what it was. We couldn't undo what happened. We had no control over the past or the future, only the present.

My father didn't stop at the back pew, as I expected; he went up to our regular pew in the second row. The rest of us followed obediently.

"It will be okay," Luca whispered as he and I knelt, my knees hurting a bit against the pressure. I focused on them as I tried to tune out the not-so-quiet whispers.

A second later, the bell in the back of the church rang, signaling the beginning of Mass. We stood along with the rest of the congregation. Father Luke came down the aisle, led by Beth's little brother carrying the cross high above his head.

That meant that Beth was likely here. My face burned as I remembered the waiter from the BayTree. What had she told him? Friday night, I'd been terrified. Today, in the sunlight, next to Luca, I was not afraid—I was angry.

During the readings and homily, when I should have been focused on what was happening in front of me, I was thinking of Beth somewhere behind me and wishing I could confront her before I lost my nerve. Luca must have sensed my distraction because, as Father concluded his homily, Luca nudged me—a gentle reminder to still my mind and heart. I inhaled and exhaled, focusing on God in front of me in the tabernacle. It would be much easier if I could actually sense the change that happened during the consecration, as Luca could. I'd prayed to see the world as it was; I hadn't meant the darkness of the past. I'd hoped for beauty.

If that portion of my prayer wasn't answered, there must be a reason.

God did not allow something that could not bring at least some minuscule amount of good. He would not have allowed me to witness my father slicing his arm or the terror-stricken children just because. There must be a reason and it must be for some good.

I was in line now, on my way to receive the Eucharist. I prayed fervently to focus on God, begging him to purify my heart and mind and help me understand what he wanted me to understand, to forgive all that I needed to forgive. Luca was behind me, but even so, I could sense him fall to his knees in front of the Eucharist, a contrast to me and almost everyone else in the church who simply bowed. He rose quickly and followed me to our pew. He had not received—he wouldn't until he officially entered the Church at Easter.

He was staring at me. He did this every time after I received Communion. It had nothing to do with me and everything to do with Jesus inside me. It was a little eerie, like he was watching God's essence spread through my veins.

"How do you not simply float away?" he'd asked me the first Sunday he came with us.

I'd whispered back that some saints did levitate and a few priests even today have to hold on to the altar with one hand during Consecration to keep from rising into the air. To many, these must seem like bizarre lies; to Luca, they made perfect sense.

I slid back into the pew, Luca's fingers grazing mine.

At the end of Mass, Father dismissed us and added that there would be donuts and coffee in the parish hall. It was funny that he always announced this. We all knew there would be coffee and donuts, but I supposed it was nice to invite any visitors who might be with us.

We waited for Dad to exit the pew. The rest of us would follow. He didn't move. He was staring at the crucifix.

After another few minutes, he shifted his body to face the rest of us sitting in the pew. "I think we should go eat some donuts," he said.

"I don't want any," Avi said glumly.

"I meant at the parish hall," Dad said, his voice reflecting it was more of a question. He thought this was what we should do, but wondered what the rest of us thought.

Luca was the first to speak. "I'm always up for donuts."

"It would certainly cause a stir," Gigi said, a bit of her old spunk returning.

"I need to talk with Beth anyway," I said, aware of Luca eyeing me.

Lisieux said, "I guess if nobody talks to me, I could read my book."

"You have a book with you?" Luca asked.

"In my purse," Lisieux said, like it was a strange question.

Luca's eyes twinkled. "Of course."

Avi was the only one who didn't say anything.

Dad took her hand. "Come on, you can stand by me. One donut, and then we'll leave."

He led her from the pew. Each of us genuflected as we exited the pew. Luca went down on both knees and bowed so that his head almost touched the floor. By the time we left the church, those going to the parish hall were already there and the rest were in their cars, streaming out of the parking lot.

"This will be good," Gigi announced. "Good to make a grand entrance."

Twenty-Seven

The hubbub inside the hall was as loud as ever. The gawking stares were new, but part of our life these days. I felt my dad tense beside me; he wanted to run. I didn't blame him. I did too.

"Avila, let's get you a donut," he said, swallowing the discomfort.

We went, in a clump, to the table that held open boxes of donuts on one end and white foam cups of coffee or orange juice on the other.

I stuck to Luca's side, his presence providing me strength as I sensed Beth and Chastity glaring at me. It was Avi I felt the worst for. Some of the kids she used to play with started toward us, their parents quickly stopping them.

From the edge of the hall, the young mom from the funeral who had sat in front of us, blocking the glares and frowns, came to us with her daughter. She was a few years younger than Avi.

"Good morning, Avila. My little girl, Elle, has been missing you." The mom, Jody, leaned in closer to Avi like she was telling a secret. "You know how shy she is. Can you get her to play? You've always been so sweet with her."

Avi loosened her grip on our dad's leg.

"I think it's a good idea," Dad said gently. "After all, you don't want to hurt Elle's feelings."

Avi twisted the toe of her shoe on the linoleum floor. "Okay. If it will help Elle," Avi said, letting her arms fall to her side.

Jody winked at Avi. "It will, thanks," she said in a whisper.

"Come on, Elle," Avi said, taking her by the hand. Avi led her to the side of the hall where there were some hula hoops and jump ropes laid out.

Dad exhaled in relief. "Thanks," he said to Jody.

"It's the truth. Elle hasn't played with the other kids since you all stopped coming in here. I'm glad you're here today," she said with a kind smile. She left us to rejoin her husband and son at a square card table where the little boy was busy getting donut icing all over his face.

"That was very kind," Gigi said.

"She and her husband have always been kind. They keep to themselves, both quiet but sincere," Dad said, his voice stronger. "Lisieux, did you notice the twins over there?"

Lisieux's former best friends were sitting at a far table, each reading a book while their parents chatted nearby. "I doubt they'd mind if you sat with them."

"It is the quietest table in the room. That's why we always pick it," Lisieux said. "And it's not like they own it."

Gigi said, "They don't own it, though I'm fairly certain they'd be happy to have you join them and not say a word."

"My feet are sore, anyway," Lisieux said. She bravely made her way to the table, digging through her bag for her book. When she reached the table, both girls looked up, offered the slightest of smiles, and returned to reading without saying a word. That was their equivalent of a welcome home party. Lisieux looked more relaxed than she had in weeks as she took her place between them and opened her book.

Dad put his hands in the front pockets of his slacks; his face showed an expression of gratitude. "I'm going to get a donut," he said, stepping away.

A guy greeted him with a slight nod. Dad stood beside him as he ate his donut and drank some coffee.

Gigi said, "There's Maribelle. I've been wondering if her granddaughter had her baby. I think I'll go ask." Gigi wandered off.

"I guess it's just you and me," Luca said.

"That's how it always was before," I said. "Not the you part, but the me part. All the rest of them had their people. I never did."

"That's because I didn't know where you were. Now that I do, you've got me. But I, ah …." He was focused on the donuts.

"You want a donut, don't you?" I said.

"Can I bring you one or maybe two or three?" His eyes twinkled.

"One would be great," I said, touching his arm briefly before he, too, wandered off.

From the corner of my eye, I caught the stares of Beth and those surrounding her. I met her glare and went toward her. I felt like Daniel walking into the lion's den, but it had to be done.

"I need to speak with you," I said abrasively to Beth.

"She doesn't *need* to speak to you," Chastity shot back.

I ignored her. "I get that you hate me but you sending that goon after me Friday night, that's crossing a line."

"Is your whole family as crazy as you?" Beth said. "Do all of you make stuff up or is it just you?"

"Keep your jerk friends away from me," I said.

"Trust me. My friends want nothing to do with you," she said, turning away.

I stepped between her and Chastity. "I'm serious. Tell your waiter friend to stay away from me."

"I don't even know any waiters," she mumbled, trying again to get away.

I wouldn't let her. "The waiter at the BayTree. You don't know him?"

She stopped for a second. "Are you talking about Chase?"

I nodded.

"He might even be a bigger jerk than you. I haven't talked to him in years."

"Then why did he say I was just as you described?"

Beth and Chastity snorted. "Oh, I've posted a ton about you. He probably meant that," she said, eyes alive with hateful satisfaction.

This time I let them walk away. How much had she posted about me? What had she said? I shook my head. It didn't matter. She could say whatever she wanted to on social media; I couldn't stop her or let it bother me. That was what evil wanted

… for me to be so distracted by her hatred that I'd begin to hate. I would not let her win. I would not let *it* win.

Luca came beside me with two glazed donuts in his hand. "Looks like that went well," he said sarcastically.

I crossed my arms. "Yeah, super great."

"Come on, there's room at Lisieux's table," he said, taking a large bite of donut.

I looked over. The twins were gone, and Lisieux was reading by herself at the card table.

"Good idea," I said as I followed him to my sister.

"What did Beth say?" he asked once we sat down.

I could tell him about the posts, but why? How would his knowing something like that help either of us?

"She said she didn't specifically tell the waiter anything. She doesn't seem to be close to him. He'd just heard gossip."

"That does seem most likely," Lisieux said while still looking at her book.

Luca grinned at my bookworm sister. "There you go. The most likely option," he said, taking a sip of orange juice.

I mouthed to Luca, "Does she even know what we're talking about?"

He shrugged and finished his last donut.

"Sorry your friends left," I said to Lisieux.

She lifted her eyes from the page for a second. "They had to go. At least they didn't get up as soon as I sat down."

I glanced around. The twins and their parents were gone, so they probably did have to go. I saw Dad near the door. He gave me the signal.

"Dad's ready to leave," I said as I arose.

Lisieux and Luca followed, Lisieux reluctantly closing her book to walk through the mess of pulled-out chairs.

"I'll grab Avi," Luca said, and disappeared to the side where Avi was playing with two little girls along with Elle and her baby brother.

"I think she had fun," I said to Lisieux.

"It's good Thomas's parents weren't here," Lisieux said.

"Yes, that would've made things more complicated."

Dad held the door open for us as we left the parish hall. We'd been here long enough that those coming to the next Mass were starting to fill the parking lot. On the way to our vehicles we dodged several cars that were parking. When we were almost there, a familiar BMW passed us; it was Phil's car.

"He didn't even try to run us over," Avi said jubilantly.

"You're right, Avila. It is the little things in life that we must be grateful for," Gigi teased.

"Being not run over is not a little thing. It's a big thing," Avi said.

Dad took Avi's hand. "You're right about that," he said as he helped her into his car.

Next to Dad's car was Gigi's Mercedes. There wasn't enough room in the Range Rover for all of us plus Luca. He and I got into the Mercedes.

"I'm thankful for not being run over and for a car with solid doors and windows and, most of all, for heated seats," Luca said as I started the car.

I giggled. "Those are nice things."

"They are *nice* things in Florida. They're practically essentials for survival in Maine," he said, pushing his hands against the hot air blowing out the air vents.

"What's my dad doing?" I asked as his brake lights turned red in front of us.

"Maybe he forgot something," Luca said.

A second later, his car door opened and so did his trunk. He stepped out of the SUV, removed a bag of garbage from the back, and went to the church's dumpster. He tossed the bag into the dumpster and got back into his car. His trunk started to close as the vehicle inched forward.

"That was the kitchen trash," I said.

"He must have wanted his stash out of the house so he wouldn't be tempted," Luca said. "The next several days aren't going to be easy for him."

"Many things aren't going to be easy."

We drove for a bit without talking. I was mindlessly following my dad back to our castle-like home. The trees appeared distorted from the condensation on the side windows.

Luca asked, "What are you thinking about?"

What *had* I been thinking about? "I guess I was trying to understand why I've been given these gifts, if that's what they are."

"To use for his glory," Luca said.

His faith had grown from a tiny mustard seed to a mighty oak in a few short weeks. I supposed that's what happened when God revealed himself to a person in a tangible way.

"Yes, but what does that mean?" I asked.

He was silent for a moment. "To bring light, not darkness, into the world."

I was about to ask him to be more specific, when he spoke again.

"My mom wanted to bring light. I believe that with all my heart. But she didn't because she didn't listen to God's word. She ignored the instructions he's given to us through Scripture and the two thousand years of knowledge contained within the teachings of the Catholic Church. That wasn't her fault," he said sadly. "She didn't know any better. But you do, and now I do. So we can do better. I've been thinking so much about the spiritual world lately—people don't understand that it's all around us. In this car, there are two humans and at least two angels, but there could be more. You and I don't have a way of knowing that, which is probably a good thing. That level of truth would be too much for us … too much for most people," he said, his voice becoming quiet.

The image of the little girl I'd seen on the trail entered my mind. I thought of her, this child I didn't know. Somehow I understood such gifts wouldn't be too much for her.

"I think some people could handle it," I said, remembering the beauty that radiated from the child with the wavy brown hair and amber-speckled eyes.

"Yes, that's probably true," he said. "I wondered about stuff my whole life. About why I was different, why my family was different. Then, when your gifts appeared …."

"And they freaked you out," I said.

"And they freaked me out, I realized I had to understand more. So I spent last night searching through your dad's books."

"He has a ton," I said.

"Most didn't pertain to any of this, but some did. Did you know some theologians believed that these sorts of spiritual gifts were meant to be part of the general human experience, but because of the fall, they were stripped away and weakened?"

"Umm … no, I had no idea." I didn't add that it would never have occurred to me to read the writings of theologians or saints to try to understand the odd abilities Luca and I had.

"Reading that and all the other things I found," he said, "helped me understand even more that these gifts are not from evil. No gifts are. Everything we are given is from God. But like everything else, we can choose to use it for his glory or not."

"Right, but how do we do that?" I asked, wanting to get away from the philosophical and focus on the practical.

"We ask him," Luca stated.

I lowered my head. I'd hoped for an actual answer.

Luca said, "Have you done that? Have you asked God what you're supposed to do with the memories you've seen?"

He was right. I hadn't done that.

Twenty-Eight

Sam pulled two cinnamon-scented casseroles of apple puff pancake from the oven. My sisters shed their coats. There was chattering around me. Happy chattering. It was a nice change. Outwardly, I tried to engage with the rest of my family as they prepared for Avi's favorite breakfast.

Inwardly, I was asking God why he'd given me the abilities I had. Why did I see terrified children who had been dead almost a hundred years? My dad's scar made more sense. He was my dad; the sin happened on our property. Whatever darkness he'd brought into his life, he'd brought into mine and my sisters'. Plus, he was still alive; he could be different … our lives could be different.

None of that was true for the children. They were gone; even those who had mourned their loss were gone after a hundred years. I was not going to bring them back or tell their loved ones what happened to them. I didn't even know their names. Perhaps I would recognize their pictures, but pictures from that long ago often weren't clear. Besides, it was the terror I saw, the terror that I would recognize, not the face of a happy child in a family photograph.

If their families were still alive, if I could bring them closure, it would be worth the pain of the vision. But they were not alive. Their nieces or nephews would be as old or maybe older than Gigi. I was sure they carried the scars of their ancestors, but I couldn't track them down. When the children died, any darkness surrounding them left. Our Lord would've taken them straight to his heart. There was no time spent in purgatory for the children who were tortured in this life, not if they had even the faintest understanding of God's love for them.

I could change nothing in their lives or their families' lives, and they were safe in heaven, so why had I seen them?

Bring them to the light, the quiet voice in my heart said.

"Siena, would you like some?" Sam asked. She held the spatula, ready to dish a golden-brown square of appley goodness onto a plate for me.

I came back to all that was happening in front of me. "No, thank you," I said, hanging up my coat.

As conversation bubbled and forks clinked against plates, I slipped into the hallway and then into my dad's office. Despite what Dad had done in this room the last few weeks, it still felt like the holiest place in the house to me. It was where we prayed every night and the place Luca saw the holy souls coming toward us. It was the place I'd often find my mom folding laundry when I woke up from a nap. She and my father would be discussing the growing business. We gathered around the fire here. Aside from the kitchen, this room felt most like home in our cavernous castle.

I went to the window behind the desk and pulled the drapes open. The warm morning sunlight poured into the room. On my dad's desk lay a simple wooden cross. It was a gift from my mother, but I hadn't seen it in years. I picked it up, the wood smooth from where his hands had rubbed the edges away. I held it tight for a moment and then returned it to the spot next to his keyboard. Where had it been the last several years? Luca was in here last night, combing through Dad's books. Did Luca find it and put it here? Or did Dad find it when he searched his office?

I touched it gently with the tips of my fingers. I felt goodness. My hair fell into my face, the strands of red creating a striking contrast against the light wood.

"Are you all right?" Dad asked, entering the room.

Gigi was behind him. I didn't mind their presence—now that he'd returned to being the father I'd always known and she to the grandmother I loved. Things had returned to the right order of things.

I said, "It's good you threw the kitchen trash out."

"I'm only so strong," he said, sitting down on the couch, his hands wringing in anxious movements, his dark hair glistening with sweat. He'd been calm during church and afterward—a grace given to him—but now the effects of drugs leaving his body continued … and would for many days.

"How are you, Siena?" Gigi asked, never wanting to acknowledge my father's addiction.

"What do you suppose *bring them to the light means*?" I asked.

Dad leaned back, his right leg subtly bouncing. "It could mean a few different things. To shine an actual light on something, to make something known, or if you think of The Light as a metaphor for God, then it might be to bring something to him, to present it to him."

My fingers slid across his polished mahogany desk, the desk his parents worked at when creating the empire he now controlled.

"Why do you ask?" Gigi said from beside my father.

"That's why I've been shown things," I said.

I sat in my father's high-back leather chair. I picked up the wooden cross, my left hand clasping it, my right thumb rubbing against the smooth wood—the spot where Jesus's feet would've been pierced by a nail.

Dad said softly, "Yes, that makes sense."

"Does it? Because it doesn't make sense to me," I said. "Maybe with the memory of your … of your arm, it might make sense. But not the children."

"Prayers always make sense," Gigi said. "Even when you don't know what else to do, you can pray. You can bring your worries for those kids or your dad or anyone else, to God."

"They've been dead a long time," I said somberly. "My prayers can no longer help them."

Dad shook his head. "Don't limit yourself by placing limits on God, Siena. You're thinking about time as linear, and for us it is. One thing happens, then the next thing, then the next. For God, it's different. God exists independently of time. There are no limitations, no past, no present, only now. Your prayers for those children would help them in their darkest moments, even if those moments happened a hundred years ago. God will take the prayers you offer for them now and grant them that strength when they need it, whenever that may be."

Gigi said, "You can also pray for all those who loved them and never received any form of closure or peace in this life. I'm sure they would appreciate your help during those torturous years."

"Why doesn't God grant them that strength, or better yet, protect innocent children?" I said, trying not to be angry at God for allowing precious children to suffer like that.

Dad answered, "God created the world with physical laws, laws we witness every time plants grow, or heat cooks food, or rain falls. The spiritual laws are just as real, but we can't see them—or most of us can't."

"Your father makes it sound so simple to grasp," Gigi said, sounding tired. "It isn't. Life is full of suffering—there's no escaping it. It is never God's desire for us to suffer, but sometimes it's the suffering that brings us closest to him. Though he never creates it. That's part of the law. He creates only good because he is good—he cannot give what he does not have, just as evil can never give good because it has none. That's how you can know what's from heaven and what isn't. Though at times, what is good can be unclear, at least for a while."

I thought of Luca's mother, who believed she was doing good though she wasn't.

"I don't believe my gifts are evil, even if I see the evil that has been done," I said, my voice sounding so mature it was almost unrecognizable to my ears.

"You're not evil and neither are your abilities," Dad said, rubbing his hands together.

Sweat was dripping down the side of his face. He was suffering, but it was suffering he'd brought upon himself. I didn't blame God for the pain he experienced—at least not these pains.

"Though like anything, they could be used for evil," Gigi cautioned.

"Sometimes, people do what they believe is right, what they believe is good, but it isn't," I said. The fear of the truth, the fear of turning out like Luca's mom, was evident in my voice, if only to me.

"It can be complicated," Dad said, his voice weak. "It becomes more complicated when people use their feelings to determine good from evil."

Gigi said, "You have the teachings of the Church to guide you."

"And you have Luca," Dad added. "He's like your mother, in that way."

"And your grandfather," Gigi said.

I felt the truth of their words, both of Luca's goodness and his equivalence in my life, as my mother had been to my father, and my grandfather to my grandmother. There were no sly smiles on their part or blushing cheeks on mine. They were speaking a simple fact. Luca was created for me, like those who were no longer here were created for those who sat across from me.

"I don't want his fate to be theirs," I said, with the same unrecognizable voice.

My father's eyes lowered. "I, along with my grandmother, created my father's fate … and your mother's." His voice was severe. "I entered into a promise sealed by blood." He rubbed his right hand over the sleeve of his left arm. "That blood was washed away when Thomas threw the box with the stone in it into the ocean."

"Flowing water has the ability to dissolve curses," Gigi said in a tired voice. They'd discussed this before.

"You believe Thomas ended the curse?" I asked, hope seeping into my soul.

"Yes," Dad said. His shirt was discolored from perspiration.

Gigi said, "Thomas's actions—combined with decades of prayers, both the prayers offered on earth and the prayers of those who love us in heaven—have helped to remove the darkness."

I replied, "Sam said the darkness remained."

"Some amount of darkness does remain," Dad said. "It always will, but with Thomas throwing the blood-soaked stone into the ocean came the cleansing of the blood."

"The demons in Thomas almost killed Luca too," I whispered.

"Almost," Dad said.

I ran my fingers along the cross on the desk. It wasn't fair that Thomas died. It wasn't fair my mother or my grandfather died, either. Each of those deaths rested on my father's shoulders, his and his great-grandmother's. Though he never wished it, he entered freely into a promise, a promise of evil. There are consequences for such promises, spiritual laws that, though unseen, are as real as those holding us to this earth. It doesn't matter if the one making the promise is a foolish young boy. Children are not given a free pass. Playing with fire in this world or the spiritual one will end in destruction, often death. Those are the laws … these were the consequences.

"Do you know what happened to them? The children, I mean. Did your mother tell you?" I asked, afraid Gigi may be able to answer me.

She folded her hands in her lap. "I don't believe anyone knows for sure. Back then, news traveled slowly. Horrible crimes can still be gotten away with, but it was easier then. No one in town even realized there were missing children from surrounding areas, until weeks after he fled."

"Did they find them once he was gone?" I asked, my hands wrapping around the wood of the cross.

She shook her head. "People realized what happened after it was too late." She lowered her head in sadness. "He was seen throwing something into the bay one night. The next day a little boy's body was discovered. The tide must not have gotten as high as he'd expected. When the sun rose, a precious child was lying on the rocks."

Dad placed his hand on Gigi's upper back. She appeared so frail next to him. She leaned a little closer to him, grateful he was finally present enough to offer comfort.

"Later that day, he was accused," she said. "Before they could officially arrest him, he was gone and his wife and son were dead. They searched his house and found traces of people having been in the attic. It wasn't until much later that they put the pieces together and figured out he'd been behind a series of kidnappings, all young children of color. Right after that happened, my mom left. She never said that was why she left, but the way she linked the events when she told me … I'm not sure.

"When we returned years later, she was so sick. We weren't thinking about what happened in that house, only how to keep her alive. After she was gone, I was in a daze and then I left. I never thought to ask anyone about those children. Once your grandfather and I settled here, I asked a few people about it, but no one knew anything more than I did. Most didn't even know *that*. It was thirty years in the past, at that point, and from what I could gather, it had been kept pretty quiet, even when it first came out."

"Why?" Dad asked.

Gigi raised and lowered her shoulders. "I think he was sort of prominent, maybe even the mayor, at some point. I can't remember. But it was something like that. And his wife was some big deal too, and …."

"And the children weren't white," I said, their dark sunken eyes appearing before mine.

Gigi nodded with sorrow. "All of that made people want to pretend it never happened."

"If I don't tell people, am I doing the same thing?" I said, wondering if *bring them to the light* meant more than prayer.

"If you're asked to do more, you'll know it," Dad said. "Until that point, prayer is the most powerful thing you can do."

Gigi said, "Prayer is always the most powerful thing you can do."

"Your grandmother's right," Dad said.

I let go of the wooden cross and stood up. I was ready to leave the office. I had survived Mass, survived confronting Beth, and now survived talking about my gift and the pain it brought me in the memories I had witnessed. The day had been long enough and it was still morning. My stomach gurgled. "I'm going to take Sam up on her offer for breakfast."

"You'd better hurry, or Luca will eat it all," Gigi said, with a twinkle in her voice.

How she loved him … how we all did.

I began to leave, when Dad asked, "Where did you find my cross?"

I turned. He was holding it in his hand, gazing lovingly at it.

"It was on the desk when I came in," I answered, not telling him that Luca had spent most of the night in his office searching through books and must have found it.

He stroked it. "Hmm, I'll have to ask the others who found it. It's been missing for years."

"Luca might know. I'll ask him," I said as I left the room. The aroma of apple puff pancake was calling me.

Twenty-Nine

"Can I come in?" Luca was at my door.

"Of course," I said. I pulled my arms up and arched my back in a stretch. I'd come up to my room right after breakfast. The last several days, the last several weeks, hadn't been good for my grades. I had a lot of assignments to finish before the end of the quarter. The beauty of homeschooling—extreme flexibility. The downside—extreme flexibility. It was easy to get behind.

"How's it going?" he asked. He went to my fireplace and grabbed hold of the flat shovel.

"You don't need to do that," I said, feeling guilty as he began scooping ashes into the metal bucket.

"I'm the one who starts most of the fires in here. Besides, it's a good excuse for me to be here," he said, giving me a wink.

"You don't need an excuse."

"I need to give myself an excuse when you're working. I've been trying not to bother you, but you've been up here for …"—he checked his watch, another gift from Gigi—"five hours. So I decided to interrupt you by cleaning your fireplace," he said with a satisfied expression.

I yawned and stood, flopping down on my bed. "I needed a break," I said, my eyes tired from so much reading. "I could fall asleep right now." I pulled the quilt my mom had made, up around my shoulders.

"Don't do that. You'll miss dinner, and Lisieux and Uncle Jace have been cooking all afternoon. Even your dad's been helping."

I snuggled into my bed. "I'm so glad you moved in with us and brought Jason. The meals were good before, but he's taken them up to a whole new level."

"Maybe after we move out, Lisieux will keep up the cooking," he said.

I frowned, though I doubted he saw me. He continued to clean the fireplace. I didn't want him to move out. Our house, our family, was better with all of them in it. "How long until your house is done?"

"Probably four months, depending on the weather."

Then I'll hope for lots of bad weather, I thought, pushing myself up into a sitting position, the quilt wrapped loosely around my shoulders.

"We all like having you here," I said, hoping they could stay, or at least he could. This was his home—I was sure of that.

"We like being here," Luca said, closing the ash bucket and putting the shovel back in its holder. As he stood, he touched one of the pictures on the mantle. It was a family picture, all of us, even Avi, having a picnic in our backyard. Gigi had taken it for us.

"It isn't fair," Luca said, sliding his fingers along the frame.

"What?"

"You aren't supposed to get the girl of your dreams and have three beautiful daughters with her, only to have her taken away from you. That's not how life is supposed to go."

The air suddenly felt chilly. I pulled the quilt up around me. "This life isn't perfect. God's plan for us … we aren't going to experience that in this life. The next one will be better," I said, thinking not only of my parents, but of Luca and me, of our life together. We had already experienced more sorrow than most. I wondered if our future would be any different.

Luca came and sat beside me. "The next one *will* be better," he said with the sort of acceptance that told me he felt something ominous about our future too.

It was strange to have these thoughts, to know these truths when we'd never even kissed. Yet, somehow I knew Luca was mine and I was his. He'd love me all the days of his life and I'd love him. But how long that would be? That was where the sinking feeling came in.

I took his hand in mine. "At least you found the girl."

He squeezed my hand, his face sad. He felt everything I did. He knew everything I did, maybe more.

"It will be a great life," he said.

"Just too short," I said, staring into his golden eyes.

He forced a smile. "We'll make it amazing."

"I don't think other people have to face these truths when they're so young," I said.

He smiled, this time more easily. "Other people aren't like us."

"No," I said with resignation. "We're gifted."

He kissed me on the forehead. I leaned into him.

"We are gifted," he whispered, his body close to mine.

After a moment that I hoped would never end, he released me. "And you need to graduate from high school, so get back to work." He pulled me up and seated me at the desk.

I groaned. "I'm so tired."

"Dinner will be ready soon. I'll come get you when it is," he said, kissing me again on the top of my head.

"Okay, fine," I said, staring down at the various open textbooks strewn across my desk.

"Oh, hey," I called to him.

He stopped in the doorway.

"Where did you find my dad's cross?"

"What cross?" he said, puzzled.

"The one on his desk. He'd been missing it for years."

He shook his head. "It wasn't me."

"Weren't you in his office all night?"

"Yeah, but I never saw a cross on his desk. There's one on the wall by the door, but that's the only one I've ever noticed."

"Hmm," I said. "It must've been one of my sisters."

He watched me and I him, both of us knowing it was not my sisters.

"It would be odd to go through life only believing what's right in front of you," Luca said, touching the doorframe as an example of the physical world.

"Yes," I said, "that would be odd."

Luca smiled. "I'll come get you when the food is ready."

"Thank you," I called.

I leaned back in my chair, my gaze stopping at the distant picture frame on the mantle. The quilt my mother had made draped from my shoulders.

"Was it you?" I asked into the air.

There was no answer. To hear one would have been too bizarre, even for me. But not for some, I realized. Some people who were so tuned in to the world beyond this one would have asked that question and heard the answer. Not the false answer of demons, but the true answer of angels.

Did I envy such a person?

No, I decided. Those would be extraordinary gifts for an extraordinary person. Far more extraordinary than me or even Luca.

I thought again of the girl in the woods: her green eyes speckled with amber watching me as intently as I watched her. She was extraordinary. I thought of my mother, of how she must have longed to stay on this earth with her children and the man she loved. How short her time had been.

Would I be given more time? Would Luca? I wondered if our child would grow up in a world without us, a world changed beyond either of our imaginations—a world in need of the gifted.

End of Book Two

Also by Jacqueline Brown

The Light, Book One of The Light Series
Through the Ashes, Book Two of The Light Series
From the Shadows, Book Three of The Light Series
Into the Embers, Book Four of The Light Series
Out of the Darkness, Book Five of The Light Series
"Before the Silence," a Light Series Short Story
Awakening, Book One

If you enjoyed *Gifted*, please consider leaving a review. You can learn more about the author at <u>www.Jacqueline-Brown.com</u>, where you can get your free e-copy of "Before the Silence" and join the mailing list.